"HOW DOES THIS FEEL?"

Jacob's reply was muffled by the pillow. "Mmm. . . ."

"I take it that means good." Smiling seductively, Leah continued her sensitive massage up and down the length of him.

"Leah . . . do I really look like your husband?"

Her hands stilled. "I s-suppose so. Does that matter?"

"Not really, except—" he rolled over to look at her "—I worry that you might be making love to him through me."

"Oh, Jacob," she said, a tremor in her voice, "believe me, I know who's in bed with me." And she began sensuously to convince him.

Jacob groaned. "Do you know how long I've waited for you?"

Gently she nibbled at his bottom lip. "My dear," she murmured tenderly, "you don't know what waiting is. . . ."

For Bill . . . and Bill B., Debbie,
Bob, Laura and Susie.

◆

BARBARA KAYE
is also the author
of this title in
SuperRomance

COME SPRING

and in
Love Affair

CALL OF EDEN

HOME AT LAST

Barbara Kaye

A *SuperRomance from*
HARLEQUIN
London · Toronto · New York · Sydney

First published in Great Britain in 1986 by
Harlequin, 15–16 Brook's Mews, London W1A 1DR

© Barbara K. Walker 1985

ISBN 0 373 70161 6

11–0386

Printed and bound in Great Britain by
Cox & Wyman Ltd, Reading

PROLOGUE

ALL DAY LONG Leah had grappled with the feeling that something was terribly wrong. Now, as she shifted restlessly on the living-room sofa, awakening from her nap by slow degrees, the feeling returned. Heavy-lidded with sleep, her eyes opened, closed, then opened again. Afternoon naps had never been part of her life, but now, as she entered the final month of her pregnancy, she found it easy to drop off almost anytime.

She lifted her arm and looked at her watch. Four-thirty. She had slept for more than an hour. Her father would have left for the bus station long ago and wouldn't have wanted to waken her. Jim would be home soon, thank goodness. Just knowing he'd be with her tonight made her feel better, because she'd missed him more than she would have imagined possible. An odd uneasiness had settled over her as she'd watched that smoke-belching bus pull away from the station the day before, and it had stayed with her ever since. She chided herself. Foolishness! They had been apart only one day and night, but it was their first separation since their marriage, and the time had passed much too slowly.

Yawning lustily, she shoved herself to a sitting position, then stood up and slipped on the low-heeled shoes she'd kicked off earlier. Her swollen stomach seemed grotesquely huge to her, for she was a slender, small-boned woman and was carrying the baby low. *I'm tired of being pregnant*, Leah thought. *I'm anxious to be a mother. Anxious for a lot of things, actually—for Jim to get home, for us to move into our own place, for the baby....* Leah was just shy of her twenty-second birthday; it was easy to be impatient for the future.

Brushing away an unruly lock of raven hair, she crossed the old-fashioned farmhouse's parlor to look out the window at the overcast March sky. The grounds, so lush and green most of the year, looked bleak and rather forlorn at the end of winter. The big white house belonged to her veterinarian father, the only home Leah had ever known. She and Jim had stayed on after their marriage, partly because her father had wanted the company, partly because it was so convenient for Jim. And mostly because the young couple had had so much trouble finding a suitable place of their own.

Soon everything would change. Five months ago they had found the charming place in Sedona, which they were still renovating. Now it was almost finished, in plenty of time for the baby's arrival. That was the reason Jim had gone to Flagstaff—one last buying trip to purchase all the little things needed to complete the job.

Leah left the window and prowled restlessly. She paused at the wooden loom that occupied one corner of the parlor. Her half-finished tapestry beckoned to her, but she'd been too edgy all day to concentrate on it. This feeling of disquietude made no sense, and again she attributed it to Jim's absence. A small laugh escaped her lips. Good Lord, from the way she was carrying on, he might have been gone for weeks instead of one day and night.

The house was too empty and silent, and unaccountably, she felt chilled to the bone. Hugging herself and rubbing her arms briskly, she went into the kitchen to brew a cup of tea. It was as empty and quiet as the rest of the house. She called the housekeeper's name. "Tee?" There was no answer. Then Leah remembered that Tee had promised to take soup to a sick neighbor. She filled the kettle with water and set it on the stove to boil.

A car door slammed just then. Her heart leaped expectantly. Turning off the stove, she hurried out of the kitchen and into the parlor in time to see her burly father walk through the front door. "Dad! Where's...?" The words died in her throat when she saw his expression. His face was ashen.

"He wasn't on the bus, Leah," her father said in a shaken voice.

Her hand flew to her throat. "He had to be! You just missed him," she said irrationally. "Let's go back."

"Jim wasn't there. I waited until the last passenger got off."

"He...only missed the bus. He'll be on the next one."

"The next one isn't until morning. He would have called. You know he would have called, Leah. Jim wouldn't let us just sit here and worry."

She knew what he was thinking, and it was unthinkable. "No, I—" Her lips began to quiver as panic took over. Her eyes stinging with tears, Leah did the first thing that came to mind. She rushed to the phone, reaching for it with trembling fingers. "I'll call the motel in Flagstaff. There's an explanation. There has to be."

Her father moved quickly to her side and took the receiver from her hand. "Here, let me do it." His very real concern for his daughter was evident, as was his own fear. "You go sit down."

"I can't sit down! How can I sit down?" Stepping back, she watched as her father placed the call. From his end she caught the gist of it. Jim Stone had never put in an appearance at the motel where he had made a reservation. Anguish ripped Leah apart, and the tears splashed and spilled, running down her cheeks into the corners of her mouth. *I knew I should have gone with him!* She made a little sound like a choked scream. *We'll find him. I know we will. Jim can't go away now, not now, not with the baby, the house. . . .*

But even at that moment, watching her father slowly replace the receiver in the cradle and summon up the strength to look at her, Leah knew hope was useless. They would never find him. Jim was gone. The thing they had all dreaded—sometimes privately, sometimes openly—had finally happened.

Leah clutched a nearby table for support, placing her hand on her stomach as the baby began to kick violently. . . .

CHAPTER ONE

JACOB SURRATT was in an uncharacteristically happy frame of mind when he stepped through the starkly modern bank's smoked-glass doors. Occasionally he experienced such brief moments when he felt young and unfettered instead of old and restricted. He never knew what inspired the moments, and they never lasted long, so he had learned to enjoy them.

He glanced around the unfamiliar bank lobby, unable to recall ever using this downtown branch; usually he conducted his business at the smaller one near the clinic. This morning, however, he had attended an early breakfast meeting at a downtown hotel with some of Phoenix's civic leaders. The bank happened to be nearby, and he was short of cash.

It was early; there were few customers, so he walked directly to one of the teller windows. The smile on his face was, for Jacob, an unusually warm one.

"Good morning, sir. May I help you?" The woman who smiled back was young, not too many years out of high school, Jacob guessed, and wholesomely pretty. The nameplate beside the window informed him that she was Donna Pierce.

"Good morning, Ms Pierce. I'd like to cash a check. I assume I've come to the right place."

"You sure have if you have an account with us." She glanced at the check he pushed toward her, then back at Jacob. "Dr. Surratt?"

"That's right."

"Are you the Dr. Surratt of the Surratt-White Clinic, by any chance?"

"Yes, I am."

"My boyfriend and I drove by your new place yesterday. It's really something!" She punched Jacob's account number into the computer on her right.

"Thank you. Dr. White and I have been waiting for it for some time."

"I told Doug—he's my boyfriend—that I sure would like to see inside the place, but I wouldn't want to be sick . . . or visiting someone who's sick."

Jacob smiled. "We're having the grand opening Saturday night. Why don't you and your young man drop by? I must warn you, though, it's a black-tie affair."

Donna Pierce laughed lightly. "Then I guess that leaves us out. Even if Doug had a tux, I'd have a devil of a time getting him to put it on." Her bright eyes raked her customer appreciatively.

Jacob Surratt was a tall, darkly handsome man in his late thirties, impeccably groomed and dressed in an expensive gray suit. His hair was thick and dark, as were his well-shaped brows; his eyes were a smoky gray, incisive and penetrating. The lean bone structure of his face played up its angles and planes, giving him a brooding, mysterious look that many women seemed to find irresistible.

Long ago he had grown accustomed to the kind of admiring glance he was receiving from the pretty young teller. Such attention neither pleased nor displeased him, for he was by nature very reserved, not given to flirting or idle chatter. Though as a well-known internist he was readily accepted within the upper reaches of Phoenix high society, most of his socialite acquaintances admitted they didn't know him well. Jacob, they said, was just too unknowable.

Donna Pierce finally tore her eyes from her customer and returned to the computer. Jacob propped an elbow on the counter, absently studying the lobby. The bank building was impressively beautiful, full of polished marble, wood and brass, great expanses of glass. Typical of modern downtown Phoenix, it screamed of money.

His eyes moved on—and that was when he spotted the tapestry. He was aware of a quickening of his pulse. An inveterate collector, particularly of southwestern art, Jacob occasionally could "feel" a piece, and he felt this one. Being drawn to a particular painting, a piece of sculpture, anything unique and lovingly handcrafted, was not a new experience for him, but it was always exhilarating, something impossible to explain to anyone who had never known the sensation.

He stood transfixed for a moment, almost mesmerized. Yet the emotion the tapestry inspired was not entirely pleasant. He felt...for want of a better word, "anxious" in a very personal way. Something he had never felt when looking at a piece of art. Frowning, he kept his gaze fastened on the wall.

The weaving was large, possibly eight by ten, and it dramatically dominated one wall of the main lobby. The colors the artist had chosen were earthy southwestern hues; the design a lone saguaro cactus set against towering buff, pink and crimson buttes. A cloud-filled summer sky backlighted the whole. The tapestry seemed to capture the heart, the spirit, the very essence of Arizona. The weaver had to be a native of the state, Jacob decided, someone who felt one with his or her environment.

He stared at the tapestry until the young teller's voice

snapped him out of his reverie. He turned with a start. "I'm sorry, what did you say?"

"I asked how you wanted this. Will twenties be okay?"

"Yes, that'll be fine." While she methodically counted out the bills, Jacob commented, "I was admiring that stunning tapestry over there."

"Yeah, gorgeous, isn't it? I look at it all day every day and never get tired of it. Mr. Fletcher—he's the bank president—commissioned the weaver, then had to wait months for her to finish it. It's supposed to be quite valuable, but I don't know much about that sort of thing. I just know it's nice to look at."

Jacob took the bills, counted them and reached for his wallet. "I'm looking for something exciting and dramatic to hang in the clinic's reception room. I'd been thinking of a painting, but the tapestry is so much more eye-catching. Do you happen to know the artist's name?"

The young woman frowned thoughtfully. "Funny, I can't remember it, but I think she's famous, at least in Arizona. There's a little plaque on the wall, though, and her name's on it."

"Thank you, Ms Pierce."

"Don't mention it. Have a nice day, Dr. Surratt."

"Same to you. And if you and your boyfriend change your minds about the opening, you'll be more than welcome."

Jacob's long-legged stride took him across the lobby to stand in front of the weaving. It was magnificent. The work was meant to be viewed from a distance, but up close he could study the fine detail, the superb craftsmanship of the tight, even weave, the meticulously finished edges. The weaver obviously had been practicing the craft for some time. One didn't learn to do this kind of work in a few months, or even a few years.

He had to have one like it. No, something even grander. With any luck the artist was still active. His eyes traveled to the small brass plaque hanging unobtrusively next to the tapestry.

Designs by Leah Stone
Exclusively Through
The Alexander Trent Gallery
Sedona, Arizona

Once again something stirred inside Jacob, something so fleeting it took no form. Suddenly alert, he stared at the plaque. Did one of those names have meaning for him? Leah Stone? Alexander Trent? He waited for something, anything to take hold of him, but nothing did. Perhaps it was the place. Sedona? As an art lover he had heard of the community, but he'd never been there. At least, not that he knew of. . . .

Jacob gave himself a shake and passed a hand wearily over his eyes. He often wondered if he'd been wise to call a halt to the sessions with his partner. Charles White, the psychiatric half of the Surratt-White team, seemed to think so. "We gave it our best shot, Jacob, and failed, so do your psyche a favor and drop it." Finally, trusting Charles, he had terminated the therapy, convincing himself he was only wasting valuable time—his and Charles's. Yet occasionally the longing persisted, the longing to know. . . .

Jacob reached into his breast pocket for the pen and small note pad he always carried. Jotting down the information off the plaque, he turned to leave the building, but not before pausing to study the tapestry once more.

It called to him, as ridiculous as that was; it held a fascination for him he was powerless to explain. He owned a century-old Navaho rug, one of the most valuable items in his extensive collection, yet it had never moved him the way this weaving did. Why did the piece affect him so profoundly? Why had it aroused this peculiar feeling in the pit of his stomach? Why, on a day when twenty minutes one way or another would totally wreck his schedule, was he wasting precious time gaping at this weaving?

Jacob pushed open the doors and stepped out into the bright morning sunshine. Ms Stone doubtless had many admirers; well, now she had a new one. Artists intrigued him, anyway, since they were as different from scientists as light from dark. Sometimes he sought out one who particularly captured his attention. He knew he wouldn't rest until he'd met Leah Stone.

THAT NAME HAUNTED HIM for the remainder of the day, as names often did. This one, though, was different. He had seen or heard the woman's name somewhere; he just knew it. Later, in the solitude of his own home, he picked up some magazines and rifled through them until he found what he was looking for. There it was in last month's issue of *Art News Magazine*—a four-color advertisement for the Alexander Trent Gallery in Sedona. Superimposed over a shot of the showroom was the announcement that the Trent Gallery was the exclusive representative for Leah Stone. Beneath that a quote appeared from a review in the *San Francisco Chronicle*. "Leah Stone may well be the most gifted and original American weaver currently at work."

Jacob relaxed and closed the magazine. That was where he'd seen the name. He chuckled to himself and rubbed his eyes. He was going to have to stop overreacting to names and places, to almost everything that struck a responsive chord in him. All sorts of people had trouble with names and places, not only those with amnesia.

CHAPTER TWO

LEAH PULLED THE ROCKING CHAIR into the center of the porch, sat down and sipped a glass of ice tea. Late May, and already the weather was very warm, portending another scorcher of an Arizona summer. She hated to see it come, for then the house would have to be closed up and air conditioned most of the time. She much preferred the windows open wide, the earthy outdoor aromas pouring in.

Every afternoon, weather permitting, she sat on the porch and watched for the yellow school bus to come rumbling down the road. She still found it difficult to believe Nina would soon have completed the first grade. In some ways the first six years of her daughter's life had flown by; in others, they had plodded along.

"My God, you take motherhood seriously!" Alex Trent had said once when he stopped by unexpectedly and found her waiting for the bus. Leah chuckled, recalling her friend and mentor's reaction. Yes, she took her parental responsibilities very seriously, and with good reason. She herself had been a product of a one-parent home, but although she had been motherless since the age of five, she hadn't felt in the least deprived. Whit Haskell, her father, had always given her one priceless commodity—his time. She was determined that Nina would someday say the same about her.

Leah's gaze swept her surroundings. The view in all directions was of red rock spilling into evergreen hillsides. There was nothing subtle about the landscape; it was explosive, magnificent, and had served as a background for countless television commercials and Hollywood films. Often called "Zane Grey Land" because the famous author had lived there while writing *Call of the Canyon*, it was an area of sharp contrasts and incredible beauty.

"Where do you find your inspiration?" people often asked, and Leah always answered, "On my front porch." Something of the Red Rock Country found its way into most "Designs by Leah Stone," and the rug she had just completed, commissioned by a group of Michigan tourists last winter, was no exception. Small wonder so many professional artists had chosen to live in Sedona. The entire countryside—streams winding beneath cottonwoods, red-sandstone buttes thrusting out of the earth, the smell of cedar and ponderosa permeating the air—was a natural work of art.

She never tired of it. Her quaint studio-home, which had once been a one-room frontier schoolhouse, was tucked way into the cedars, blending in with the landscape. The high-pitched roof afforded Nina the luxury of a loft bedroom to call her own. Otherwise, the house consisted of one huge room, a bathroom and a small kitchen alcove beneath the loft. In another more-conventional community, Leah's house might have been an incongruous sight, but in Sedona, where million-dollar mansions coexisted with rustic cabins and vacation cottages, it fit in just right.

Leah thought she would have hated a conventional house with a manicured lawn and a busy paved street in front. She much preferred the quiet country lane that was the only access to her front gate. "That is a miserable chassis-rattling excuse for a road, Leah," Alex often complained. "I don't know how you stand living out here."

Her inevitable reply was, "It suits me."

Leah had been born nearby in the Verde Valley, raised by her veterinarian father, so she was a country person at heart. As a child she had often accompanied her father as he made his rounds of the farms and ranches. Her earliest ambition had been to be a "horse doctor," just like him.

In her midteens, however, the artistic side of her nature burst into full flower. At an arts-and-crafts fair she watched a Navaho woman working at a primitive loom. Fascinated, she stood there for over an hour simply watching the weaver, unable to understand the fascination but knowing it existed. That very week she purchased a small hand loom and produced a set of place mats. From that time on Leah was hooked; she wanted to weave.

When she entered college at eighteen, it was to major in textile design and weaving, not veterinary medicine. After college she continued to live with Whit in the old family home, serving as her father's receptionist, answering the phone, scheduling appointments. But mostly she practiced and perfected her craft, weaving to her heart's content.

Her life had followed this orderly, peaceful course until Jim had come along.

Leah's thoughts braked, as they always did when she dropped her guard and allowed his name to enter them. The old emptying sadness washed over her. So much time had passed, but still the hurt remained. To be able to love only once was a character flaw, she thought. A heart should have room for more than three people— Whit, Nina. . .and Jim.

Always Jim. She could go for several days without thinking about him, but eventually something would trigger the memories. Now she supposed it was the time of year, the weather. You could smell summer in the air, and it had been a summer night eight years ago when she had first seen him. Closing her eyes, she expelled a shaky breath. Unbidden images filled her mind. Eight years ago might have been yesterday.

"You can't live in the past, Leah," Alex told her over and over again. Dear Alex, the gallery owner who had given her just the push she had needed five years earlier when her professional career was beginning. In the interim she had grown so fond of him, and he quite plainly adored her. She knew their mentor-protégée relationship would quickly change to something more intimate if Alex could have his way, but for Leah such a change was unthinkable. Too much of her was tied up in love and memories of the man she had married.

Once, when Alex had been totally impatient with her, frustrated by his inability to pierce her shell, he had shouted at her. "What is the matter with you, Leah? I find it impossible to believe you can remain so devoted to a man who left you just before your child was born!"

The strained, icy silence following that exchange had alarmed Alex; such an incident hadn't been repeated. They had reached a tacit agreement: her marriage was never to be mentioned. Leah discussed Jim with no one but Whit, because her father had been there and understood. He was the only person on earth, save Leah herself, who knew what had actually happened.

Enough of this, her mind scolded. *Stop thinking about it. Stop longing for what can't be.*

At that moment she welcomed the telephone's shrill ring; normally the sound intruded on both work and solitude. Getting to her feet, she hurried into the house.

"Hello."

"Leah, I want you to get over here right away." Alex sounded elated, the way he did whenever negotiations with a wealthy buyer had gone well, or whenever he stumbled onto a particularly fine acquisition.

"What's up?"

"I'll tell you about it when you get here."

"Alex, you know I like to be home when Nina arrives."

"This is important! Call your neighbor and have her intercept Nina. A very important client is on his way here from Phoenix, and he's anxious to meet you. There's a tremendous commission in the offing."

"Can't it wait an hour or so?"

"No, it can't. The client is a busy physician, but he's taking time from his schedule to come up here for the express purpose of meeting Leah Stone. He saw the tapestry in the Phoenix bank and wants you to do something for him. I think you're going to be very excited. Please...."

As always Leah experienced a twinge of guilt over balking at doing something he wanted her to do. Alex was so generous with her, so enthusiastic about her career. It wouldn't hurt to expend more energy on being generous and enthusiastic in return, even when she didn't much feel that way.

She glanced down at her working clothes—jeans, T-shirt and sneakers. It wouldn't do to meet an important client dressed like that. "Give me a few minutes to change, then I'll be there."

"Thanks, Leah. We'll be waiting."

First Leah called Sandra Martin, a neighbor whose daughter, Ann, would be on the bus with Nina. Sandra was also a single parent, also an artist, a sculptor. The two women had established a satisfying friendship, each knowing the other could be counted on for last-minute baby-sitting. Sandra had been married to a domineering, stultifying businessman known to Leah only as "that bastard," and her friend's unhappy memories of her marriage had given her a bitingly humorous view of love and life. Leah had come to depend on Sandra's cynical observations and colorful language for comic relief.

Once assured that Sandra would meet the bus and take Nina to her house, Leah quickly changed into a pair of off-white slacks and a softly tailored peach blouse, then slipped on a pair of low-heeled pumps—expensive, understated clothes that were typical of the unaffected Leah. Giving her appearance a cursory glance in the mirror, she picked up her handbag, leaving the house.

A short time later she strode across the sun-dappled, tile-paved courtyard of Tlaquepaque, the unique arts-and-crafts village in Sedona, designed in a Mexican style. Her heels tapped sharply on the tiles as she passed a fountain surrounded by potted marigolds.

Leah loved Tlaquepaque, as anyone involved in the arts would. There was no hustle and bustle; no one hurried. The charming complex of galleries, shops, archways, stairs and balconies invited strolling, browsing, lounging and sitting. This afternoon, however, she had no time for such leisurely pursuits. She wanted only to get this business over and done with so she could go home. Climbing a narrow handcrafted stairway, she ducked into the serene elegance of the Alexander Trent Gallery.

The first thing that always caught her eye when she entered Alex's showroom was *Gemini*, her maiden effort as a professional weaver. It had captured Best of Show at a fair five years earlier, but more importantly, it had captured the attention of Alexander Trent, one of the judges. When he had purchased it, naturally Leah had sought him out, introduced herself and told him about other work she had done. That simple gesture had spawned an association that had been enormously profitable for them both.

Alex often declared he would never sell *Gemini*, not in a million years. Leah smiled wryly. He would when the price was right.

A well-dressed, middle-aged woman was seated at the Queen Anne reception desk. Beth Thompson, Alex's secretary, glanced up and smiled warmly. "Good afternoon, Leah. I believe he's waiting for you."

"Thanks, Beth." Leah walked through the main part of the gallery to a door at the end of a short hallway. It was open, so she entered Alex's private domain.

"Well, here I am," she announced brightly. "As ordered."

Alex was standing on the balcony, hands clasped behind him, staring down at the courtyard below. He turned and smiled, then advanced toward her. Taking her gently by the shoulders, he bent his head and kissed her lightly on the lips. "Thanks for coming, Leah."

Leah glanced around. "Hasn't the doctor arrived yet?"

"Yes, but he had to call his clinic, so he's using the other office. Sit down and let me get you something to drink. I'm sure Dr. Surratt will be with us in a minute."

"Just ice water, Alex, please." She took a seat in a comfortable armchair facing a glass-topped desk, while Alex walked to a wet bar concealed behind louvered doors. "Surratt?" she asked. "The name sounds familiar."

"The Surratt-White Clinic. I'm sure you've heard of it."

"Ah, that Surratt. Of course I've heard of it." She was impressed. In the Southwest, Surratt-White was as well-known as the Mayo Clinic. This doctor who had taken a fancy to her work must be a VIP of the first order.

She watched as Alex took ice cubes out of a small refrigerator and plopped them into a glass. He wasn't a tall man, something under six feet, but he was trim and straight and gave the impression of greater height. His wheat-colored hair now showed definite traces of silver. At forty-three, he was fifteen years Leah's senior, urbane and utterly charming, a man of flawless good taste. A quick glance around his office, at the quiet elegance of the furnishings and objets d'art he'd chosen, attested to that. "Sophisticated" was a word often associated with him. In ten more years, Leah supposed, "distinguished" would be added.

Leah knew how much she owed Alex. She'd been blessed with talent and expertise in the technical aspects of weaving, vaguely aware of her work's worth, yet totally ignorant of the business side of the art world. By the time she met Alex, Leah had begun to realize she was going to need someone knowledgeable to guide her career if she intended supporting herself and Nina. She had introduced herself to him with high hopes and plenty of doubts. That he had placed considerable monetary value on *Gemini* had thrilled her. That he had wanted an exclusive association with her had been almost too good to be true, and she had seized the opportunity without hesitation. Never for an instant had she regretted that move. She could trace the beginning of her career's rise to the day she had approached Alex.

"Here you are, dear." Alex handed the glass to her before taking a seat behind the desk.

"I suppose you know I'm about to pop with curiosity," she told him, smiling over the rim of the glass.

Alex returned her smile with one of immense satisfaction. Leah knew that smile. It meant he had just struck an advantageous bargain. For all his polish and sophistication, for all his love of art for art's sake and his professed disdain for commercialism, there was some of the horse trader in Alex.

"As I told you," he began, "Dr. Surratt has seen the tapestry in the bank, and he called to ask if I had anything else you'd done. I explained you rarely have time for speculative work anymore, because commissions keep you so busy." Alex's smile broadened. "The doctor then informed me he would pay any price for an exclusive Leah Stone design."

"Oh? I'll bet your ears really perked up at that," she said with a grin. "Does he want something for his home?"

"Eventually the tapestry he wants you to do will become part of his private collection, but for now he wants it for his clinic. Surratt-White is moving into new ultramodern quarters, and he wants something for the main reception room. Fifteen by twenty."

Leah frowned. "Fifteen by twenty? I've never attempted such a large piece, Alex, you know that. I don't even know if it's possible on a ten-foot loom."

"I'm sure you'll be able to do it," Alex said confidently. "Dr. Surratt wants something dramatic, since the physical plant itself is so dramatic. He brought two photographs with him...." He reached for a manila envelope, which he handed across the desk to Leah. "I want you to have a look at them. You have to be impressed."

She opened the envelope, withdrawing the photographs. The first was an exterior shot of the clinic; it was a space-age architectural marvel, a sleekly modern glass-and-steel structure. Beautiful, she supposed, if that type of architecture appealed; her tastes ran more to renovated schoolhouses. The second photograph was of the reception room, and it was also impressive. The vaulted ceiling rose two stories high, partly supported by one intensely dramatic—and stark—stone wall.

"According to Dr. Surratt, the wall on your left is where the tapestry will hang," Alex said. "As you can see, anything smaller than fifteen by twenty would be lost."

Leah nodded. Moreover, she thought, the tapestry would be the room's focal point, the first thing anyone entering the clinic would see. For a moment she dismissed the complexities of weaving such a large piece and visualized the design. Not clearly, of course, since she didn't know what the doctor had in mind, but it would have to be a bold design done in bold colors. Nothing subtle, nothing pictorial. The excitement that always accompanied a new effort began to bubble inside her.

"Dr. Surratt mentioned that the price is inconsequential, since he fully expects the tapestry to increase in value considerably. He's right, it will. I explained how long it would take you to complete such an ambitious work, and he seemed perfectly willing to wait as long as necessary. An agreeable man, I must say. Leah, this is exciting! Do you have any idea how many people must troop through that clinic in any given week? Far more than frequent galleries and museums, I assure you."

Alex's enthusiasm was met with silence. He waited a moment, but when Leah said nothing he demanded, "Well?"

"I'm thinking. I wonder... Perhaps it could be done piecemeal, then the pieces joined together. Of course, it mustn't look that way, but I learned a lot from repairing torn rugs and tapestries. Eventually I learned to make repairs not even experts could distinguish from the original weave. Why couldn't I sew together pieces of my own weavings?"

"Working out the technicalities never worried me for an instant. I knew you could do it." Alex glanced toward the open door. "I wonder what's keeping Dr. Surratt."

"Don't you ever watch those doctor shows on television? They're always making urgent phone calls or receiving urgent phone calls. I don't see how they ever get any doctoring done."

Alex faced her. "I might as well warn you about something, Leah. Dr. Surratt has invited us to the clinic's black-tie opening in Phoenix Saturday night. Why don't you get your finery out of mothballs, and we'll make an occasion of it."

Leah slipped the photographs back into the envelope and groaned. "Oh, Alex, you know how I detest that sort of thing!"

"I know, and you know I ordinarily accede to your wishes and shield you from such affairs, but this man is an admirer of yours, obviously one who knows a thing or two about quality and art. Who knows how many dealings I might have with him in the future? I'm also a businessman, fortunately for you. Surely you can forsake your hermitlike existence for one weekend to do a favor for me and give the doctor a thrill. He's paying plenty for the honor."

"I'd really rather not. Make excuses for me if he mentions it. Nina—"

Alex waved an impatient hand. "You can't plead parental responsibility with me, darling. I know Nina can spend the weekend with your father. Loves to, in fact. Do you have any idea how often you use the child as an excuse for not going places?"

"I never use my daughter," Leah protested. "I simply would rather be at home with Nina than at one of those silly, shallow cocktail parties you're so fond of."

"I'm no more fond of them than you are, but they're a necessary part of doing business. I've acquired more clients at those 'silly, shallow' parties than I ever have sitting here in this gallery."

"You're a businessman, of course, but I prefer to let my work speak for me."

"Don't be stuffy, Leah. Clients who pay through the nose for a work of art enjoy meeting the artist."

"I'm terrible at those parties, anyway," she persisted stubbornly. "I always find myself lurking in corners, trying to fade into the woodwork."

"Actually, you're delightful in social situations. People take to you even if you don't take to them. I suspect if you'd relax you might even enjoy some of those 'silly' parties. Look, I'm going to insist you go this time. You really should see the room. A photograph only shows so much. This is an important commission, the most important of your career. For once I took the liberty of accepting the invitation for both of us, so when the doctor mentions it, please be gracious. He's making reservations for us at the Biltmore. Why don't we drop Nina off at your father's place early Saturday morning and get down to Phoenix in time to enjoy some of that luxury?"

Leah shrugged resignedly. Alex was difficult to deny. In fairness to him, she admitted he normally bent over backward to get her out of such situations. The fact that he hadn't this time could only mean the opening was important to him. "Oh, all right," she said with a sigh. "I'll tell him how delighted I am to be invited. The Biltmore, hmm? The doctor goes first-class."

"Oh, he's a first-class type, all right, no question about that. Very nice and . . . well, 'refined' is the word, I suppose. I hope you'll like him."

She wouldn't get to know the doctor well enough to like or dislike him, Leah was sure. She rarely socialized with the wealthy clients who might have welcomed her into their social circles. She got just close enough to ascertain their wishes and tastes, then retreated to her studio and let Alex handle the rest. "If I was to lead a wildly exciting social life," she had once asked him seriously, "when would I weave?"

"You simply need something else," he had replied just as seriously. "Your life needs other dimensions. I do believe you'd live like a hermit if I allowed it."

Usually Leah dismissed such remarks with "You don't understand." He didn't, not really. Alex probably wouldn't have recognized the Leah Stone of earlier times, a carefree, lighthearted young woman who had lived only for the day. Time and loss had changed her, as they change everyone.

Yet the changes, as far as she was concerned, weren't particularly undesirable. Was there something basically wrong with being a loner who preferred a solitary hillside to parties and people? Apparently Alex, who thrived on socializing, thought so. He could become so exasperated with her. He accused her of wearing melancholy like a cloak, of living on memories.

Leah realized she tended to be quiet and thoughtful, less than outgoing, but to define that as melancholy was going a bit far. And if she clung to memories. . . well, they were her memories, and she would have been lost without them.

Alex got to his feet. "Come over here, Leah. While we're waiting for Dr. Surratt, I'd like you to see a collection of porcelain miniatures I've just acquired."

Leah stepped over to a display table behind Alex's desk. The two bent over the miniatures, so they didn't see Jacob walk quietly into the room. He opened his mouth to speak, then quickly shut it when he saw the woman standing beside Alexander Trent. She had one hand propped on the display table, the other on her hip. Her back was to him so that he couldn't see her face, but the view from behind was of a lithe body that would feel good in a man's hands. She walked a few steps down the length of the table and picked up something. The movement of her hips beneath the fabric of her slacks elicited a sharp sensation in Jacob, reminding him that his responses were still in good working order.

Could that possibly be Leah Stone? Who else would it be? Ridiculously, he was content to simply stand there and watch her for a moment. Her erect carriage, her smooth arms, her glossy hair, those shapely hips, all came under his scrutiny. She made a little half turn, and the profile of a firm breast came into view. Trent said something to her just then, and she laughed—a lovely, lilting laugh that brought a smile to Jacob's face. Anticipation welled up inside him. He could hardy wait to get a good look at her.

Leah was intently studying one of the exquisite miniatures when she got the distinct feeling she was being watched. Carefully she set down the porcelain and turned. Alex turned, as well.

"Ah, doctor, there you are. Leah and I were just discussing the tapestry. She's very excited about it."

"Wonderful. I'm sorry it took so long, but there was a minor emergency at the clinic—monetary not medical." Jacob settled his gaze on Leah Stone. Her face intrigued him; he had met many women who were more beautiful, but this was a face he would remember forever. Perhaps it was her eyes—dark, haunting, compelling eyes that had a slight downward slant. They riveted him in place. That the person whose artistry he admired so much should turn out to be such an arresting woman was unbelievable. He had been expecting someone much older. How old could Leah Stone be? Less than thirty, he'd wager.

Leah froze as she watched the tall, beautifully dressed man advancing on her, hand outstretched. She went absolutely cold for an instant, then hot, and everything inside her coiled into a tight, painful knot.

"I'm Jacob Surratt, Ms Stone, and I can't tell you how delighted I am to meet you."

That voice! A knifelike pain shot through her. The past couldn't resurrect itself without warning, she thought senselessly. For a moment the room spun in a sickening revolution. How often she had imagined this very moment, but now that it was upon her, she felt as though she was hallucinating. This couldn't actually be happening!

Though everything inside her churned with turmoil, though her heart thudded against her ribs, Leah's only outward show of emotion was a sudden draining of color, a rigidity to her stance. Her hands clenched at her sides, but to the two men in the room she looked ill rather than agitated. Feeling so much, she could say nothing. In fact, at that moment she couldn't have spoken a word if her life had depended on it.

Jim.

CHAPTER THREE

WHEN SHE DIDN'T IMMEDIATELY ACKNOWLEDGE Dr. Surratt's greeting, Alex looked at her quizzically. "Leah? Leah, is something the matter?"

Jacob's brows knitted. The woman looked ghastly. Instantly the physician in him took over; he quickly closed the space between them. "Ms Stone, are you ill?" he asked with concern.

Leah thought she was choking. "No, I—"

Alex had moved closer to her. "Leah? What's the matter?"

Dazed, disoriented, she gave a little shake of her head. "I...don't know...."

"Please, Ms Stone, sit down," Jacob said quietly. "You're very pale." Taking her gently by the arm, he led her to the armchair she'd been sitting in earlier. Too weak to protest, Leah sank into it, only dimly aware of the two men hovering solicitously over her. She pressed the palm of one hand against her stomach, and she swallowed rapidly, fighting down nausea.

"Let me get you a glass of water, Leah," Alex murmured, frowning. She had been fine a minute earlier. He knew Leah better than he'd ever known anyone, and he suspected she wasn't ill. Sensing something very complicated was going on in her head, he shifted his worried gaze to Dr. Surratt, and his frown deepened.

Jacob rubbed her hands between his. "You're trembling. Do you feel light-headed? Have you eaten to-day?''

Leah nodded distractedly, avoiding eye contact with him. Her mouth was bone-dry. She would have welcomed that drink of water, but she feared she'd never be able to swallow it. She was ashamed of herself for losing control, but she had reacted so suddenly that there hadn't been time for thought.

Don't be ridiculous, Leah, it isn't him! How many times in the past six years have you seen someone you thought was Jim? Dozens! Pull yourself together, take a good look at him, and you'll see he isn't Jim!

Alex didn't bother with the water. He stood at the desk, staring at Leah's bent head, and a ridiculous sense of forboding swept over him. Something was very wrong. She had taken one look at Jacob Surratt and fallen apart. What the devil was this all about?

Jacob knelt in front of Leah, and from somewhere she mustered the courage to look at him again. He was so much thinner than Jim and looked so much older. Compared to her Jim, this man was gaunt.

But, after all, six years had passed. The eyes were the same, only sadder; the mouth was the same, only harder. Jim had smiled all the time. This man looked as though he'd never known a mirthful moment in his life. The thick dark hair she had loved to feel between her fingers was now threaded with strands of gray at the temples.

Everything was the same, only different. The differences, however, were superficial, the products of the passage of time and a changed life-style. Leah's breath escaped in short, agitated puffs. This was one time she wished she was prone to fainting. If she could simply collapse, she'd come to in a few minutes and discover this all had been nothing but a wild, cruel flight of imagination.

But he was Jim, all right. The memory of his face was emblazoned on her brain. And he didn't know her at all. Dear God, to have been spared this.

Once her father had asked, "How do you think you would react if you were suddenly to come face-to-face with him, Leah? If he's from around here, you might. You'd be a stranger to him, you know."

She had answered, "I don't know, dad, honestly I don't. I guess I'd fall to pieces."

Which was precisely what had happened. She was in a million pieces.

"Ms Stone, are you feeling better now?"

That was definitely Jim's voice. Sometimes it seemed she remembered his voice most of all. By an act of will, Leah forced herself into some semblance of calm. "I...yes, I think so," she said too softly. "I'm... sorry."

Relieved, Jacob expelled his breath. "Well, you certainly gave me a scare. For a moment there I thought you were going to faint. I don't normally prompt such a dramatic reaction in beautiful women." No one chuckled. The attempt at levity had been feeble, and Jacob regretted it. Leah Stone was obviously in distress. "Do you feel nauseated?"

"N-no." Which wasn't entirely the truth, but Leah knew her upset stomach had no physical basis.

"Then the doctor in me insists on asking if you have a chronic medical condition. Heart trouble? High blood pressure?"

Leah stared at her hands and shook her head. "No, no."

"What about that water, Mr. Trent?"

Alex tugged thoughtfully on his chin. "I don't think Leah needs a drink of water. How about a shot of brandy?"

Jacob was emphatic. "No, I don't think brandy would be such a good idea right now."

"No, I don't want anything, thank you," Leah muttered. "I'm all right." Jacob Surratt was so close she could feel the heat emanating from his body. He wore a tangy, woodsy, masculine fragrance very different from the scent Jim had always liked, and his clothes were expensive, possibly tailor-made. He made some kind of motion with his hand, and a flash of gold from his wrist caught her eye. He still had that watch. . . .

Tightly she clasped her hands in her lap to keep herself from reaching for him. It wasn't fair! To be so near to him and unable to touch him wasn't fair at all.

Jacob stood up. "Mr. Trent, do you have a place where Ms Stone could lie down for a few minutes?"

Leah got to her feet and discovered she was almost in Jacob's arms. Flustered, she moved away. She needed time, time to think. She was a wreck. "No, I don't want to lie down. If you'll just excuse me, I . . . I think I want to go home. It's late. My daughter—"

"Leah, Dr. Surratt has driven all the way up here to discuss the tapestry with you," Alex reminded her firmly.

"I'm sorry, I . . . can't. Not today."

"Leah, please. . . ."

"No, Alex," she snapped, more harshly than she intended. "Not today."

Jacob was surprised to realize he didn't want her to leave. He wanted to get to know her better. Never had he been instantly attracted to a woman—frankly he had suspected such an attraction was impossible. Yet he had responded to her immediately. Combined with that unforgettable face and those mesmerizing eyes was an air of fragility that made him want to comfort her. He, who normally held others at arm's length, felt a tenderness for her that made no sense. The sensation was peculiar but not unpleasant.

It had been so long since he'd felt much of anything, he reflected ruefully. Concern for the patients who came to him for help, of course. And a certain proprietary pride in his clinic. Otherwise, a wearying sort of sadness he had spent six years trying to shake. It felt good to want to be near this woman, to talk to her, to want to find out what she thought about...everything.

Then something occurred to Jacob. Trent displayed a decidedly possessive attitude toward her, and his concern right now was evident. Did they have some sort of special relationship, or was it based purely on business? And Leah Stone had a daughter. She was married...or had been married, maybe. One never knew anymore.

God, she excited him in ways he didn't completely understand. He was disappointed because she wasn't feeling well, but if they didn't discuss the commission today, he would have a perfect excuse for seeing her again, provided there was no husband in the picture.

"Ms Stone, I can see you aren't feeling well, so of course we'll arrange to discuss it some other time," he said quietly.

"Doctor, I can't tell you how sorry I am—" Alex began.

"Think nothing of it, Mr. Trent. It can't be helped."

Leah's head was pounding. There was no way on earth she could do that tapestry, and Alex was going to have a fit. Just how she intended explaining all this to him was the least of her problems at the moment. She couldn't look at her friend and wouldn't look at Jim again, so she simply stammered a goodbye, made for the door and left the gallery as quickly as possible. It wasn't until she was in her car and driving away from Tlaquepaque that she allowed the first tears to fall.

ALEX PULLED TO A STOP in front of Leah's house. Pushing open the front gate, he hurried up the path and mounted the porch steps. He rapped loudly on the door, then entered without waiting for her summons. Quickly his eyes surveyed the place. No noise, no activity. Only Leah huddled on the sofa. "Where's Nina?" he asked abruptly.

"Sandra Martin invited her to stay for dinner. Or rather, I asked her to invite Nina to stay for dinner." Thank God for Sandra. No questions, just a "Sure, Leah. Give me a call when you want her home."

Leah wasn't the least bit surprised to see Alex. She had known he would be along the moment he could get free. Less than half an hour had elapsed since she'd fled the gallery.

Alex crossed the room and faced her implacably. "Dr. Surratt stayed awhile after you left, or I would have been here sooner. I think I convinced him you simply had been working long hours and had probably skipped lunch. Frankly, I don't think your health was uppermost in the good doctor's mind. Mostly he quizzed me about your private life. All right, Leah, out with it. What's going on?"

"Leave me alone, Alex, please," she said wearily.

"You've been crying."

"Yes."

"Good God, what's all this about? You took one look at that man and.... What is there about Jacob Surratt that made you go to pieces?"

"I want to be left alone!"

"No dice. Not until you tell me what that man

means to you. I know you like the back of my hand, Leah, and I've never seen you so rattled. Who is he?''

Leah sighed, closed her eyes and leaned her head on the back of the sofa. She had known all along that when Alex started quizzing her, she would tell him the truth. He would have sensed in an instant whether she was lying. "He's my husband," she said numbly.

Alex frowned and stared at her a moment. He had expected anything but that. "That's preposterous!" he finally said. "That man didn't know you from Eve."

"I realize that."

"You realize that? That's it?"

"Jacob Surratt is the man I knew as Jim Stone, the man I married, Nina's father. You asked me, and I told you."

Shaken to the core, Alex again simply stared at her. His sense of foreboding returned, stronger than ever. He turned on his heel and paced, hands clasped behind his back. "If Jacob Surratt is your husband, why didn't he recognize you?"

"The answer is simple. Jim Stone was an amnesiac. I married a man who knew nothing about his past. I was always aware that his memory might come back, and if it did he probably wouldn't remember me. But I loved him, and I married him, anyway."

Alex digested this. "Why haven't you ever told me before? I thought your husband was a creep who'd deserted you. I never could understand why you clung so tenaciously to his memory, why you never filed for divorce."

She stared at him blankly. "Why would I file for divorce?"

"Dammit, you might want to remarry!"

"Never. In another year he'd be declared legally dead, anyway, so what difference would it make? Alex, I don't like talking about this!"

"Well, you're going to have to talk about it. I want the whole story, and I'm not leaving until I get it."

And he wouldn't, Leah knew. Lifelessly her shoulders rose and fell. "All right. I guess I owe you that much. I put on some water to boil a while ago. Make us some coffee, will you? There's instant in the—"

"I know where it is." Alex shrugged out of his suit jacket and threw it across a nearby chair. Loosening his tie, he made for the kitchen alcove tucked into one corner of the house. Within a few minutes he was back carrying two cups. He set them on the coffee table, then took a seat beside Leah on the sofa and waited until she was ready to talk.

When she began, it was in a tired, emotionless voice. "It was summer, eight years ago. I was twenty.... I had just graduated from college and was living with dad. One night we were sitting on the porch after dinner, when a pickup truck stopped in front of our house. A young man got out of the passenger side, and the truck moved on. The man had thumbed a ride, he told us. He needed a job and had heard dad was looking for someone he could train to be a veterinarian's assistant. For some reason he thought he would like that kind of work."

Leah paused to take a sip of coffee. "He was handsome, clean-cut and personable, and he said his name was Jim Stone. I remember wondering what such a prosperous-looking man was doing combing the countryside for work, but dad was immediately impressed with him and asked him to sit down and have coffee with us. Then Jim Stone told us more about himself.

"He wanted us to know he was a victim of amnesia. Several weeks earlier he'd woken up in a small valley hospital unable to recall his name or what he was doing in the Verde Valley—or in Arizona, for that matter. Two policemen were at the hospital with him, and they filled in a few details.''

Leah sighed, struggling with her memories. Struggling, too, with her feelings for Alex. This was going to hurt him.

Alex watched her carefully; it was on the tip of his tongue to tell her to forget about the rest of her story. Obviously she was finding the recollection painful. But he was too interested, unwillingly fascinated. Silently he waited for her to continue.

''During a late-night stop at a grocery-gas station on a desolate stretch of highway, Jim had been struck on the head from behind by a person or persons unknown; his car had been stolen, too. The store owner ran outside when he heard the screech of tires in the driveway— he thought someone was leaving without paying for gas—but all he saw was Jim lying facedown near one of the pumps. He didn't witness the crime nor see the car.

''The victim had no money or identification on him; apparently everything had been in the car. He'd been wearing an expensive watch with the initials 'JS' engraved on the band, thus the name Jim Stone, the first thing that had come to mind. His clothes were casual but expensive. He remembered nothing, knew nothing of his past. He'd been doing temporary odd jobs around the valley, but he really needed permanent employment. For one thing, he had a hospital bill to pay. He wanted to know if dad would take a chance on him.''

''And Whit did?''

Leah nodded. ''Dad just took a liking to Jim for some reason. I had reservations at first. We knew so little about him. I reminded dad that the man could be an ax murderer for all we knew, but dad liked him, so he put him to work.

"Jim turned out to be almost too good to be true. He seemed to have an instinct for working with animals. He got along with their owners, too, which wasn't always easy. He didn't mind the odd hours and wasn't the least bit squeamish about even the nastiest medical task. Dad gave him a room in the back of the big house, and in a few weeks it seemed he had been with us for years."

"And in all that time he hadn't remembered anything?"

"No, nothing. At first we were certain his memory would return, but weeks passed, then months, and nothing happened. The police didn't have much to go on, since they didn't know what kind of car to look for. We hoped the watch might be a lead, but though it was expensive it was also a brand name sold in many jewelry stores throughout the country. Nothing turned up in Arizona at any rate, so where did we go from there? Jim could have bought the watch years before, almost anywhere in the world. About all we could do was monitor the missing-persons bulletins and hope something turned up. Nothing did, though, and Jim finally admitted he'd lost his enthusiasm for the search. He was happy and content. Besides...." Leah faltered.

"Besides," Alex finished sagely, "he'd fallen in love."

Her lips trembled. "Yes," she said quietly. "And so had I."

It was impossible for Leah to tell Alex about falling in love with Jim. That was the most private, intimate part of her life. In retrospect, the attraction seemed to have been immediate, although in the beginning they had only been good friends. He had simply been the nice young man who worked for her father, and she had sympathized with his emotional stress, with his need to know about his past. Sometimes he had reminded her of a rewarped loom or a blank canvas, waiting for a loving hand to give it shape, form, meaning.

Together she and Jim often speculated on what kind of life he'd led before the accident. He hadn't been a laborer; she could tell that much by his hands. He must have made a good living, though, judging from the watch and his clothes. His manners were gracious, almost courtly, and his speech was educated. He hadn't grown up on the streets, that was for sure. Since he didn't know how old he was, they settled on a vague thirty.

Jim was such a gentle and sensitive man. He admired her work; in the evenings he was content to sit silently and watch her weave. They often took long walks together, and she taught him to ride a horse. A country vet, she laughingly told him, needed to know how to ride a horse, because sometimes that was the only way to get to the patients.

The first time Jim kissed her, they were riding along the riverbank. She felt as though she'd never been kissed before, and in that instant she knew she wanted to stay with him forever; there wasn't any doubt in her mind. As their lovemaking progressed, he opened up a brand-new world of sensuality to her. . . .

Leah felt a fresh supply of tears welling up then. She sat mutely for a few minutes, staggered by the memory of all she had lost. Presently Alex touched her gently on the arm, and her eyes flew to him; she had completely forgotten he was there. "Oh, I'm sorry."

"That's all right, Leah. No more."

"No, I want to tell you everything." Collecting herself, she went on. "By the time Jim had been with us six months, we were in love and talking about marriage. We discussed it with dad, and the three of us agreed it was risky. After all, Jim's memory could return at any moment. What if there had been a wife and family in his former life? Jim argued that someone would have been looking for him in that case. We'd stayed in close touch with the police, and no one fitting his description had been reported missing. Jim's theory was, he'd been moving from one town to another, had broken all ties in the old place and not yet made any in the new. It was as good a theory as any, I suppose, and I was ready to accept almost anything.

"Then dad came up with another problem. He had discussed Jim's condition with a physician friend and had learned something about amnesia. Jim was going through what was called a 'fugue state.' So that if his memory did return, it was entirely possible he wouldn't remember anything that happened during the fugue period. Highly likely, in fact. Dad was worried about where that would leave me."

"Weren't you?" Alex asked sensibly.

Leah shook her head. "I was young and in love, and Jim was so sure nothing could happen to keep him from me. Anyway, in the end love won out...and Jim and I were married. By late summer I was pregnant. We decided we wanted a place of our own, and that's when we found this abandoned schoolhouse. It was farther from dad's house and Jim's work than we had originally intended, but we fell in love with it and were determined to have it renovated before the baby came....

"I've never been as happy as I was then. I was wildly in love with my husband and could hardly wait to become a mother. My work was going well. About that time I started *Gemini*."

Again she faltered, and Alex grew tense. He sensed she was coming to the conclusion of her incredible story. Her eyes were distant and vacant. Deliberately she picked up the coffee cup, took a sip, grimaced and set it down again. Taking a deep breath, she began to speak in a voice that, to Alex's ears, didn't sound quite like Leah's.

"A month before Nina was born, the house was almost finished, but we needed a long list of items we couldn't find in the valley. Traveling had become an ordeal for me, so Jim decided to take a bus to Flagstaff for one last buying trip. He planned to be gone a day and a night. He was carrying three hundred dollars in cash and a small suitcase. I stood at the bus depot, waving goodbye, so upset because it was our first separation. And...that was the last time I saw him until this afternoon."

Leah's body sagged. The silence that descended was like a third presence in the room. Alex, tight-lipped, exhaled on a ragged sigh. Considering the story he'd just heard, he thought Leah had handled her confrontation with Jacob Surratt rather well. What a jolt it must have been! He was surprised she hadn't dissolved into hysterics.

No, that wasn't true. Alex couldn't imagine Leah in hysterics, ever. He turned to her, wishing he could take her in his arms, knowing it would be the worst thing he could do. She seemed bereft, beyond his reach. "Surely you tried to find him."

"Oh, of course," she said sadly. "I was frantic when he didn't come back. Dad and I met every bus from Flagstaff for days, which was ridiculous, but we had to do something. I kept telling myself he'd simply been delayed, but that was also ridiculous. He would have called. We telephoned the motel where he'd made reservations and was told he'd never shown up. So dad and I drove to the bus station in Flagstaff and discovered his suitcase hadn't been claimed. His wallet was inside with the brand-new driver's license I had finally nagged him into getting. He hated carrying a wallet, so he kept his cash in a money clip, which was probably the reason there had been no identification on him when his car had been stolen."

Leah's voice broke. She flicked at a tear with a forefinger. "I had to face it—Jim's memory had somehow returned, and he'd gone back to his former life, having forgotten me entirely. Dad and I checked with the police for months afterward, but I never really held out too much hope. I knew what had happened."

"Didn't you circulate a photograph of him to the newspapers?"

"I didn't have a photograph, only a couple of not very good snapshots taken at a Fourth of July picnic. And, too, we didn't know what kind of life he'd gone back to. If he had a wife and family, broadcasting his face all over the place might have been a terrible embarrassment for him. Think of the dilemma—two families. Jim wouldn't have even known me. Dad and I discussed it and decided against it."

"What . . . did you do then?" Alex asked quietly.

"I stayed with dad until after Nina was born. He was so worried about me, and I wasn't in the mood or condition to live alone. When I felt up to it, I finished this house and moved into it. Nina was four months old. Dad thought I ought to get rid of it entirely, but I wouldn't hear of it. Nina and this house were all I had left of Jim. Eventually I finished *Gemini*, entered it in that fair, and . . . well, the rest you know."

"Ah, Leah...." Alex sighed, shaking his head. "Are you absolutely sure Surratt is your husband? A lot of time has passed, and the mind can play tricks."

"Yes, I'm sure. I remembered everything—the shape of his eyebrows, the tiny mole to the right of his mouth. But his voice most of all. Voices just don't change. The worst part was not knowing what had happened to him. I used to think...if I just knew he was all right, that he was well and happy, it would be better. But it isn't. Seeing him again was awful. He didn't recognize me at all, yet I wanted to throw myself into his arms. I...."

"Nina looks like him," Alex mused.

"Wh-what?"

"Nina. I always thought the girl looked exactly like you, but now that I know, I can see a lot of Jacob Surratt in her."

"Oh, Lord!" Leah faced Alex, her eyes earnest and pleading. "Alex, I can't do that tapestry. I simply can't! And I certainly don't intend to go to Phoenix this weekend. You understand that, don't you? I can't undertake a project that might bring me into contact with him again. He's probably married and has a family. I don't want to know anything about Dr. Jacob Surratt. I just want to be left with my memories of Jim Stone."

Alex slapped his knee and got to his feet. "Leah, as a man who loves you, I'm so tempted to forget the tapestry, but that would be dishonest of me. As the man who has guided your career, I can't let you refuse this commission. It's much too important."

"I won't do it! Make excuses for me. Say I have too much work, say I need a vacation and am going away. Say anything, I don't care, but get me out of it. I can't do it."

"Leah, darling, listen to me. I've always known what's best for your career, and I have a feeling about this tapestry, that it will lead to such grand things for you. Forget about the opening. It isn't that important, but the tapestry is. I'll act as go-between. You'll never have to see Jacob Surratt again, I promise, but don't turn down this commission. My God, more than ever I should think you would want to stay busy."

Leah put her head in her hands. Alex was right. School would be out for the summer in a few days, and Nina would want to spend most of her time at Whit's, playing with the animals and accompanying her grandfather on his rounds. This was a sacrifice Leah made for Nina, for she much preferred having her daughter with her. However, she thought it imperative that Nina acquire a deep sense of family, particularly since the child's family consisted only of a mother and a grandfather.

So summer would be a time of even-greater solitude than usual. If ever she needed to stay busy it would be then, and a project like the tapestry would require months of eight-hour days, working four hours at a stretch. Usually when she was working she forgot everything else; only Nina came before the interplay of warp and weft. She supposed Dr. Surratt's weaving would actually be a blessing...provided she didn't have to see him.

She had to remember that Jacob Surratt was not Jim Stone. Jim was gone forever now, and she didn't even know Jacob. "All right," Leah said quietly, "but only under those circumstances. I don't care what you have to do. Tell him I'm a temperamental artist who throws tantrums if a client comes near while I'm working. Just keep him away from me, Alex."

"Oh, my dear, you can be very sure I'll do that."

Leah lifted her head and shot him a quizzical look. Alex smiled sadly. "You fell in love with him once. You might again. He. . . he isn't married."

"How do you know that?"

"He told me. Quite casually in conversation he mentioned he was a bachelor. And he asked if you're married. I. . . wonder if it was wise to tell you that."

Leah's eyes clouded; it seemed as though her heart weighed fifty pounds. "It doesn't matter, Alex. Dr. Surratt isn't Jim."

CHAPTER FOUR

LEAH SUPPOSED she should have invited Alex to stay for supper; ordinarily she would have. But tonight she wasn't in the mood for food and conversation. She hoped he understood. He was so good and patient with her, and he deserved more than she could give him. If she had accepted one of his many proposals of marriage two, three years ago, how would she feel now after seeing Jim again? She didn't even want to think about that.

She heated some soup and made do with that for supper, then called Sandra and waited for Nina to come home. She forced herself to be cheerful for Nina's sake, but apparently she didn't do a very good job of it. Nina immediately sensed her mother was upset.

"What's wrong, mama?"

"Oh... I'm just a little sad, honey, that's all."

"Why?"

"I, ah, saw someone today, someone I used to know."

"And that made you sad? Why?"

"He's... changed a lot."

"Oh," Nina said, and shrugged away incomprehensible adult behavior.

Her daughter's usual bedtime routine took Leah's mind off the day's incredible events for a time, but finally it was late, Nina was asleep, and Leah was alone with her thoughts.

So often in the past she had fantasized about seeing

him again, and the fantasies had taken many forms. In a favorite, she first spied him from afar. After recovering from surprise, she approached him. He stared at her in startled confusion; then recognition slowly dawned. Their reunion was so poignant.

In another, less-pleasant fantasy, a wife and children were in the picture.

Now Leah had actually seen Jim, and neither of her fantasies had materialized. He hadn't recognized her, and he wasn't married.

He isn't married. . . .

They had guessed his age fairly accurately eight years ago, she mused. He must be in his late thirties now, and every bit as handsome as she remembered. But so urbane, so elegant, so somber. Jim had been casual and relaxed, jovial. Leah recalled the sadness she'd seen in Jacob Surratt's eyes. What had put it there? He wasn't a man at peace with himself.

A doctor. No wonder Jim had taken so readily to his job as Whit's assistant. No wonder the fine manners, the educated speech, the expensive watch and clothing. And he was no ordinary doctor, either, but the Dr. Surratt of the famous clinic bearing his name. Leah frowned. The clinic had been open for years, originally known as merely the Surratt Clinic, probably begun by Jim's—Jacob's relatives. A prominent physician didn't simply disappear for two years. The event ought to have been headline news; in the area, at least.

Why hadn't anyone been looking for him? What had happened on that bus, or in Flagstaff, to cause his memory to return? What a jolt that must have been! Had he ever tried to find out about the two years missing from his life?

Leah sighed. So many questions, and she would never know the answers to any of them.

It had grown late. The house was completely dark, but she hadn't bothered to turn on any lights. Slowly she paced through the house, thinking of the past six years she'd spent alone, longing for what she had had with Jim, raising their daughter. They had been difficult, uncompromising years with only a few bright spots. Nina, of course, was the joy of Leah's life, and her own father had admirably tended to parenting duties above and beyond the call of duty. And there had been her work, a source of pride and satisfaction. Yet a void had remained that nothing and no one could fill.

Odd, she had sometimes experienced an eerie feeling he was near. Perhaps he had been. She often went to Phoenix for one reason or another. They might have been in the same shop or restaurant—

The ringing of the telephone startled her. It would be Alex, of course, calling to see if she was all right. Everyone should have such a friend, Leah thought as she walked to the phone beside the sofa bed. Steadying herself, she picked up the receiver, determined not to worry Alex anymore.

"Hello."

"Feeling better, Ms Stone?"

Leah's heart plummeted to her feet. "Dr. Surratt."

"Why, you recognized my voice. I'm flattered."

"It's...it's distinctive," was all she could think to say.

"You sound much better."

"Yes, I feel much better, thank you."

"Ms Stone...ah, may I call you Leah?"

"Of course."

"Leah, I took the liberty of getting your number from directory assistance. I hope you don't mind. It occurred to me that I neglected to mention the clinic's official opening Saturday night. I wondered if perhaps Mr. Trent told you about it.''

''Yes...Alex mentioned it, but I'm afraid I won't be able to make it, Dr. Surratt.'' She couldn't even come up with a plausible excuse. Her mind wouldn't function properly. This was terrible! When she couldn't see him, when she only could hear his voice, he became Jim. Leah sank to the edge of the sofa.

''Oh? I'm terribly disappointed. Won't you please reconsider? I thought that would be the perfect time to discuss the tapestry.''

''I'm sorry, but...I can't.''

Jacob persisted. ''Another time, perhaps? The clinic is closed on Wednesday afternoons. That's tomorrow. I normally play golf, but I can easily cancel that. I could be at your place by one o'clock.''

This was unlike him. He couldn't imagine how he'd mustered up the courage—or gall—to be so persistent. A no from a woman had always meant just that; never before had he been sufficiently interested to pursue a reluctant female. But the desire to see Leah Stone again was so strong he would even risk seeming obnoxious. Until that afternoon he had never given credence to the existence of an instant bond between two people. Chemistry was one thing, but all that ''across a crowded room'' nonsense only existed in sentimental love songs, or so he had believed. So how else could he explain this attraction to her? ''Would one o'clock be all right, Leah?''

Oh, God. What could she say? Too many tangled emotions were bundled up inside her, too many conflicts she was incapable of dealing with rationally. To have him in this house, the house the two of them had spent countless hours building, would be more than she could handle.

Suddenly something in Leah's head snapped, and her mind simply made a 180-degree turn. Her resolve never to see him again crumbled like clay. Why not invite him to the house? What if he remembered? Was it even reasonable to think he might? If seeing it jogged his memory she might have Jim back again. He had loved this funny little house so much.

But he had loved her so much, too, and seeing her hadn't brought on a flicker of recognition.

"Leah?"

Did she dare? Did she even have the right to tamper with something she didn't at all understand? Wasn't it worth the chance...? "Oh, I, well, I suppose tomorrow afternoon would be fine...Jacob. I'll wait on you for lunch if one o'clock isn't too late for you to eat." Her pulses were pounding.

She thought she heard him breathe a relieved sigh. "That sounds wonderful. I'm looking forward to it. Could you give me directions to your house?"

Leah did; then they said goodbye. When she hung up she was trembling all over.

Six years of being a single parent had made her self-reliant, she had thought. She was accustomed to making her own choices, her own decisions. She set her own hours, disciplined her time and depended on no one for support or assistance. Save for allowing Alex to handle the marketing of her work, she controlled her life.

She didn't feel in control now. Events were swirling unchecked all around her. She had just made the decision to see this doctor, her husband, again, and somewhere in the dim recesses of her mind she suspected she would want him to eventually recognize her, to remember, to love her the way he once had. If they could recapture that, she might erase the haunting sadness from Jacob Surratt's eyes.

Leah could only pray she was doing the right thing. She would never want to harm him. In a daze she stood up and took the cushions off the sofa, stacking them nearby before folding out the bed. In the dark she undressed, putting on a pair of tailored pajamas and recalling how long it had been since she'd felt the urge to wear something frilly and feminine to bed.

What she needed was a good night's sleep. She would be able to think more clearly in the morning...she hoped. "Cope" would be the watchword, although at this particular moment, Leah had never felt less able to cope with anything, least of all Jacob Surratt's bewildering appearance in her life.

At some point during a fitful night of reenacting her marriage to Jim, something had occurred to Leah: even if Jacob recalled their life together, did she think for a minute he would prefer it to the life of a prominent, respected, sophisticated physician? Of course not, but her easygoing, private existence with Jim was what she still longed for. So what on earth had prompted her to invite Jacob here?

A sensible part of her brain reminded her that human nature being what it was, she probably would have found it impossible not to do so.

Leah climbed out of bed filled with an inner agitation that twisted her stomach into a knot. All of the instant clarification she had hoped would come with the new day didn't materialize. In a few hours Jim would be here—here! Only he wouldn't be Jim. She wondered how she was going to get through the day.

Somehow she managed her and Nina's usual early-morning routine, and the moment she had seen her daughter off on the school bus she telephoned Whit, only to be told he was out making calls and would be gone most of the day. Leah didn't leave a message for him to return the call. On second thought, she decided it might be better to talk to her father later, after she'd seen Jacob and had some clear-cut idea, she hoped, of what she was going to do—if anything.

Trying to stay busy, she vacuumed the house, dusted everything in sight, arranged and rearranged pillows and knickknacks. Still she had time on her hands. So she couldn't have been more delighted by Sandra Martin's impromptu visit shortly before eleven. The front door was open; her friend knocked twice, then peeped in. "Am I interrupting anything?"

"Not at all. I'm happy for the company. I'm just killing time until one."

Sandra stepped into the house. "What happens at one?"

"A . . . new client is coming to see me."

"Oh? That's unusual, isn't it?"

"A little," Leah admitted.

"Important commission, huh?"

"Yes, very."

Sandra strolled across the room and flopped down on the sofa, her copper-colored curls bouncing with each step. There was a pixielike quality to Sandra that Leah found adorable. She had an elfin face and a round body that the more-angular Leah sometimes envied. Sandra, however, constantly complained about her weight and was forever just on or off a diet of some sort.

Leah usually could count on her friend for a laugh or two, but this morning Sandra looked completely humorless. Leah eyed her speculatively. "Want something to drink?"

Sandra shook her head. "I've spent the morning drowning my sorrows in the coffeepot. My caffeine level must be at an all-time high."

"Something wrong?"

Sandra's mouth drooped. "You might say that. My darling ex-husband dropped by to thoroughly spoil this beautiful day."

So that was the reason for the visit. "Ah," Leah murmured sympathetically. "I'm sorry."

"I don't know why he doesn't just leave me alone!" Sandra said with an unusual degree of irritation. "That man gave me eight of the most miserable years you can imagine. When I think of the time and money I spent with my shrink just trying to get up the nerve to leave him...."

Leah remembered Sandra had once mentioned seeing a psychiatrist. At the time it hadn't made much impact on her. "I'd forgotten you were in therapy."

"I don't often talk about it. People can bore you to tears with the details of their hours on the couch, and I've never been able to talk about it casually, as if it's as natural as going to the dentist. Sheer desperation sent me to see Dr. Graves, but therapy saved my life."

"The psychiatrist—you think he helped you that much?"

"She," Sandra corrected. "She helped me. Did she ever! I would never have gotten up the courage to leave that bastard if it hadn't been for Dr. Graves."

Leah was intrigued. "I've often wondered how psychotherapy works. What does the doctor do exactly?"

Sandra frowned. "Now that I think about it, she didn't seem to do much but ask questions. The object is to get you to talk, really talk, and sooner or later she'd ask the right question, and I'd open up and chatter for the rest of the fifty-minute hour. First thing I knew I was looking at myself fully and honestly for the first time in my life, and I wasn't especially thrilled by what I saw. Sounds simple, doesn't it? Well, it isn't. It's painful. . .and revealing.''

Leah regarded her friend with new interest. Of all the people she knew, Sandra seemed the least likely candidate for therapy, but then she recalled that she'd met Sandra after the woman had undergone analysis. She crossed the room to sit on the sofa beside her friend. "What did you find out about yourself? I'm not being too nosy, am I?"

"Oh, no, I don't mind talking about it. Most people aren't really interested, though."

"I am, really."

"Well, eventually I discovered I had married a man exactly like my father, because that was the only kind of man I could relate to. Imagine that, Leah. I married at eighteen in order to get away from my father, and I walked straight into the arms of a man exactly like him! My dad wrote the book on domineering male chauvinism, and Sam might have been his disciple.''

"Sam," Leah mused irrelevantly. "So that's his name."

"Samuel T. Martin," Sandra said with exaggerated hautiness. "A self-made man, blessed with endless self-esteem and the sure knowledge that he was always right and I was always wrong. Dr. Graves reminded me that no one is always wrong. I mean, even a stopped clock is right twice a day!"

Leah smiled. "True."

"Anyway, I came to realize that my ideas had just as much value as Sam's did. I wasn't being ungrateful or selfish by wanting to pursue art and live a life of my own. When I finally left, Sam couldn't believe it. I think he thought I was bluffing. When he realized I was serious, he was somewhat pissed off. He predicted all sorts of dire consequences. He knew I'd come crawling back—but now he can't stand knowing I'm doing just fine without him, thank you. I think he'd love it if Ann and I were starving. Then I had my father to contend with. He was 'mortified.' My divorce had 'disgraced' the family.'' Sandra paused. ''Sam says he's changed.'' She scoffed. ''That things will be different if I come back to him, but I'm too smart to fall for that.''

Leah wondered. She had often detected a wistful note in Sandra's railing against her ex, and she sometimes suspected a love-hate relationship, the classic ''can't live with him, can't live without him'' syndrome. ''You'd never go back?'' she asked slyly.

''Hah! Double hah! Bound and gagged maybe, but that's the only way. I'm no fool. I'll tell you something, Leah....''

For the next twenty minutes or so, Leah listened while Sandra let off steam. Leah interjected a remark here and there but mostly just listened. This was a catharsis the woman seemed to need from time to time, and Leah was flattered to be entrusted with so many confidences. When Sandra finally wound down, she turned to Leah with a sheepish smile. ''Sorry for the monologue, but that's something else analysis does for you—teaches you to open up. I used to be scared of my own shadow. I couldn't put together three coherent sentences if Sam was around. No more. A good shrink can work wonders, believe me.'' She shoved herself off the sofa. ''Well, I have a date tonight. Maybe he can snap me out of this foul mood.''

Leah smiled. She envied Sandra in a way. Her friend had a lot of dates and seemed to enjoy them. Which was the way it should be, she thought, all the while remembering a few disastrous dates of her own. She could enjoy a man's company only so long, until the time came for romance. Then all she could think of was Jim, the way she had felt in his arms, the way his kisses set off a series of involuntary responses that were exquisitely torturous, and she would stiffen, freeze. A few disappointed and hurt suitors had marched away from her door, never to call again. Sandra was fortunate to have developed a much-healthier attitude toward man-woman relationships.

Leah walked her friend to the front gate and watched her until she disappeared from view. And she pondered what Sandra had said. She thought of Jacob Surratt and tried to imagine how he had felt when he discovered he'd lost two years of his life. If he had ever seen a psychiatrist, why hadn't it helped?

WHEN THE EXPECTED KNOCK sounded at promptly one o'clock, Leah jumped. A few seconds passed before she crossed the room to answer it. Her hand trembled as she reached for the knob. When she swung the door wide, she felt the knot in her stomach tighten.

He stood on the porch, his eyes alight and a half smile softening his somber features. "Good afternoon," Jacob said, and his eyes roamed over her in a way that made Leah catch her breath.

She would have been astonished, he thought, to know how good she looked to him. She was wearing crisp khaki slacks and a bright yellow shirt; her hair was twisted on top of her head. Foolishly, he wished he could see it tumbling down, caressing her shoulders, swinging around her face.

She looked so fresh, alive, young and vital—exactly the way he remembered her. That's what confounded him, that he'd remembered her so clearly from their first meeting; that some powerful feeling grabbed hold of his senses. No one had ever made such a profound, immediate impression on him, and he was quite prepared to believe no one ever would again. He had actually been nervous while dressing this morning. Nervous as a kid. It made no sense. But then, he conceded, such things weren't supposed to make sense.

"Good afternoon," she replied in an amazingly normal voice considering what the sight of him did to her. She felt weak and disoriented. He looked beautiful, debonair even in casual slacks and a short-sleeved knit sport shirt. Not very much like Jim, who had been earthy. This man would always stand out in a crowd, no matter how much he might try to withdraw from it.

Would she actually be able to treat him like a new acquaintance? Her hand gripped the doorknob as she stood aside. "Please come in."

The woodsy, masculine scent she had noticed in Alex's office assailed her as he brushed past her into the house. "Beautiful day, isn't it?"

"Yes, lovely. You're missing a perfect day for golf."

"I don't mind in the least. There will be hundreds of perfect days for golf."

Leah closed the door. Well, that hadn't been too bad, she thought with relief. The anticipation mingled with dread subsided somewhat. She was more in control than she would have imagined possible. Sometimes her own poise surprised her.

Turning, she found herself staring at the back of his broad shoulders, his trim waist and hips, his well-remembered stance more on the left foot than the right. The shape of his derriere was as appealing as ever. Jim had had the cutest fanny. Everything about him was so damned familiar, while she was a complete stranger to him. Keeping that in mind was going to be the hardest part of the whole charade. A certain formality was called for, yet her arms ached to reach for him, to hold him to her.

She realized he was intently studying the house, not merely giving it a cursory look. Nervously she skimmed her tongue over her bottom lip. What would she do if seeing the house triggered his memory? What if he began asking questions? How much should she tell him? Perhaps she should have discussed this incredible situation with someone knowledgeable before seeing him again. But who? She waited silently while his scrutiny continued.

Jacob's eyes swept the big room that constituted virtually the entire house. It was an unusual structure, with one large picture window and high-pitched roof that added to the illusion of space. Every square inch had been ingeniously utilized; storage space existed where there seemed to be room for none. Rustic and quaint. Through artful placement of furniture and the use of area rugs, the room had been divided into three distinct sections: living room, dining room and a studio. An upright wooden loom stood in front of the big window. The machine itself was a work of art. Certainly it hadn't come off an assembly line.

Jacob's gaze moved on. A kitchen alcove was at one end of the room; a ladder rose to a loft above. One door led, he assumed, to a bathroom. Simplicity itself, yet so appealing. The house had personality, and it was perfect for Leah Stone, he thought with satisfaction. Having some preconceived and rather romantic notions about artists and their life-styles, he would have been absurdly disappointed had Leah lived in a conventional house.

"Charming place, Leah," he finally said. "Did you have it built to specification?"

Only then did Leah realize she'd been holding her

breath. Silently it seeped out of her. "No. As a matter of fact, it was once a schoolhouse. We...renovated it ourselves."

"By 'we' I assume you mean you and your husband."

"Yes."

"You did a good job. A schoolhouse, of all things! How on earth did you come to find it?"

"Oh, we were just looking around for something out of the ordinary and happened upon it quite by accident."

"Well, it's charming, but I believe I've already said that."

Leah couldn't give a name to what she was feeling. Neither she nor the house had jarred his memory, so nothing was likely to. Jim really was gone. Except for the wonderful good looks, she could see no traces of him in Jacob Surratt. The finality of it squeezed at her heart.

Just then Jacob made some sort of motion with his left hand, and that flash of gold again caught Leah's eye. She stared at his wrist. Surprising that an affluent man would keep the same watch all these years. "Your watch," she murmured. "It's very attractive."

Jacob glanced at it quickly, then back at her. "Thanks. I've had it some time now, almost ten years. I bought it during a trip to Hong Kong, and I wouldn't trade it for a dozen new ones."

Hong Kong, of all places! It was a good thing they hadn't wasted more time trying to trace Jim through that watch.

Jacob crossed the room to the loom in front of the window. It was bare. He appreciatively moved his hand along the polished wood. "An heirloom?" he asked.

"It will be someday, I'm sure, but actually it's only eight years old. A man in New Mexico built it, a master woodworker. You'll notice there aren't any metal screws or bolts in the frame. The workings are as tight and strong as they were the day the loom was delivered to me. Do...." She hesitated. "Do you know anything about woodworking?"

"It was my hobby before medicine claimed all my time." He turned to her with a smile. "I still love the smell of sawdust."

Leah's heart thumped. She and Jim had often speculated on his talent with wood. He had built every cabinet in the house, the fence and front gate, too. They had wondered if he had made his living that way....

"You're not working on anything right now?" Jacob asked.

"No."

"Then may I assume my tapestry will be the next work in progress?"

"Y-yes. I'll warp the loom when I've created a design for your piece." It hadn't been wise to undertake the project, Leah was certain now. She had said she would do it, and she would, but it would be difficult, knowing it was for him. The most demanding work of her career. She would want it to be special, a masterpiece. Fixing her gaze at a point somewhere above Jacob's right shoulder, she miserably pondered the impossible situation.

Jacob seemed unusually fascinated by her loom. "What prompted you to take up weaving?"

Leah told him about the weaver at the fair. "I just made up my mind right then and there. I knew that's what I wanted to do."

"At sixteen? Lucky girl. Some people never find out

what they want to do. How does one get started on a tapestry, or a rug or whatever?'' he asked, his eyes scanning the apparatus. "What do you do first?"

Leah snatched at the slender thread of conversation. Moving closer to him, she said, "First I draw the design, then I make a pattern draft to guide me in dressing the loom. I don't suppose that means much to you."

"Not really, no."

"The draft is to a weaver what a recipe is to a cook or a pattern is to a dressmaker. It specifies exactly how the loom should be warped in order to achieve a particular design. In pioneer days the drafts were treasured and handed down from generation to generation."

"I see," he said in a vague tone that told Leah he was interested but didn't really understand.

"The Indians did the same thing, but the drafts were in their heads. Now, as the elderly weavers pass away and with fewer and fewer young Indian women wanting to take up the ancient craft, some of the classic designs will soon be gone forever."

"I own a century-old Navaho rug."

"Really? How fortunate you are!"

"It's not in the best condition but still quite valuable." Jacob glanced at her with admiration. "It's a noble craft you've chosen to keep alive."

"Yes," she said simply, for it was true. When she worked at her loom she felt an almost mystic kinship with the Navahos, with the Scottish weavers of Hebridean tweeds, with the makers of Turkish rugs and the priceless Persians, to say nothing of the uncounted legions of pioneer women who labored over simple looms to produce enough fabric to clothe a family.

"Do you look on your work as an art or a craft?"

A question she had been asked many times. She shrugged. "Good craftmanship is vital—who wants to own sloppy work?—but the designs are all mine and set my work apart.''

He grinned charmingly. "Marvelous answer, Leah.''

His untouchable nearness was slowly eating away at her poise. Having him here was at once thrilling and terrible. He looked like Jim, sounded like Jim, but he wasn't Jim at all. Maybe she shouldn't ever see him again. She wanted something that no longer existed.

But he was here now, and the time would have to pass somehow. Leah gestured toward the kitchen. "Lunch is ready. I'm sure you must be starved.''

He sniffed the air. "If the taste is anything like the aroma, I'm in for a treat.''

"My homemade vegetable soup. I've been told a person could live happily on it and never want anything else.''

And who had told her that, Jacob mused as he followed her to the table, already set for lunch. Her husband, of course. He had noted the slight twitch of her facial muscles when he'd mentioned her husband earlier. For a fleeting second there had been pain and longing in her eyes, not anger or resentment. She was still in love with him. Not surprisingly, Jacob wondered what had happened. From the information he had pried out of a reluctant Alexander Trent, he knew she'd been married, no longer was, but wasn't widowed. So that meant she was divorced. The husband must have been the one who had wanted out; otherwise, why the longing? Another woman? Hard to believe.

Only a short breakfast bar separated the dining table from the tiny kitchen. Jacob slipped into a chair at the table and watched Leah as she poured glasses of ice tea, then ladled steaming soup into bowls. She worked with economy of movement in the neat, efficiently organized kitchen. He noticed the way she reached for things without looking, and he guessed she could walk into the kitchen blindfolded and put her hand on the paprika jar. He admired organization—he himself couldn't begin work until everything was at hand and in place—but had never equated it with the creative mind. But Leah wasn't just an artist; she was also accomplished in a technical skill.

She was such a soft, fluid woman, and she excited him in a way that went beyond the obvious, the physical. Her loveliness was unstudied, almost ethereal, with an underlying current of sensuality. No, he couldn't believe a man would leave her for another woman. It was easier to imagine her marriage had fallen by the wayside for more complex reasons: a woman intent on a career and a man jealous of his wife's phenomenal success. Perhaps a clash of personalities. Almost anything was easier to believe than another woman.

"THAT WAS DELICIOUS, LEAH," Jacob said after two helpings. "Isn't a good pot of soup supposed to be the proof of a cook's ability?"

Leah smiled. Lunch had been a pleasant interlude, full of talk about inconsequential things. Slowly, without being aware of it, she had been lulled into a pleasant sense of well-being. He was a thoughtful and interesting conversationalist. To her utter surprise, she discovered she had forgotten Jim Stone for a few moments, having found it amazingly easy to concentrate on the fascinating character of Jacob Surratt.

The haunting quality she had sensed the day before lurked just below the surface, giving him an air of brooding mystery. It made a woman want to plumb those dark depths. Were the two blank years of his life responsible, she wondered. Wouldn't something like that prey on one's mind constantly?

The word Alex had used to describe him, "refined," suited him to a tee. He was reserved, too. Very reserved. She couldn't imagine him opening up and spilling the story of his life. What was the story of his life? It came to her with a start that Jacob could tell her all the things she had never known about Jim.

He had a straightforward way of looking at a person that was unsettling until one got used to it, as though he could see more than the person wanted to reveal. Not an easy man to get to know well. He didn't talk about himself at all, and Leah was too concerned about saying the wrong things to ask many questions. Yet he radiated confidence, a necessity for a doctor, she supposed. "Just put yourself in my hands," his manner said, "and everything will be all right." She imagined him standing in front of an auditorium full of distinguished physicians presenting a paper, or whatever it was doctors did at those meetings. Dr. Surratt, a recognized authority in his field.

What was his field? Leah asked him, and he told her he was an internist. "Not a dramatic specialty," he added modestly. "There are those who'll tell you I'm nothing but a glorified GP."

She could tell he was interested in her as a woman, and she certainly wasn't immune to masculine appreciation. Particularly not when the handsome face across from her was the dearest on earth. She could feel the old magnetic pull between them, just as she had eight years ago; she knew she wasn't imagining it. "I must admit to being a pretty good cook," she said, returning to their earlier conversation. "Cooking is the creative side of housekeeping, it seems to me. When I'm not weaving I enjoy cooking and working in the garden, but housework...." She wrinkled her nose in disdain. "Fortunately the house requires very little care. It was designed so there would be a place for everything."

Jacob glanced around. "It's exceptionally neat, especially when you consider there's a child living here."

"Nina's neat, too. Just the two of us have lived here for a long time, so perhaps she's always sensed the need for keeping clutter to a minimum. At least she's good about keeping her clutter up there." She used her thumb to indicate the loft above their heads.

"How old is your daughter?"

"Six."

"You must have been very young when you married."

Leah's expression altered; instantly the most vulnerable part of her was alerted. *Stay away from that subject,* she warned. *Don't let him ask questions.* "Not really. My marriage...was a brief one," she said stiffly, and got to her feet in a jerky movement, gathering up their dishes. "I'll rinse these and put them in the dishwasher. It won't take but a minute."

Jacob remained at the table, staring across the room while tugging thoughtfully on his chin. Whatever her relationship with her husband had been, it had left scars. She definitely didn't like to talk about her marriage. In fact, she froze at the mention of the word. So, although he wanted to know more, although he burned with curiosity about this woman, he wouldn't ask any more questions.

HE STAYED MOST of the afternoon. He seemed loathe to leave, and Leah sensed he was starved for companionship. His reserved manner coupled with his lofty position probably made it difficult for him to form close friendships. There was a hint of entreaty in Jacob Surratt's manner that she found appealing. She imagined he would like nothing better than to relax and loosen up a bit, but simply didn't know how.

Try as she might she couldn't detect any of the easygoing Jim Stone beneath Jacob's controlled exterior. How could one man be two such different people? And how could one woman be so enormously attracted to both of them? And how, dear God, could she sit here and calmly distinguish one from the other? That was what she was doing, with greater ease than she would have dreamed possible. Without effort she could recall Jim holding his head one way, while Jacob held his another way.

Their conversation was politely friendly, befitting a meeting between two supposed strangers who were taking first hesitant steps toward getting acquainted. Most of his questions concerned her career, and he seemed especially interested in her relationship with Alex.

"How long have you been associated with the Trent Gallery?"

"Five years. When I first met Alex I'd been weaving for a number of years, but I had no clear-cut notion of where I thought my weaving would lead me. Alex took me in hand, pointed me in the right direction, and the rest, as they say, is history." She smiled slightly.

"You've enjoyed tremendous success, I understand. I guess you feel you owe it all to Trent."

"Most of it. Of course, I have to give myself a little credit, too. I'm the one who has to produce."

"He's fond of you."

"Alex? Yes, he is, and I'm fond of him. Besides being sort of my business manager, he's probably the best friend I've ever had. Leah paused before concluding, "But that's all he is." She felt compelled to add that, and the look on his face clearly told her how glad he was to hear it.

At last Jacob got around to mentioning the ostensible reason for his visit, the tapestry. Leah sketched a tentative design for him—a bold, impressionistic view of the Red Rock Country that he professed to like very much.

"This part of the state offers a lot in the way of inspiration, but if you'd prefer a desert scene...."

"No, I want to leave the design entirely up to you. I want you to do what you feel. I know I'll like anything you come up with."

They were sitting side by side on the sofa, deep in a discussion concerning colors, when the front door flew open and Nina burst into the room with childish exuberance.

"Mama, why weren't you waiting for me on the porch?"

Leah's eyes flew to the clock on the wall. She hadn't been aware of the passage of time, and she had vaguely expected Jacob to be gone before her daughter—his daughter—got home from school. Her heart thudded painfully as she cast a sidelong glance at Jacob, then looked at Nina's winsome face.

"I'm sorry, honey. I've had company and completely forgot the time."

Nina eyed Jacob with candid curiosity. "Hi."

"Well, hello," he said with a smile.

Leah stifled a wave of panic. "Nina, I'd...I'd like you to meet Dr. Surratt. Jacob, my daughter...."

Jacob, courteously and with all the gallantry usually reserved for adults, uncurled his lanky frame and got to his feet. "It's very nice to meet you, Nina."

The child crossed the room and stood in front of him, tilting her head. "Are you a people doctor or an animal doctor like my grandpa?"

"I'm a people doctor."

"Well, I'm going to be a vet when I grow up."

"Are you? How wonderful, Nina. I hope you actually do it."

"I will. Grandpa says he'll need me."

Leah reminded herself to keep breathing, slowly, evenly. She couldn't fall apart now, though her reserve of inner strength seemed dangerously depleted. Jacob and Nina were intent on each other, so she was free to study both of them. Father and daughter. How could they not see it? To Leah's eyes, Nina was reminiscent of the tall dark man in many ways. Perhaps her eyes and mouth were more like her mother's, but the rest was Jacob all over again.

Jacob stood over the girl, smiling down at her. "Nina, you look exactly like your mother."

Nina nodded solemnly. "That's what everybody says."

Leah expelled her pent-up breath. No, of course they wouldn't see it. Nina was much too young, and Jacob was seemingly too removed from them for such a thing to cross his mind. People saw what they expected to see. To Jacob, Nina's dark hair and eyes would seem to have come from her mother.

But had a third party entered the house at that moment—say Sandra—Leah feared the common genes would have been all too apparent. If Jacob Surratt became a part of her life, what kind of problems would that present? How could she even think of such a thing at this stage? She wouldn't.

The uncomfortable moment passed. Only Leah

seemed to be aware of the awkwardness. Jacob sat down, and Nina shifted her attention to her mother. "Can I go to Ann's house, mama?"

"May I go," Leah corrected.

"May I go?"

"I suppose so, but change your clothes first...and hang up that dress. It can be worn again."

"Okay." Nina scampered away and was up the ladder leading to the loft in a flash. Leah stared wistfully after her daughter's darting figure.

"She's an adorable girl, Leah."

"Thank you." She drew a few unnecessary lines on the sketch pad in her lap, thoroughly spoiling the design.

"She must be a lot of company for you."

"Yes."

"I think I'd like having children. I'm not sure I'd be a great father, though. I'm afraid I wouldn't have the slightest idea what to do with a child."

"I have news for you, not many first-time parents do. It's strictly on-the-job training. You...never married?"

"No. I guess there was never time. At least, that's the excuse I've always used. Actually, I suppose the problem was I never found the right person. Had I found her, I'm sure I would have found the time."

"Yes, of course," Leah said distractedly, pretending absorption in the mess she had made of her sketch. "Have you ever regretted not marrying?" The words were out before she remembered her decision to avoid the subject.

"Sometimes." Jacob paused, then said, "No, not sometimes. Often."

Leah's breath caught in her throat. It was a touching admission, and one that seemed to embarrass him. Only the greatest exercise of will prevented her from reaching out to touch him. "Well, you've plenty of time."

"I'm galloping toward forty."

"That's not so old."

"I wonder. I'm pretty set in my ways. I wonder if I could adapt."

"Of course you could. Don't be fatalistic about it. It's important to...have someone to share things with. You'll find out...someday." Leah swallowed rapidly. Why was she saying these things? Why was she discussing marriage with him? She knew he was staring at her, and she couldn't turn to meet his gaze.

Jacob was puzzled. Here was a woman with a failed marriage behind her, one that apparently had left deep scars, yet she seemed to be encouraging him to give marriage a try, even though the very subject bothered her. Best to find something else to talk about. Nervously he cleared his throat. "Your father is a veterinarian?"

"Yes, he has a practice in the Verde Valley."

"Is that where you grew up?"

"Yes."

"So you're a country girl?"

"Through and through."

"I've often thought I might like living in the country."

He had. Jim had loved country life, and he had abhorred crowds. Leah had attributed that to the fact that he'd never quite lost his feeling of alienation from the rest of society. He had been an amnesiac; therefore "different."

She felt oddly detached from everything that was going on around her, as if she were a third person viewing the scene from afar. That she could sit and make idle small talk, exercise all the social graces when her nerves were stretched to the snapping point, astonished her. Jacob was sitting in a house he had personally renovated, on furniture they had purchased together. He filled the room with a masculine vitality she had once been so accustomed to but had since almost forgotten. When he left this afternoon his presence would be missed, just as Jim's had been six years ago. Leah glanced at his strong hands with their slender, sensitive fingers and didn't want to look away. She noticed the way his trousers fit so smoothly over muscular thighs and tried not to remember his naked legs sliding sleekly along hers....

For a moment her throat closed completely, and a warm flush crawled up her neck. He had always possessed more than his fair share of sex appeal, and they had been passionate, responsive lovers. No other man had even come close to touching her heart. During the years Jim had been gone, she had come to accept emotional emptiness as a way of life.

But inevitably there would have been other women in Jacob's life during the past six years, and she wondered what he looked for in a woman. Beauty? Sophistication? Well schooled in all the social graces? Had there been one special one? Had anyone ever broken his heart? Good Lord, if she thought about such things she would drive herself crazy!

In only a few minutes Nina was hurrying back down the ladder, dressed in shorts, halter and sneakers. She hugged her mother, favored Jacob with a little wave and bolted out the front door. The house seemed deathly quiet in her wake, and the one thing Leah couldn't cope with was silence. Abruptly she stood up. "I promised Nina I'd make spaghetti for supper. I need to start the sauce. Just make yourself comfortable...."

With apparent reluctance Jacob also got to his feet. "I really should be going. I've taken up far too much of your time as it is."

"I...didn't mind. I enjoyed it." Which wasn't entirely the truth. The pain had overshadowed the enjoyment.

"Did you, Leah? I'm glad, because so did I."

Bold, intense eyes captured hers, forcing Leah to look quickly away. If she didn't look at him she could almost forget he wasn't the stranger he was supposed to be. "I...ah, I'll be starting the tapestry in a few days, I imagine."

"Will I be allowed to view the work in progress?"

He was asking, in a roundabout way, if he could see her again. And of course her answer would be yes. How could she not see him again? Now that she knew where he was, she would gravitate to him, irresistibly drawn. "I have no objections to a client seeing an unfinished work," she said, although normally she did. Alex was the only interested party who was allowed to visit her while she worked.

Hearing that, Jacob fully relaxed for the first time that afternoon. From the moment he had stepped into the ridiculous, wonderful little house, throughout lunch, all the while he was making the sort of small talk he usually despised and executed so poorly, he had been planning how to see her again. The tapestry was the obvious bond...for now.

To Leah's consternation, he stepped closer to her. The clean male scent of him filled her nostrils, making her light-headed. Casually he took her hand and held it in both of his while saying, "You know, I've never put much stock in fate or Kismet or whatever, but...." He groped for words, finally settling for, "I had never been in that bank building before. Never in my entire life." His eyes begged her to understand how momentous that simple act now seemed.

Leah didn't know what to say, so she said nothing. He left quickly then, with a smile and a chaste handshake. For long moments after she had closed the door behind him, she simply stood with her forehead pressed against the cold, hard wood. It took some time for the confusing mixture of emotions inside her to run their course, then subside.

She had no idea when she would see him again, but she knew she would. When the opportunity came along she would seize it. Her life had been diverted into a new channel, and there was nothing she could do but go with the current. It was useless to try to pretend the day hadn't changed everything. For now she couldn't be bothered with wondering what she hoped would come of all this—finding Jim again or getting to know Jacob. There would be plenty of time for introspection later.

A long sigh left her lips. She was exhausted by the extremes of emotion that had assaulted her all afternoon. Honestly, she didn't know how she had gotten through it.

CHAPTER FIVE

JACOB SLID BEHIND THE WHEEL of his Corvette, after removing his billfold from his hip pocket and tossing it onto the console between the seats. That was a habit of his that many people found idiosyncratic, but he simply disliked sitting on a wallet for any length of time.

Absently he patted the dashboard of the flashy, luxurious automobile before turning the key in the ignition. His acquaintances also found the car uncharacteristic of Jacob Surratt, and he admitted it was the one frivolous aspect of his eminently sensible life. The vehicle was totally impractical, with room for two people and nothing else, but its very impracticality was probably the reason he loved it so.

Leisurely he drove away from the picture-postcard community of Sedona, out of the deep abyss of Oak Creek Canyon, and headed south for Phoenix. For once he took the time to notice and appreciate his surroundings. Puffy pillows of cumulus cloud drifted overhead in a sky of such brilliant clarity that it hurt the eyes. The air was pure and crystalline. He rolled down the car window and sniffed deeply of it. The perpetual haze that hovered over Phoenix seemed light-years away. He was caught up in an extraordinary sensation of well-being, hardly a usual state of mind for him, and the feeling remained with him throughout the trip home.

Two hours later he turned into the driveway of his

home in the swank Phoenix suburb of Scottsdale. Leaving the car in the drive, since he fully intended going to the clinic after dinner, he entered the house by way of a side veranda. The interior smelled of soap and polish, as always; all was peaceful and serene, as always, for the big house remained impervious to the trials and tribulations of the man who owned it.

He strode through the dining room and into the tiled foyer. There he was met by a tall, spare, gray-haired man, his butler.

"Good evening, sir. I hope you had a pleasant day."

"Very pleasant, thank you, Davis. Are there any messages?"

"None, sir, but George would like to know when you wish dinner served."

Jacob glanced at his watch. "Eight or thereabouts. And please tell George to keep it light. I had a substantial lunch."

"Very good."

Taking the stairs two at a time, Jacob went to his room on the second floor, stripped and stepped into swim trunks. Within moments he was back downstairs, heading for the pool at the rear of the big house. Diving in, he swam his customary daily laps with even less enthusiasm than usual. It had been years since he'd thought of swimming as recreation. Swimming and golf were his ways of staying fit; he despised jogging and calisthenics. Inside his house, in a converted attic, was an exercise room full of the latest equipment, but it was seldom used. In fact, there were many rooms in the house that were seldom used. He often wondered why he bothered keeping the place. Because it was easier to stay put, he supposed.

Swimming with precision, he performed the daily

chore with the air of a man doing penance. Then he lifted himself out of the pool and went to lie facedown on a poolside lounge. The sun was warm on his back, and as he gradually relaxed pleasant languor took hold of him. Not surprisingly, his mind strayed to Leah Stone.

He felt so drawn to her, as though he knew her better than he actually did. Not the facts of her life exactly, since he had barely scratched the surface there. What they shared was more like a communion of souls. At this Jacob chuckled derisively. That was quite a conclusion for a man who held others at arm's length.

Thinking about Leah now, he realized that his first impression was of having met her before. But realistically wouldn't she have remembered and mentioned it? She was as curious about him as he was about her; he had seen that much in some of the quizzical looks she'd cast in his direction. A plus for him. He had captured her interest, and that was half the battle.

So that first impression of a rare bond must have been nothing more than another of his overreactions. In spite of his resolve not to dwell on his memory loss, he still harbored the hope that he would someday meet someone who had known him, someone who would tell him about the lost period of his life.

He didn't know why resurrecting the past was so important to him. Wherever he had spent those missing years, whatever he had been doing couldn't possibly measure up to what he had now. Just looking around he could see it. See what? Incredible comfort, the trappings of affluence and success, an outward display of social status? All that, of course—and he was suddenly struck by his lack of interest in what he owned. If he couldn't be happy with all this, he definitely had a problem.

Yet he wasn't, not really. Most people labored a lifetime to attain only a measure of what he had; still there were times when he would have gladly given up all of it just to find out where he'd been, what he had done during the thirty-first and thirty-second years of his life. How often he had tried to push all thoughts of those years to the back of his mind, but they relentlessly inched forward, until there were days when he thought of almost nothing else. When that happened he felt completely fragmented.

Charles had told him to give up. After fruitless months in psychotherapy with his partner, it had occurred to Jacob that he might be better off not knowing. Why possibly complicate his life? "The mind is a wondrous thing," Charles liked to say. "It can block out the unwanted." Jacob, calling upon his own knowledge of psychiatry, liked to think of the mind as a sort of cold-storage vault. Everything that had ever been put into it was still there, and would stay there until someone or something took it out.

Ah, forget it! He would concentrate instead on Leah Stone, the first woman in years who had elicited a spark of interest in him—and in Leah's case it was more like a full-fledged flame. She was lovely, artistic, intelligent. Quiet, too. Jacob had always appreciated quietness in a person. So many people talked too much and said too little. Leah listened to what was being said to her and gave some thought to her own reply. Refreshing.

If he had ever known her before he would have liked her; of that he was sure. Today he had longed to stay in that funny little house with her forever. Even the house clutched at him in some peculiar way.

Lazily he sifted through what he knew about Leah. She had been weaving professionally for five years, and Trent was her mentor, nothing more. Jacob suspected the gallery owner would have welcomed a more intimate relationship—he had gathered that much at Tlaquepaque the day before—but if it hadn't happened by now, after such a long association, it wasn't likely to. Trent wouldn't be a rival.

His potential rival—how odd to be thinking in such terms already! But it was the other man in Leah Stone's life who could be the formidable obstacle. Her marriage had been brief, yet years later she was still in love with her husband. There was the little girl, too. A child could be a problem, particularly if the girl was possessive of her mother. Jacob hadn't seen signs of that, but one never knew.

Forget that, too. He would worry about that later, if indeed it needed worrying about. Leah wasn't married anymore, and this afternoon had only whet his appetite to get closer to her. Abruptly he sat up. Damn, he shouldn't have left without making arrangements for another meeting. He might have read too much into her apparent interest in him. He knew, to his everlasting regret, that he wasn't a man who projected warmth and charm. He often found it impossible to express what he felt. She might just have been behaving courteously...then again, her apparent interest might have been genuine. What the hell— Nothing ventured....

Without giving it too much thought—for if he had, he probably would have done nothing—Jacob stood, threw a towel around his shoulders and went into the house. On the desk in his study he found the phone number he had jotted down the evening before. Dialing, he was aware of his accelerated heartbeat, of his sheer excitement as he waited to hear her voice on the other end of the line. He felt as callow as a schoolboy, and curiously, that felt wonderful!

"Hello."

"Leah?"

"Jacob?"

"Yes, I.... I've been thinking. You really should see the clinic itself before you begin the tapestry. Won't you please reconsider Saturday night's opening?"

"Well, I...." Leah was hesitant about accepting eagerly when she had so adamantly refused the night before. But she wanted to go. Oh, how she wanted to go!

"Of course your friend Trent is invited, too," Jacob added hastily. "And I'd like both of you to stay at my house, not at the Biltmore. We won't have to do much more than put in an appearance at the party. I think you'll enjoy it." This was a new role for him, and he wasn't the least certain how well he was playing it.

"I... why, thank you, Jacob. I'm sure I will. I'll tell Alex in the morning."

"Are you familiar with Phoenix?"

"Yes, I went to school there."

"Anytime Saturday afternoon. I'll be home," he assured her before he gave her directions to his house.

"I'm looking forward to it."

The elation Jacob felt when he hung up was an alien sensation. Foolishly, he admitted to dangerously high expectations. A pity he had felt compelled to invite Trent along. That had just popped out, a gesture at propriety. He would have liked nothing better than to have that charming woman all to himself, but he doubted that she would have come if he'd left Trent out of the invitation.

Tugging on both ends of the towel, Jacob went upstairs to shower. He couldn't remember the last time he had looked forward to a weekend, to much of anything, for that matter. He longed for an end to the sameness of his days, an end to evenings passed without meaning or purpose to him personally. It would be wonderful if Leah Stone turned out to be the one who finally carved a niche in his life, erased the loneliness and brought peace to his mind and soul. How wonderful if she was the one who finally made him stop caring about the missing years.

JACOB NEVER DID GET AROUND to going to the clinic that evening. He ate his solitary evening meal and retired early, only to awaken in a cold sweat in the middle of the night. He had had the dream. Four years or more had passed since the last one, but tonight it had returned, unchanged. He saw a house, not clearly, and a front door. It opened; a woman stood there. He could never see her face, and the dream always ended abruptly when she appeared. The same dream, never varying.

Flinging back the covers, he went to stand at the window. His chest was heaving. Dammit, why now? Why had it come back to haunt him now, when he had finally found someone who excited him? When he longed to concentrate on someone else for a change. He passed a hand over his eyes. His amnesia had always embarrassed him, as though it was a weakness of character, although his subsequent knowledge of the subject assured him that wasn't so. For a time he had also worried about his actions during the fugue. Maybe he had done something illegal or immoral. Again, he had learned that wasn't likely.

But what of the people whose lives he had touched during those two years? No one existed in a vacuum. That bothered him most of all—the possibility that he might have left someone "out there" six years ago, someone who needed him. What if the dream was a warning, a warning not to get involved again until loose ends had been tied up?

That scared the hell out of him.

LEAH TELEPHONED ALEX the following morning. Beth informed her that he hadn't put in an appearance at the gallery, so he first learned of their upcoming visit to Phoenix when he stopped by her house that afternoon, something he usually managed to do a few times a week. He knocked twice, called her name, then came in to find Leah in the kitchen.

"Something smells good," he commented.

"Stay for supper?"

"I'd love to, but I can't. I'm due in Flagstaff for dinner. I'm meeting a marvelous new watercolorist from New Mexico. Her show in Taos drew raves."

"You're always so busy," Leah said with a smile. "I don't know how you stand all that gadding about."

"Well, I'm not going to be busy Saturday night, so let's do something. I'll take you out to dinner."

"I'm afraid we have other plans," she said slyly, then told him of Jacob's invitation.

"You what?" he exclaimed, his tone and expression registering alarm. "Leah, what on earth prompted you to do such a thing?"

Leah wasn't the least surprised by his reaction. She had anticipated it, down to the firm set of his mouth and the furrow in his brow. He would protest mightily, but he would go. "I told him we'd be there," she repeated. "He invited us, and I accepted. It was something I had to do."

His eyes narrowed questioningly. "Why did you have to do it?"

"I can't explain it, Alex, and I shouldn't have to. I want to go, that's all."

"And if I refuse to tag along?" he asked, sounding as pettish as a small boy.

Leah shot him a wry smile. "Would you?"

He regarded her levelly for a second. "No," he said finally, firmly. "No way."

Under no circumstances did he want her going alone. The situation was rife with potential disaster for more than one interested party. Leah's husband's surprise reappearance had Alex filled with dread, but he had been encouraged by her refusal to see Jacob Surratt again. Now this. Leah, it seemed to him, was asking for trouble and heartache. Surely she was aware of that. Perhaps she simply didn't care, and that in itself alarmed him.

Alex had no illusions about his place in Leah's affections; it was solid, impenetrable, exclusive—but not based on romantic love. That he had accepted. His ambitions concerning her now centered on their closeness and shared interests, their common goals. One day, he hoped, Leah would marry him, not because she was wildly in love with him, but because she wanted and needed his support and companionship. He had been willing to wait for that day.

Peculiar that he hadn't considered the possibility of another man, but he hadn't. He had been watching Leah for years, had watched men turn themselves inside out attempting to attract her. All of the attempts had been met with polite detachment, leaving Alex secure in believing he was, with the exception of her father and daughter, the most important person in her life. Until now.

It was easy to see how falsely complacent he had been, but how in God's name could he have foreseen this incredible turn of events? Jacob Surratt wasn't just any man; he was the one man she had loved. Nina's father. Handsome and eligible. And Leah had never divorced him, never remarried. Alex wasn't one to give fate much credit for anything that happened, but in this case. . . .

Something had kept them free for each other. He hadn't understood why, in an age when divorce and infidelity were commonplace, Leah had remained faithful to a man she hadn't seen in six years. Now he understood. She had never quite given up hope that he would come back to her one day. Her husband may have returned in a new guise, but he had returned. Alex didn't like it one damned bit.

"What brought on this change of mind, Leah? My last instructions from you, as I recall, were to keep him away from you at all costs."

Leah smiled at him across the breakfast bar. "He came to see me yesterday, and we. . .talked."

"He was here?"

She nodded. "Most of yesterday afternoon."

"But how. . . ."

"When he called Tuesday night he asked if he could come to see me, and I said yes."

"Why on earth did you do that?"

"Because I wanted to," she said simply.

A rush of color suffused Alex's face. "Did. . .did he meet Nina?"

Again she nodded. "But the meeting was brief. It made no impact on him. Neither did the house. He remembers nothing."

"Oh, Leah." Alex sighed wearily. "Do you have any idea what you might be letting yourself in for?"

"Honestly, no. Hundreds of possibilities have crossed my mind, but I don't know which ones are valid. I can't be bothered with all the 'ifs' and 'maybes.' I know Jacob Surratt isn't the man I married, and I know he and I might not get along the way Jim and I did. But I have to know for sure, don't I?'' She waited. ''Well, don't I?''

''I don't know, Leah. I swear I don't. You were so adamant about not wanting to meet with him....''

''At first, yes. I was confused, frightened, still reeling from the shock of seeing him again. I didn't want to face the possibility of rejection. Jacob Surratt might not have given a fig for Leah Stone. But then he came here for lunch, and...I could tell he was interested in me as a woman. The spark's still there, regardless of who he is.'' Leah reached out to squeeze his hand. ''Alex, I've missed him every day for six years. It always seemed strange that I couldn't get him out of my head, but I never could. Even lately, when I could sometimes go for days without consciously thinking of him, I've missed him. Can you blame me for...anything?''

A pall of silence descended. Leah could almost see the resignation settling on Alex, and her heart ached for him. She hoped she hadn't been too frank, yet he wouldn't have wanted her to be any other way.

''No,'' he said finally. ''No, I suppose I can't. Apparently none of us has much control over the workings of the heart. It's you I'm thinking of. At least, I think it's you. I don't know...maybe I'm only thinking of myself. So, what time are we due at the good doctor's place Saturday?''

''Anytime in the afternoon. What about four?''

He shrugged. ''Four's fine with me.''

An alarming thought crossed Leah's mind. ''Alex, you do realize the importance of not saying anything to Jacob that would hint at my knowing him before?''

''Damn, Leah! Do you think I'm stupid?''

''No, but something might pop out. I really don't know how to handle this, but instinct tells me to move carefully.''

"Well, put your mind at ease. I'll be the soul of discretion. I guess we'll drop Nina off at your dad's."

"No. School's out for the summer at noon tomorrow. Nina will be like a colt let out of a pen. I'll take her down then and let her run off some of that energy on the farm." A distant look came to Leah's eyes. "Besides, I need to talk to dad. He has to know about this."

Alex didn't stay long. Leah guessed he had some emotional turmoil of his own to deal with, and she felt deeply for her dear friend at that moment. Although she had never encouraged him romantically, she imagined he had never completely given up hope. And who knew what might have happened in the future? One day she might have turned to him for solace and companionship.

Alex would cope, though, and he wouldn't let this change their professional relationship. She was sure of that. Other things would change. Perhaps it wasn't even reasonable to be so sure of that so soon, but Leah was. Lives would be altered, and all because Jacob happened to walk into that bank and spot that tapestry.

CHAPTER SIX

IT WAS MIDAFTERNOON of the following day when Leah drove through the wooden gate and up the long lane to her father's home, a large white frame farmhouse sitting in the middle of twenty fertile acres along the Verde River. At one time the Haskell property had been worked extensively, and citizens in nearby communities had gobbled up all the beans, tomatoes, corn, apples and grapes it could produce. With a two-hundred-day growing season, the produce had been plentiful. But now farming was limited to a dozen laying hens, a couple of milk goats, a few horses and a small but thriving vegetable garden. Whit Haskell's veterinary practice left him little time for other work, while Tee Santos's arthritis precluded the housekeeper doing much outside work. Farming chores were handled by two hired workers, and Whit also employed a young man to help with the clinic and kennels. Everyone resided on the premises, which meant Whit had plenty of company.

In the seat beside her mother, Nina fidgeted and squirmed with end-of-school excitement and the anticipation of a long weekend at the farm. The chief attraction for the girl, aside from her doting grandfather's shameless devotion, was the number of animals that populated the place. Dogs and cats abounded, and the queen bee among them was Bess, Whit's adored collie. Bess, now heavy in the late stages of pregnancy, ambled up to the car the moment Leah halted in front of the house. Nina leaped out to give the dog an enthusiastic hug.

"Oh, mama, Bess is so big! She's going to have a bunch of puppies!"

Leah bent to rub Bess's head affectionately. The dog's limpid eyes closed in satisfaction. "How're you doing, girl? About ready for the whole mess to be over, I'll bet."

Nina straightened and scampered up the front steps. "Grandpa says we can have one of the puppies," she informed her mother over her shoulder. "We get first pick."

"How thoughtful of him," Leah muttered sarcastically, following her daughter. "He might have discussed it with me."

"I'll take good care of it, honest."

"Hmm. I'd like a dollar for every mother who's fallen for that one. Now don't get your heart set on it, Nina. A puppy's a big responsibility."

Leah caught the screen door before it banged behind Nina. She stepped into her father's homy living room in time to witness the enthusiastic greeting between grandfather and granddaughter. Whit's pleasantly craggy face broke into a beaming smile as his burly arms enfolded Nina in a bear hug. His head, covered with a thatch of salt-and-pepper hair, bent over the child's. "How's my best girl?"

"Fine."

"So, school's out, eh? Did you get any smarter this year?"

"Lots. Grandpa, when's Bess going to have her puppies?"

"Soon. A week maybe."

"Is she all right?"

"Bess? With me here to take care of her? Of course

she's all right." His gaze swept over the top of Nina's head and fastened on Leah. "Hello, hon. What's up? You sounded kinda mysterious on the phone."

Leah cautioned her father with a frown and a slight nod in Nina's direction. Whit pursed his lips in comprehension and immediately set the girl at arm's length. "Nina, Tee's in the kitchen making chocolate-chip cookies. I'll bet if you hurry you can get one fresh out of the oven."

"Oh, boy!" Nina ran out of the room, calling the housekeeper's name.

Whit glanced at Leah with parental concern. She looked worried, or what passed for worried with Leah. She never got ruffled, which wasn't right. As far as Whit was concerned, twenty-eight was too damned young to have acquired a calm acceptance of life. That was desirable at fifty-three maybe, but not at twenty-eight. Too much inside his daughter had died when Jim disappeared. "Got something important on your mind?" he inquired quietly.

"Very."

"I thought so. Let's go out back. I was on my way to check the kennels. We'll have privacy out there."

Leah fell into step beside her father. They left the house and ambled around to the back, where the clinic for small animals and its adjacent boarding kennels were located. The moment they opened the kennel door the "guests" began barking noisy greetings. While Whit let the eager dogs out into the runs, Leah walked along the concrete path between the chain-link pens, filling the water troughs. That done, her father motioned her toward his office in the clinic. Once inside, he gave her his grave attention. "Well?" he demanded.

"Dad, I've seen Jim."

Whit was halfway to the chair behind his desk. He stopped short and sucked in a startled breath. "Jim? Oh, Leah, where?"

"Right in Sedona."

"But...how...?"

"You won't believe it. Alex called me Tuesday afternoon. He asked me to hurry over to the gallery to meet a prominent Phoenix physician who wanted me to do a tapestry for him. The physician turned out to be Jim...only his name is Jacob Surratt."

"Dear God! What did you do?"

"I almost passed out."

"I'm surprised you didn't."

"It was so...so instantaneous. I didn't have time to collect myself. I turned around, and he was just there! I thought everything inside me had exploded. Fortunately, he thought I was ill rather than stunned to my toes."

Whit's breath escaped in a whistle. He continued on to his chair and slumped into it. Leah could tell the news had stunned him, just as she had known it would. He had been unusually close to his son-in-law and had taken Jim's disappearance hard. She thought he had held out hope of finding Jim long after she had given up. Keeping her eyes fastened on her father, she pulled a chair close to his desk and sat down.

"He didn't recognize you?" Whit asked in an unsteady voice.

She shook her head. "Not at all. He didn't recognize the house, either."

"He's been to the house?"

Leah nodded.

"Has he seen Nina?"

"Yes. Oh, dad, she's the living image of him!"

"Yeah, I figured as much. My memory's not all that

good, and six years have passed, but I always thought Nina looked like Jim.''

"Jacob didn't see it.''

"No," Whit said thoughtfully. "I guess you wouldn't see a thing like that, not unless you expected to. Well, if this isn't something!" He felt so much for Leah at that moment. What a helluva blow it must have been, to turn and find her husband standing there! But if anyone could handle this unexpected development, Leah could. Even now, she looked calm and collected. An astonishing woman, his daughter. He had always admired her level head, and he supposed he admired her courage. Lord knows, he was awed by it half the time. But he wouldn't mind seeing her slam a door, yell, cry, something. "It must have been rough,'' was all he said.

"Yes, it was.''

"You don't seem any the worse for wear.''

"I've had a couple of days to recover from the initial shock—and I must be a glutton for punishment. Alex and I were invited to spend the weekend at Dr. Surratt's home. I accepted.''

A moment passed. Leah wondered if that was really why she had wanted so desperately to talk to her father. He was the only person who knew what her relationship with Jim had been like. She wanted to confess her susceptibility to Jacob Surratt, and to seek Whit's reassurance that she had done the logical thing. She was reaching out to him for emotional comfort, just as she had as a child.

"You're going?" Whit asked with a frown.

"Yes.''

"Leah, I'm not too sure. . . . It couldn't possibly be the same. . . .''

"Dad, think about it. Try to see it from my viewpoint. Admittedly my first thought was to stay away, but.... If you were me, would you be able to stay away from him?''

Whit pursed his lips. ''No, I guess I wouldn't. Still, I can't help thinking about you, about all you've gone through.''

''I'll be all right, dad, honest.''

''Yeah, probably. So...tell me about it, tell me everything.''

When Leah had finished relating the details of her two meetings with Jacob, her father sighed deeply. ''I wonder why it never occurred to me that Jim might have been medically trained. You could tell he was educated, and he took to this work the way a duck takes to water. The closest I came was to wonder if he had lived around animals, or maybe was a medic in the army.''

''I think, after a while neither of us really tried too hard to find out about Jim's past. Not really.''

''Maybe you're right. Jim got to where he didn't want to talk about it anymore, and after the two of you were married...well, I guess we kinda dropped it.''

''But dad, something bugs me more than anything now that I know who he is. Prominent people don't just disappear without a trace. Why wasn't anyone looking for him?''

Whit shook his head. ''Damned if I know, but there's bound to be a reason. Maybe someone was, and all the signals got crossed. Tell me, Leah how does he look? Is he okay?''

''Oh, yes, he looks marvelous. Older, of course. He's thinner than he was when we knew him, and he's quieter, more reserved than Jim was. But you'd recognize him if you saw him, especially when you heard his voice.''

''I'd sure like to see him again.''

"I'd like for you to. There's not much chance, but you and the farm might jog his memory."

Whit frowned. "Is that what you want?"

"I . . . I think so."

"Are you going to do anything about it, help it along by telling him something?"

"I don't know, dad. I guess I'll just have to wait and see how the relationship develops. After all, Jacob Surratt and I have only known each other a few days. I have to keep reminding myself of that. I'm so afraid of mentioning something I'm not supposed to know." A small smile tugged at the corners of her mouth. "Jacob might be a little startled if I mentioned the scar on his hip." Instantly she sobered. "Jim had no idea where the scar had come from, but Jacob knows. He can tell me all sorts of things about Jim. Isn't that weird? I really am venturing into unknown territory. I don't have any idea what I should do."

"No, and I'm not sure anyone would. The mind's tough territory to explore."

"Something haunts Jacob," Leah said, more to herself than to Whit. "It's in his eyes. It must be those missing years."

"Well, I reckon that's understandable. If I had a couple of years gone from my life, I think they'd haunt me, too."

"Yes, I suppose so."

Whit's eyes were riveted on Leah, who had lapsed into some sort of private reverie. He studied her intently with fresh interest, for he noticed something he hadn't seen earlier: a certain radiance. An inner glow had heightened her color; her eyes sparkled with a mysterious light. Excitement bubbled just below her calm surface, and she looked the way she hadn't in a very long time—vital and alive. Whit had always thought his daughter pretty, but now she looked down-right beautiful.

She was looking forward to seeing Dr. Surratt again, and Whit couldn't say for sure how he felt about that. Jim Stone had adored Leah, but what if this fancy society doctor didn't? That would kill her.

Often during the past six years he had wished his daughter would find someone else, someone who would bring a little joy into her life. He realized his values were a bit old-fashioned for the modern generation, but it just didn't seem right for a woman Leah's age to be con-cerned with career and motherhood and nothing else. A man could live alone without too much trouble, but a woman shouldn't. If that made him archaic, so be it.

But what would have happened if she had found someone else and then seen Jim? Whit shuddered almost visibly at the thought.

Just then Leah turned to look at her father. The ra-diance he had noticed intensified. "Jacob Surratt is in-terested in me, dad. As a woman, I mean."

He grinned. "Oh, you know that, huh?"

"Of course. I felt the vibrations. Any woman over seventeen who doesn't recognize that look in a man's eyes is incredibly dense."

"Yeah, I figured as much. Your mother professed to be dumbfounded when I proposed to her, but I figured she always knew she could have me if she wanted me." Whit waited a moment. "How do you feel about that?"

"I don't understand, dad."

"He has no idea you're his wife, yet he's attracted to you. Say the attraction is real, the two of you get close. Could you handle that, go on with the new and never long for the old?"

Leah thought for a moment before answering. Shrugging, she said, "I hate to keep saying this, dad, but...I don't know. I honestly don't know. Something tells me I'll always want Jim back.''

"Jim...or the life you had together?''

"The life?''

"It was a simple life, really. You both were young and hadn't known any real trouble. Except for having to grow up without a mama, you had pretty well sailed through on smooth waters, while Jim didn't even have a past.''

Leah sighed. "You're right. It was a heavenly, carefree life, and I thought it would go on forever. Sure, I want that life back. Wouldn't you?''

"Which isn't exactly fair to Jacob Surratt, is it? He's bound to have a more intricate personality than Jim did.''

"Yes...he does. Much more. But I like him, too. It's complicated, isn't it?''

"If there's one thing I've learned in fifty-three years, it's that things are always complicated when you're dealing with human beings. Nothing's predictable. Maybe that's why I like working with animals. They're so simple and direct. What you see is what you get.'' Whit got to his feet. "Let's go find out what Nina's up to. We don't want her eating so many cookies she spoils her supper. Stay for supper, hon? I think Tee's whipping up a batch of chili. Spend the night?''

"I'd love to,'' Leah said, standing up also. Tonight, more than most nights, she needed her father's companionship. "I can go home first thing in the morning and get ready for the trip to Phoenix.''

Whit rounded the desk and put an affectionate arm around his daughter's shoulders. "I'll be thinking of you tomorrow night.''

"I know.''

"And I'll be a basket case until I find out what happened."

"I know that, too."

"I wish I could tell you I'm happy you've found him again, but I don't know for sure that I am—not yet. I wish I could always protect you from trouble, but no one can do that."

"That's true, but actually I've had precious little trouble in my life. Jim was about it. In a way, I have to be grateful."

"Damned if life doesn't have a way of sneaking up on you when your back's turned!"

"Tell me about it!"

CHAPTER SEVEN

THE SATURDAY-AFTERNOON DRIVE to Phoenix was anything but a joyous excursion. Leah was as edgy and nervous as a teenager getting ready for a big date; she was amazed at the butterflies in her stomach. Alex, in turn, was morose and laconic, very unlike him. Their mutual uneasiness didn't make for sparkling conversation. There were far too many clumsy silences, a first for them.

Yet underneath Leah's nervousness lay excitement and anticipation. She had hurried home from her father's house that morning to prepare for the trip, and for the first time in so long the day carried with it a sense of purpose. It had taken her an hour to get dressed, almost as long to decide what to pack, and that wasn't at all like the decisive person she normally was.

When Alex turned onto the quiet suburban street, Leah sat up straight and glanced around in confusion, as though wondering how on earth she had gotten there. Preoccupied, she couldn't remember a single detail of the journey. He braked then, turned off the street and drove through a massive wrought-iron gate, and she stared ahead of her curiously. Naturally she had expected Jacob to have a lovely home, and she wasn't disappointed. The house was a large, Spanish-style structure, built of eggshell stucco with archways and balconies and a tiled roof. Surrounding it were well-manicured grounds studded with color from neat gardens. "Gracious" was the first adjective that came to mind. A lovely, gracious home. It had probably been one of Scottsdale's finest when it had been built—some time ago, she guessed. What would a bachelor want with all this?

Which brought another question to mind: what had happened to the house during the two years Jacob had been Jim Stone? Houses like this didn't stand alone and neglected for two years. Surely whoever had taken care of it would have tried to find out where the owner was. For days her mind had been full of questions, none she dared ask.

Leah cast a surreptitious glance in Alex's direction, trying to gauge his reaction to their surroundings. Alex wasn't easily impressed, since he was accustomed to affluence himself, and he wasn't about to admit to being so now. "Very nice," was all he said.

Poor Alex, Leah mused ruefully. He was trying hard to be good about all this and failing miserably. He didn't want to be here, and he didn't want her here. Leah wished she had left him out of it altogether. But after all, Jacob had invited him, and Alex had accepted, albeit only because he didn't want her coming alone.

The car inched to a halt in front of a walled-in courtyard, apparently the main entrance. "Well, what now?" Alex asked. "Do we appear with bags in hand, or wait for lackeys to fetch them for us?"

Leah shrugged, ignoring the bite to his tone. She had never known Alex to be anything but gracious himself, and she was sure he would be now. Yet she had a feeling she was going to be under his watchful eye every step of the way. "We can always get our things later. Let's just let Jacob know we're here."

They walked through the tiled courtyard, thick with

plants, flowers and vines. Leah spied a bubbling fountain nestled against a vine-covered wall; here and there stood cozy groupings of wrought-iron furniture. Such lush, green loveliness didn't just happen in Arizona, Leah knew. Somebody or several somebodies devoted countless hours to maintaining the courtyard and grounds. The entire impression was of a desert oasis.

Alex rang the doorbell. Only seconds passed before a white-coated manservant answered it. Leah told him who they were, and the man smilingly held the door wide and motioned them inside. "Dr. Surratt is expecting you," he said courteously.

They stepped into a gleaming tiled foyer, in the center of which stood a round mahogany table. On top of that was the most exquisite—and quite possibly the most gigantic—porcelain vase Leah had ever seen. It held dozens of yellow roses, grown on the premises, she assumed. Quickly she scanned their surroundings. On their left was a formal living room; on their right a dining room. Other rooms opened off a long hallway, while ahead of them a mahogany-railed stairway rose to the second floor. It was impossible to take in everything at once, but Leah sensed that Jacob's home was furnished more for comfort than anything else. In spite of its size and immaculate condition, the house looked lived in, not untouchable.

She lifted her eyes to Jacob, who was hurrying down the stairway with a welcoming smile on his face. He was dressed much the way he had been Wednesday afternoon—impeccably and casually in slacks, dark gray, and a white knit shirt. *He looks like a doctor,* she suddenly thought. *But that's ridiculous. What does a doctor look like?* Powerless to control the acceleration of her heartbeat, Leah could only breathe deeply. Would she ever see him without longing to be in his arms?

"That's all right, Davis," Jacob said, coming up behind the man. "I'll see to our guests. Please tend to their luggage."

"Very good, sir."

Jacob stepped forward, extending his hand to Alex. "Trent, it's good to see you again."

"Thank you, doctor. I appreciate the invitation. This is quite a place you have here." Alex's voice was coolly cordial.

"Thank you. It's been in the family for a number of years, almost twenty. It's much too large for my needs, of course, and the upkeep is a constant chore, but I've never gotten around to selling."

Leah's curiosity was further peaked. A house? A family? Concrete reasons to wonder why no one had been looking for him.

Jacob turned to her, and an anticipatory gleam he couldn't suppress shone in his eyes. For two days he had been filled with excitement, convinced that some momentous event was about to occur. He had reminded himself more than once that she was coming for the opening, nothing more. She would spend one night in his house, and her watchdog Trent would be with her. Ridiculous to think anything noteworthy would come of their meeting, yet now, as he drank in the sight of her, the excitement returned, stronger than ever.

She was wearing a simple dress the color of lime sherbet, one of those straight things—he thought they were called sheaths—that skimmed her hips and stopped just below her knees. Her lustrous hair was caught at the nape with a print scarf, and tiny gold loops hung from her earlobes. For a moment he was almost mesmerized by her eyes; a man could fall into those dark eyes, he thought. Each time he saw her he was struck again by her unusual beauty, so clean and wholesome on one hand, so exotic on the other.

"Leah," he said softly, "welcome to my home. I'm so glad you're here."

"Thank you," she murmured in return. "It's lovely."

The exchange was simple and proper, yet Leah was fully aware of the sizzling current of sensuality passing between them. She couldn't have been more affected had he swept her into his arms and kissed her passionately. The sound of her own pulse hammered in her ears. Her cheeks grew very warm, and for one horrifying second she thought she was going to blush.

As much as Jacob would have liked to continue staring at her, he shook himself free from fascination, aware of the third party who was witnessing this exchange with more than casual curiosity. He could feel Trent's eyes boring through the back of his head. Rubbing his hands together in a gesture of satisfaction, he said, "Well, let me show you to your rooms. Then feel free to pass the time any way you like. We'll be leaving for the clinic around seven, returning here afterward for dinner. I hope that suits you both."

Leah and Alex assured him it did.

"This way, then. . . ."

Leah hoped she wasn't gawking, but her head swiveled this way and that as she and Alex followed Jacob up the stairway. It was readily apparent that the house belonged to a man with eclectic tastes and a passion for collecting. Evidence of that was everywhere. Some valuable paintings in ornate frames lined the stairway, each properly lighted. At the landing between the first and second floors, a stark futuristic painting was displayed on a bentwood easel beside an antique stained-glass window. A collection of dried flowers and grasses in a handwoven basket stood on the floor beneath the window, completing the display. Alex's eyes were about to pop out of his head. He would have a field day just wandering from room to room.

The house seemed to go on and on. Leah counted at least five bedrooms on the second floor. They passed one she was sure was Jacob's. It looked like him, tailored, elegantly masculine. Next to it was the one Alex was to stay in. Leah waited in the hall while the two men went inside, her interest arrested by two portraits—one of a distinguished man, the other of a regal-looking woman. She moved closer to study them.

No one had to tell her the gentleman was Jacob's father; the resemblance was unmistakable. Handsome people, both of his parents. Nina's grandparents.... If they knew about the child, would they be as foolish about her as Whit was? Leah blinked, and a lump formed in her throat. Years ago, when pregnant with Nina, she had desperately wished she could have found out something about Jim's mother and father. She didn't know why, but it had always seemed she should know more about the genes her child would inherit. Silly. Who thought about such things anymore?

There was a movement behind her. "Leah?" Jacob's voice broke through her pensive thoughts.

She turned with a start. "What? Oh, I...I was just admiring these portraits. Your parents?"

"Yes. They died in a boating accident while I was doing my residency." Her expression puzzled him. "Is something the matter?"

"No...no, nothing." She should have guessed they had died before she met Jim; parents would have frantically searched for a missing son. So who had kept the house while he was gone? Jacob was not the man with no ties they had imagined Jim to be. "Do you have brothers or sisters?"

"No, I was an only child. The last of the Surratt line, unfortunately."

There's Nina, she wanted to say.

Gently Jacob touched her elbow. "Your room is this way, at the end of the hall."

The bedroom, like everything else she had seen in the house, was tastefully furnished, a skillful blend of contemporary and antique. A king-size bed covered with a quilted terra-cotta spread dominated the room. A love seat in a coordinating print stood against one wall, and next to it was a Jacobean secretary desk. The almond-colored carpet beneath her feet was thick and plush. "It's beautiful, Jacob."

"I hope you'll be comfortable." He crossed the room and drew aside the drapes, instantly bathing the room in a lucid light. "This room has a private bath, over there." He pointed to a door on the right. "And it overlooks the pool."

Leah placed her handbag on a nearby dresser and went to stand beside him, looking down. "That's inviting."

"Did you happen to bring a suit? I forgot to suggest it."

"Yes, I did." She had packed one just in case, for she had supposed swimming pools were as common as dishwashers in Scottsdale.

"Then let's go for a swim, shall we?"

"I'd love it."

Jacob made some kind of move, to adjust the blinds or something. The only thing Leah was aware of was his nearness, his arm brushing hers, the intoxicatingly clean scent of him. If he moved even half a step closer he would feel her trembling, and what would reserved Dr. Surratt think of that? It was definitely becoming harder and harder to breathe. And she had thought

Wednesday afternoon difficult! Getting through this, then tonight with any degree of poise should earn her a medal.

At that moment he took the half step she had hoped he wouldn't; his larger body seemed to hover over hers. Leah stood paralyzed, staring at the pulse point at the base of his throat. Slowly she raised her face to look at him. Her heart-stopping thought was that he was going to kiss her. If he did, she would kiss him back. And why not? She was his wife. She had every right to kiss him all she liked.

Dolt! He doesn't know that! You can't just fall into his arms. What would he think?

Jacob thought that in all his life he had never wanted to kiss anyone so badly. He might have been on an amphetamine high, because Leah had the most uncanny ability to make him feel reckless and a little impetuous—things he had never been, not even in his youth. He raised one hand, poised at her shoulder. Would she be offended by a simple kiss? Odd how little he knew about today's women.

Contrary to popular gossip around the clinic and the country club, he didn't get involved with a lot of women. For reasons he couldn't fathom, they seemed drawn to him, but he was rarely sexually involved with them. In younger days he had had frequent passionate needs. Even Jacob Surratt had lived through a period when "scoring" with girls had been the most important thing on earth. But six years ago he had emerged from his fugue state to find himself longing for something more satisfying than a casual romantic fling. Since then he had cautiously searched for something he privately suspected didn't exist. For that reason he had guarded against emotional entanglements. Solitude spared him disappointment.

Yet he wanted to become involved with this woman—

emotionally, sexually and every other way. Could he possibly know that for sure in such a short time? Maybe not, but having waited so long to feel this way, he wasn't about to spoil it by asking himself pertinent questions. Wanting her felt too damned good. Wanting her felt...human. His hand touched her shoulder, and he looked down at her with undisguised hunger. "Leah...."

Briefly she closed her eyes, the better to enjoy the sensation of his touch. She opened them, and the past six years simply melted away. The look on Jacob's face reminded her of ones she had received from her young husband countless times. More guarded perhaps, but basically the same. An ache stirred deep inside her, down in the lower part of her stomach. He wanted to kiss her, and she wanted him to. It was a compulsion too real to deny. She longed to melt against him, slip her arms around his waist, rest her head on his shoulder, and she seemed to have lost all hold on reality. "Yes," she said breathlessly, dreamily.

"Do you have any idea what a shock it is for a man my age to be swept off his feet?"

His frankness was so disarming that Leah took a step backward, staring up at him in surprise. The thought of this sophisticated, urbane man being swept off his feet brought forth a giggle, effectively shattering the sweet eloquence of the moment. And for that fact she was suddenly, enormously grateful. Had Jacob actually kissed her, she feared her response would have been much too eager, anything but a "first kiss" kind of kiss. And the admiration she saw in his eyes might have diminished considerably. Damn, it was so hard to remember she barely knew him!

"The young lady's luggage, sir," a discreet masculine voice said. "Where shall I put it?"

Leah turned to see Davis standing at the threshold.

He was carrying her garment bag in one hand, her overnighter in the other. Beside her, Jacob released a raspy breath. "The bag in the closet, Davis, please. And just leave the suitcase on the bed."

"Yes, sir." After following his employer's instructions, Davis quickly left the room.

Needing to put some distance between them, Leah walked to the foot of the bed and unlatched her suitcase, flipping it open and reaching for her swimsuit. "I do hope Alex thought to bring swim trunks. He probably didn't, though. I didn't mention it, and it's not the sort of thing he would think of." She chattered on. "Alex is the kind who would rather sit by a pool than dive into it."

Jacob frowned. Had he totally misread the expression on Leah's face a moment earlier? He didn't think so, but she was flustered now, charmingly so. If she was interested in him—and he had to think she was—the fact troubled her. The husband again; had to be. Ex-husband, he forcibly reminded himself. She still loved him, so showing interest in another man might seem unfaithful to her. What else would account for her skittishness where he was concerned?

So, okay, he wouldn't pounce. He wasn't sure he knew how to pounce, anyway. This was a time when he wished he was more adept at clever masculine games and come-ons. What he feared more than anything was appearing to be an insensitive clod on the make...still he knew a number of men whom he considered insensitive clods, and they seemed to do very well with women.

They wouldn't do well with Leah Stone, he thought decisively. She was different. And though they both had voids in their lives, Leah apparently wasn't as ready to let him fill hers as he was to let her fill his, so he'd move cautiously. Actually, he found her reluctance appealing; even a bit old-fashioned. But engaging nevertheless. Loyalty and fidelity weren't exactly a glut on the market these days.

Pretending nothing unusual had transpired, Jacob smiled offhandedly and made for the door. "Tell you what—I'll ask Trent if he brought trunks. If not, I'm sure I have some he can wear. Then we'll meet at poolside, the three of us. All right?"

"Yes. Yes, that's fine." Blankly Leah stared after his retreating figure. When he was out of sight she sank wearily to the edge of the bed, feeling as helpless and out of control as a lost child.

LEAH LIFTED HERSELF out of the pool and went to lie facedown on a lounge. Nearby, Jacob and Alex sat beneath an umbrella table, deep in a discussion about a new artist they both knew and admired. Leah smiled as she caught snatches of the conversation. Alex, in spite of his reservations, was enjoying himself, and Jacob seemed to be more relaxed than she had yet seen him.

She had been so aware of his eyes on her when she had first appeared at the pool. Her jade-green maillot was a modest swimsuit, but it was a swimsuit. It exposed all of her gentle curves to his avid gaze. It seemed Dr. Surratt's reserve was slipping badly. He, who knew human anatomy the way she knew warp and weft, had looked at her as though he'd never seen the female form before. Even though he had stayed at the table with Alex, hadn't joined her in the pool, she had known he was watching her.

But after her first look at him she found it all but impossible to look again. He was wearing a stark white terry-cloth shirt, unbuttoned to reveal his thickly matted chest, and light blue swim trunks. She had always thought him so damned sexy in swim trunks, a lean, bronzed man. Completely desirable. Seeing him dressed that way made her aware of her own femininity, a femininity that had been held in limbo for six years.

Davis stopped at the lounge and offered her a lemonade. Thanking him, she took it and sipped slowly, idly wondering how many servants inhabited the place, halfheartedly following the men's conversation, mostly lost in a private daze. The sun induced laziness, and she closed her eyes, lulled into a half stupor by the deep resonance of Jacob's voice. Jim's voice.... Her stomach fluttered. It all might have been a dream.

Then, when she had soaked up all the sun she dared so early in the season, she pushed herself up, swung her legs off the lounge, and found her eyes fixed squarely on a pair of muscular legs. Jacob stood beside the lounge, poised on the balls of his feet. Leah took in his stance, the perfect shape of his legs, the way his bathing trunks molded to his body and blatantly outlined his masculine form. A lump formed in her throat that she had some difficulty swallowing past.

Her eyes continued upward; she was afraid she might have to sit on her hands to keep from reaching for him. He was holding something in his hand and smiling down at her. "Lotion?" he asked. "You're still very fair. You might burn."

"Thanks," she said shakily, and took the tube from him. Squirting a little circle of cream into her palm, she nervously smeared it over her shoulders and down her arms. More cream, and she covered her thighs and calves. Glancing toward the table where he'd been sitting, she saw that the other chair was vacant. "Where's Alex?"

"Inside." Jacob cocked his head toward the pool.

Then, to her consternation, he dropped onto the lounge beside her and took the tube from her hand. "Here, let me do your back."

Her protest died in her throat. She tended to make too big a deal of everything regarding this man, and he would think her silly. His warm hand touched her shoulder blades, making her flinch. As it moved over her shoulders and back, rubbing gently, she felt goose bumps prickling her arms. Nervously she massaged them away, hoping he hadn't seen.

Abruptly he stopped and recapped the cream. "You're a good swimmer. Want to go in again?"

Forgetting she had been on her way inside herself, forgetting she had already had all the sun she should, she stood up. "All right. Last one in...."

They hit the water simultaneously, cleaving through it like two knives. Jacob, however, quickly outdistanced her and was treading water, waiting for her when she reached the opposite pool wall. Surfacing, blinking away water, she crossed her arms on the concrete edge and looked at him. Slick wet hair clung to his face and neck.

"Pretty good," he said appreciatively.

"And you're awfully good. Once a lifeguard, I'll bet." She had told Jim that several times. He, of course, hadn't known if it was true.

Jacob nodded. "A long, long time ago."

She could visualize him—eighteen or nineteen years old, a tanned young man seated on the platform, pretending to be oblivious to all the admiring feminine stares. There must have been legions of dreamy-eyed teenage girls....

"And you were a Red Cross instructor, right?" he asked.

"Uh-huh. During summers when I was in college."

The pool area was very quiet; the only sound was the faint hum of the filtering system. Jacob's gaze held hers steadfastly. He saw her lashes dip under his scrutiny, and he realized he stared at her too long too often. She laid her cheek on her folded arms. Disregarding all politeness and convention, he continued to stare at her. His hand moved beneath the water to rest at the small of her back. This need to touch her was overwhelming.

At the pressure of his fingers, Leah stiffened and raised her head, then relaxed and uncrossed her arms. While one hand gripped the pool's edge, the other reached for his solid forearm. It was true that his constant scrutiny made her nervous. Had he been a stranger she might have been offended. But there was no way he could offend her. She wanted to float right into his arms. She picked up his vibrations, and a tingling sensation shot up her legs. She closed them tightly in an effort to suppress it.

Her fingers closing round his arm encouraged Jacob to glide even closer to her. Her eyes were wide, her lips slightly parted. The look she gave him made Jacob's heart pound. *Isn't it amazing,* he thought, *that two strangers can come together like this and, with virtually no effort, establish this rapport? She feels it, too. She doesn't like it; she might even hate it, but she feels it, too.*

That knowledge sent his mind winging off on some wild, uncharted course of expectation. Beneath the water his arm encircled her waist, pulling her closer. Their thighs touched.

If he wants to kiss me now, Leah thought, *I'm going to let him. Propriety be damned.* Her hunger for him was something she could taste in her mouth.

A voice called to them from the far side of the pool. "Are you two aware of the time?" Leah and Jacob swiveled their heads to see Alex watching them with a guarded expression.

"Afraid not!" Jacob called back.

"If we're going to leave by seven, Leah might start giving some thought to getting ready."

Leah slowly expelled a controlled breath. "He's right. Not being one of you fortunate males, I can't just shower and shave and be off. It takes some time for me to put my best foot forward, especially—" she touched her drenched hair "—especially after swimming."

"Then shall we make a return trip?"

"Yes, let's."

With slow strokes, breaking the water with only a ripple, they crossed the pool. Jacob lifted himself out, then helped her. Reaching for a towel, he draped it around her shoulders, holding it there longer than necessary. His hand brushed her breast, and Leah took a clumsy step backward. "I'll see you later," she said, and feeling as unsophisticated as the woman who had married Jim Stone, she hurried into the house. She knew he watched her until she was out of sight.

Upstairs, she discovered someone had laid out an irresistible array of toiletries in the bathroom, and on the bedside stand she discovered a small carafe of wine, a wineglass, a wedge of brie and a peeled, sliced kiwi. She'd wager not even the Biltmore could surpass the Surratt house for hospitality.

Since she had plenty of time—Alex had seen to that, she reflected wryly—Leah treated herself to the works: luxurious bath, shampoo, manicure, pedicure. Sipping wine and nibbling fruit and cheese, she paid special attention to her makeup. Devoting undue time to the routine task of getting dressed was something new to her, but it was just what she needed. Her confidence bolstered, she was certain she could, with some effort, learn to regard Jacob as an exciting new man who had unexpectedly entered her life. She would stop longing for Jim, stop searching for him in Jacob. She was going to enjoy this. Jacob made her feel like a desirable woman, and she hadn't felt that way in a long time.

An hour later she stood in front of the full-length mirror attached to the back of the closet door. It wouldn't be enough to simply look her best; she wanted to feel her best, be at her best. Everything she had brought to wear to the opening—the simple black dress, the lacy black underwear, jewelry, fragrance— everything had been chosen with that thought in mind. The dress was a marvel of simplicity, and there was nothing like black to make her feel dressed up. Raising her arms, she clasped a single strand of perfect pearls around her neck. One more inspection in the mirror, then she picked up her small black clutch, left the bedroom and went to join the men.

Following the sound of their voices, she walked down the hallway and paused at the threshold of a paneled room that had to be the den. Floor-to-ceiling, book-crammed shelves lined the walls on three sides. Jacob and Alex were there, both dressed in tuxedos, both holding aperitif glasses. Since they hadn't seen her yet, she took the time to study both of them.

She had always thought Alex looked splendid in a tux, and tonight was no exception. The formal dress suited him; he was that kind of man. Often he hosted formal dinner parties in his home, and everything was done with flair—the finest china, linen, crystal, food served in proper courses with appropriate wines, ladies in long dresses and gentlemen in tuxedos. He loved that sort of thing. Leah smiled. She sometimes thought Alex would have been more at home in another era.

Then her eyes moved on to Jacob, and a shock wave jolted her. Jacob in evening dress was something to see! Tall, dark and gorgeous. He had...presence. And savoir faire, polish and the indefinable something called class. With him dressed like that, she shouldn't find it hard to forget Jim tonight. She could count on the fingers of one hand the times she had seen Jim in anything but jeans. Once she had bought him a suit, but he never had worn it....

There you go, Leah. Stop it. She straightened, shook herself free of such thoughts and stepped into the room. "Good evening," she said brightly, and both men turned in her direction.

"Leah," Alex said, moving toward her. "Why, I don't think I've ever seen you looking lovelier."

She smiled softly. "Thanks, Alex." Almost shyly she looked over Alex's shoulder, her gaze colliding with Jacob's. She saw him swallow rapidly, then his mouth opened and quickly closed again. Apparently there were things he wanted to say but couldn't. He didn't have to; his eyes said it all. A woman is as beautiful as she feels, Leah thought, and in that one spellbound moment, she felt absolutely, ravishingly beautiful.

"Would you like a drink?" Alex inquired solicitously.

"No, thanks. There was some marvelous wine in my room. What a thoughtful gesture, Jacob."

He cleared his throat, collecting himself. "I wish I could take credit for it, but actually it was Davis's idea. He has a flair for that sort of thing."

"Then I must remember to thank Davis. Have I kept you gentlemen waiting long?"

"Not long. Alex has been enjoying some of my collection. Besides, any wait would have been worth it."

Alex took her by the arm. "Come here, Leah, I

want to show you something. A signed Thomas Moran, circa 1902. Jacob has an impressive collection of southwestern artists.''

Leah smiled secretively. She noticed it was no longer ''Trent'' and ''Doctor,'' and she wasn't the least surprised that the two men had taken to each other. They were birds of a feather; how could they help liking each other? She allowed Alex to lead her across the room to view the Moran.

Jacob watched them, or rather he watched Leah. Her glistening hair was wound into a sleek chignon, giving her just a hint of stylish sophistication. The dress she was wearing was simple, baring only her smooth arms and the slender taper of her shapely legs. He couldn't imagine her ever dressing in a daring or provocative manner, yet he'd wager there wouldn't be a woman at the opening who would equal her in sex appeal.

His appreciative gaze lingered on her, and anticipation welled inside him. Tonight he felt curiously removed from his customary role of prominent physician and upstanding member of the community. Tonight he felt loose and free, like a young man on a date with a lovely woman. Unfortunately—he shifted his gaze to Alex—his date was chaperoned. He wondered if he could reasonably hope for time alone with her before the evening was over.

CHAPTER EIGHT

THE OPENING TURNED OUT to be exactly the sort of affair Leah had pictured—a large cocktail party full of shine and glitter, lavish food, laughter and animated conversation. The crème de la crème of Phoenix society was there, dressed to the teeth, anxious to see and be seen. Jacob dutifully led his guests through the throng, introducing them to acquaintances; other people came forward to introduce themselves to him. Leah knew she wouldn't remember any of their names; she was too intent on observing the stir Jacob created when he entered the place. Heads turned, all right—all in his direction. She thought it odd that a man who projected aloofness drew people like a magnet, but perhaps it was that very aloofness that made him so intriguing.

He soon became separated from them, since everyone seemed to want a word with Dr. Surratt. Alex, as usual, immediately encountered someone he knew from somewhere; Leah had never been with him when he hadn't. After a few minutes of polite conversation with Alex's friend, she left the two men deep in discussion and unobtrusively backed off, helped herself to a glass of punch and found a quiet corner where she could view the proceedings with her customary lack of interest. The party's din was deafening. Were all these people really having as good a time as they appeared to be?

Brief snatches of conversation reached her. Nearby,

two men were arguing the relative merits of several investment plans. A couple walked by, and she heard the woman say, "I'm surprised Peggy didn't leave town. I certainly would if that happened to me!"

Leah smiled, thinking how interesting the story behind that must be.

Three women moved past her just then, all of them elegantly dressed, all of them in their midthirties, she guessed. They stopped just a few feet from her, and though she wasn't in the least interested in their conversation, she couldn't help overhearing it. The women, she soon surmised, were close friends, married to doctors associated with the clinic and well acquainted with most of the guests. Leah tried to ignore them; possibly she would have if a name hadn't reached her ears.

"Surratt's something in a tux, isn't he?"

"Oh, I don't know. Kinda cold and forbidding, if you ask me."

"Joe says he runs a tight ship."

"Probably runs his house the same way. Can you imagine being married to someone like that?"

"He's pushing forty and hasn't ever been married, which makes you wonder about him right away."

"Well, looking at him tonight...damned good-looking, I must say."

"Too cold. Bet he makes love like a robot."

"Hell, I'll bet he could knock your socks off if he took a mind to."

The women moved on, and Leah flushed, hating the picture of the mechanical, unresponsive lover that had formed in her mind. Jim hadn't been cold, far from it, but she wondered about Jacob. She thought she had seen a side of him that was anything but.

Her gaze moved to the huge wall where her tapestry would hang. Quietly contemplating the space, she changed her mind about the design. Alex and Jacob had been right to insist she actually see the room and the wall. She decided on something bolder than she had originally envisioned, something that would draw the eye upward....

AT THAT MOMENT, across the room a door opened and a stocky, sandy-haired man of about forty walked through. Though dressed in evening clothes, he was no imposing figure. He had the uncomfortable look of a man who is someplace he doesn't want to be. He tugged at his shirt cuffs, pressed his bow tie with thumb and forefinger. He paused, and his eyes swept the room, settled for a moment on the large group surrounding Jacob, then moved on.

Dr. Charles White was late, but his arrival caused no stir. In fact, barely half a dozen people seemed to notice him at all. Of those who did, only one stepped forward to greet him, a stout, stylish matron. Extending a bejeweled hand, she beamed at the psychiatrist.

"Dr. White, how wonderful to see you again!"

Charles took her hand and searched his brain for the woman's name. To his dismay, nothing came to him. "Why, hello, there. So glad you could come."

"I wouldn't have missed it for the world. Surely you know that."

Charles's mind remained blank, but some inner sense told him he should know who the woman was. "Quite a turnout, wouldn't you say?"

The woman eyed him suspiciously. "Yes, it is." A perfectly manicured fingertip tapped the side of her mouth. "Dr. White, you don't remember me at all, do you?"

"Oh, of course I do. I—"

"Clarice Hall," the woman said with a cool smile.

"Certainly, Clarice. Wonderful to have you here."
Had it been physically possible, Charles would have
kicked his own fanny. Clarice was the wife of one of the
clinic's chief benefactors, a local philanthropist whose
donatons had been more than generous. She prided herself on being a well-known local figure. People like
Clarice Hall expected to be recognized. He had just
committed a social faux pas of considerable magnitude,
which he did far too frequently.

Damn! And it would be useless to try to make
amends; the woman had seen right through him. Chagrined, he acknowledged her curt goodbye with as much
aplomb as he could muster, watching her stiff, regal
departure. His damaged composure was hardly helped
when, a few seconds later, he saw Clarice Hall approach
Jacob and distinctly heard his partner say, "Clarice,
how wonderful you look!"

Shrugging away his ineptitude, Charles moved to the
refreshment table to pour himself a cup of punch. Sipping it absently, he surveyed the throng, his eyes darting
aimlessly about . . . until they fell on the slender young
woman in the black dress standing apart from the
crowd. They fastened on her, widened, then narrowed
in a thorough inspection. Slowly he moved away from
the table to stand against a wall, but his eyes never left
the woman. . . .

LEAH'S THOUGHTS WERE INTERRUPTED when she had the
distinct feeling she was being watched. Turning abruptly, she saw a sturdy-looking man lounging against a
wall several yards behind her. Apparently he'd been
staring at her, and there was the strangest expression on
his face. When she caught his eye without warning, he
immediately straightened and looked away, flustered.
For a moment he seemed to want to turn and walk

away. Then he recovered and shifted his eyes back to her. A nervous smile crossed his face. Hesitantly he moved toward her, and Leah braced herself for a typical come-on, albeit not a very smooth, expert one. The look on his face was unmistakably curious. She wouldn't have been at all surprised if he had begun his overture with something as hackneyed as, "Haven't I seen you someplace . . . ?"

Curiously, she thought she might very well have said the same thing to him. His face looked vaguely familiar . . . or did it? Something made her think she had seen him before.

"Good evening," he said as he approached. "Forgive me for staring, but you seem rather bored."

On second thought, Leah decided he just had one of those faces, ordinarily pleasant, unspectacular. He looked like dozens of people. "Do I? Well, I'm not. Actually, I was studying that wall over there." She indicated it with a wave of her hand.

The man looked at the wall, then back at her. "It's rather large, isn't it? But frankly, apart from its sheer size, I see nothing particularly fascinating about it."

Leah smiled. "No, perhaps most people wouldn't, but it holds special interest for me."

The man made a show of giving that some thought. "Now I'm wondering what would cause a lovely young woman to be so interested in a wall. I have it! You're an architect."

"Not even close. I'm a professional weaver, and Dr. Surratt has commissioned me to do a tapestry for that very wall."

The man's expression changed. "You know Jacob?" he asked in disbelief.

Leah wondered why her words had evoked that response. "Yes, I do."

"Have you known him long?"

"As a matter of fact, I only met him a few days ago." She frowned. "Why?"

The man seemed to give himself a shake. He extended his hand, and the smile returned. "Had you known Jacob long, I'm sure I would have either heard about you or met you by now. I'm Charles White, Jacob's partner."

"Oh, Dr. White." She juggled her punch cup and shook his hand. "How nice to meet you. I'm Leah Stone."

"The pleasure is mine, Leah. So...you met Jacob through your work?"

"Yes, he had seen one of my tapestries and contacted me."

"Interesting. Well, what do you think of our little place?"

"From what I've seen, it's impressive. And it isn't little."

"No, it isn't. But it is impressive. This clinic is unique in many ways. For one thing, our physicians work for a salary. Would you have imagined that?"

"No, I wouldn't have. But why...?" She hesitated.

"Why would a physician want to work for a salary when private practice is so lucrative? That's what you were going to ask, wasn't it?"

Leah nodded.

"Many reasons. One, the beginning salaries are generous. Two, the facilities are superb. Working here, a doctor has all the latest technology available and doesn't have the responsibility of maintaining an office, hiring and firing and all that. You'd be surprised how attractive a feature that is. Since you don't seem enormously interested in this—" he made a sweeping gesture with his arm to indicate the packed reception room "—human circus, why don't you let me show you around?"

Leah's eyes quickly scanned the room. Jacob was standing in the middle of a group of people, most of them women. She guessed it would be some time before he was free. "Why, thank you, doctor. I'd like that."

She slipped her hand into the crook of Dr. White's elbow, and together they left the party. For the next twenty minutes or so they peered into treatment rooms and offices, X-ray centers and laboratories. Leah understood little of the psychiatrist's explanations concerning the complicated equipment. All she saw was a gleaming, modern clinic that would probably be a good place in which to find out what ailed you. Finally, at the end of a long corridor, Dr. White pushed open a double door, and they stepped into an entirely different world.

"My bailiwick," he informed her. "This is the psychiatric unit."

There was nothing clinical about this part of the building. The reception room was furnished very much like an elegant study, subdued. There was a music room, a small snack bar and a library. There were no treatment rooms, only half a dozen offices, all beautifully decorated, all with the obligatory couch, even if for appearances only. The largest and most elegant of these was set off from the others by a paneled vestibule. "My office," Charles White said, opening an ornately carved oak door. "Please come in."

Leah stepped into a room anyone would have enjoyed occupying, decorated with thick taupe carpeting, grass-cloth-covered walls, several paintings that had been chosen more for their color scheme than for artistic value, and three enormous plants. One wall was given over to glass-front bookcases. "Lovely," she murmured. "Restful."

"It was meant to be. Patients who come to this office need to forget everyday turmoil, for fifty minutes, at least. I have sherry. Would you care for some?"

"No, thanks. The punch was enough. We'll be leaving soon, I imagine. Jacob is having dinner for us at his house."

"You're Jacob's houseguest?"

She nodded. "Alex and I are spending the night there, yes."

"Alex?"

"He owns the gallery that handles my work."

"Are you married, Leah?"

The question was abrupt, taking her by surprise. "No, I... not anymore."

Charles pursed his lips and studied her intently. Too intently, Leah thought. His manner was unusual to the point of being unnerving. She was being placed under a microscope, but with none of the usual man-woman interest. The old cliché about psychiatrists being at least as odd as their patients popped into her head; then she dismissed it. He was curious about her, but so what? Wouldn't it be only natural for Dr. White to wonder about his partner's new woman friend?

Pretending to be fascinated by the psychiatrist's large collection of books, she idly wandered toward the bookcases. "Have you actually had time to read all these?"

He chuckled. "Most of them. Parts of all of them."

"You have several books on hypnotism." Her eyes scanned the titles. "Does that sort of thing really work?"

"It can be an effective tool, yes."

"Do you use it?"

"Sometimes."

"It looks as though memory is another of your interests. Improving it, retaining it, abnormalities...." Leah turned to Dr. White. "Like amnesia?"

"Yes." He moved to stand beside her. "Fascinating subject. I once wrote a paper on amnesia, which, I'm happy to say, was published."

She wondered if Charles White knew of Jacob's condition, if that was something he would have told his partner. She had no idea how long the two men had known each other. For sure she wasn't supposed to know about the amnesia, but Dr. White was the knowledgeable person she had been wishing for. He could answer some of her questions, if she proceeded cautiously....

"I can't imagine forgetting a huge slice of your life," she commented casually. "Does a person just forget...everything?"

"Everything, no. Names, places, time, events—those things are forgotten. But not things like speech, manners, traffic laws, motor skills. All those things that are so heavily overlearned throughout life are normally retained."

"If you've published a paper on amnesia, you must have treated many cases."

"Many short-term cases. A few long-term ones. My main interest is in psychological amnesia."

Leah turned abruptly. "Psychological?"

"Yes. Amnesia can be caused by illness or injury, of course, but then there's the complex world of psychological amnesia, where a patient professes to want to remember but actually doesn't. Fascinating. I've found, in most cases, that the patient's present life is so pleasant, he fears memory return will only complicate it."

Dr. White had confirmed an earlier suspicion. Once she and Jim had fallen in love, he had stopped trying to find out about his past. Could Jacob be doing the same thing? "Interesting," she murmured. "What are the chances of a patient's recalling things that happened during the fugue?"

He looked startled. "You know the name for it?"

"I, ah, once knew someone with amnesia. That's what he called it." Leah bit her lip. Dumb thing to say. It didn't jibe with all the questions she'd been asking. Oh, well. Maybe he wouldn't realize that.

"I see." The psychiatrist rubbed a forefinger across his mouth. "The chances are, frankly, poor. And the more time that passes, the poorer they become. Even good memory dims with the years."

"One more question, doctor, and then I really should go back to the party. Alex and Jacob might be ready to leave."

"Of course. What's the question?"

"If you had a friend with amnesia, and if you knew what had happened to that friend during the period of memory loss, would you tell him what you knew?"

Charles White frowned darkly, staring at the floor a moment. Then he looked up. "No," he said decisively, "I wouldn't."

"Why not?"

"Because it would require too swift an adjustment on the amnesiac's part. And it would do nothing to restore memory, only add to the confusion. Besides...there's always the chance you could be dealing with psychological amnesia. By telling the patient something he or she doesn't really want to know, you might be doing irreparable harm." He emphasized the word "irreparable."

Every nerve in Leah's body seemed to tighten. Instinct had warned her against saying anything to Jacob, so in that respect she had been right. She could accept the fact that he wouldn't be able to immediately adjust to the knowledge. But psychological amnesia? She'd never heard of it. She couldn't believe that Jacob subconsciously didn't want to remember her or their brief life together. That was too much to ask of her already overburdened heart.

"Amnesia must be handled delicately," the psychiatrist went on. "Certainly it isn't something for a lay person to, er, fool around with. I'm sure you understand that." His eyes bore down on her as if to underscore the warning.

Leah nodded mutely.

"What happened to your friend?" Charles asked.

"Friend?"

"The friend with amnesia."

"Oh, I . . . I don't know," she said lamely. "He went away, and I lost track of him."

LEAH RETURNED TO THE PARTY to discover Jacob and Alex were indeed looking for her, both of them anxious to leave. Conversation on the way back to the Surratt house was mostly limited to offhand remarks about the party, the food, the beautiful new clinic, but Jacob seemed mildly surprised to learn that Charles White had taken the time to show Leah around.

"Charles?" he asked.

"Yes. Why?"

He shrugged. "Oh, no reason in particular. That kind of hospitality doesn't sound much like Charles, that's all."

Once they returned to the house they were immediately ushered into the dining room and treated to a superb dinner. Afterward they adjourned to the den for after-dinner drinks and more conversation.

Alex was in a wonderful mood, for this type of evening was his cup of tea—plenty of food, people and talk. Leah feigned rapt interest in everything being said, but she actually heard little of it. Her interest was centered on their host, and a vague sort of restlessness gripped her, along with disappointment. She hadn't had a moment alone with Jacob all evening. She knew no more about him than she had before, only that he seemed the antithesis of Jim Stone. Whatever she had hoped this visit would accomplish—and she wasn't at all sure what she'd expected—hadn't come about.

Her eyes wandered around the den, then collided unexpectedly with Jacob's. She thought he telegraphed his own disappointment, and her heart skipped a beat. Quickly she glanced at Alex, who, it seemed, intended talking half the night. Jacob politely returned his attention to his guest, and the minutes continued to tick by.

It was almost midnight when Alex finally got to his feet. "Well, Jacob, this has been a great evening, but I guess I'll call it a day. How about you, Leah?"

She was in the rather awkward position of having to follow him upstairs and end the day, too, or simply saying something like, "In a minute, Alex. I'll see you in the morning." She chose the latter and suffered the look she received from her friend.

Jacob walked with Alex to the foot of the stairs; the two men exchanged a few more words. Once Alex had gone upstairs Jacob returned to the den. He looked at her with unrestrained pleasure. "Nice gentleman, but I thought he'd never leave."

Leah laughed lightly. "I don't think I've ever seen him in a better mood. He had a wonderful time."

"And you?"

"Yes. I did, too."

"That's good. More brandy?"

"No, thanks."

Jacob moved across the room to the liquor cabinet, where he refilled his snifter. He had tried hard throughout dinner and the postprandial session not to stare at Leah, but he had made certain observations. At some point after dinner, she had kicked off her shoes and slipped the pins out of her hair. He remembered watching her toss her head casually as the silky stuff fell in a cascade to her shoulders. A simple act that transformed her from sleek sophisticate to charming ingenue. She never looked the same twice! Taking her features one by one, Jacob supposed she wasn't more than usually attractive, but in his eyes she was distinguished from all other women, and he couldn't have explained why.

Across the room, Leah watched as he poured brandy. He was wearing his tux trousers and the starched, pleated white shirt, but his tie had been discarded, and his shirt sleeves were rolled to his elbows. A sudden self-consciousness took hold of her, and she fleetingly considered getting to her feet, saying good-night and going upstairs. But the longing to talk to him, to probe and pry into his background, was too insistent. She sat quietly, almost primly with her hands folded in her lap, waiting for him to sit down beside her.

He didn't. Instead he said, "Come with me, Leah. There's something I'd like to show you."

Interested, she got to her feet, slipped on her shoes and followed him out of the den, down a short hallway to oak double doors with etched-glass panels. "My study," he explained, opening one of the doors and standing aside for her to enter. "The one room in the house I feel is personally mine, aside from my bedroom, of course."

The study had a mellow, masculine appeal, with

warm wood tones and a soothing neutral color scheme, furnished with predictable objects—a floor globe, an antique stand holding an enormous dictionary. An elaborately carved wooden desk was the focal point. At the other end of the room was a long sofa, and on the wall behind that—Leah gasped—was obviously what he had wanted to show her. The priceless Navaho rug. She moved closer to study it.

"Oh, Jacob, it's a treasure!"

"Isn't it? A shame it's not in top-notch shape."

Leah's fingers sought and found the half dozen frayed spots and tiny holes that marred the rug's perfection. "I know of someone who can repair it for you."

"You?"

"Oh, goodness no, not me. I can repair rugs and tapestries, but not one like this. I don't have the knowledge of natural dyes needed for this kind of restoration. But there's a woman in New Mexico. I have her card. I'll get it for you."

"Thanks, I'd appreciate that," he said, seizing any means of keeping them in contact. "Here, let's sit down." The study was illuminated by one small lamp, leaving most of the room bathed in soft shadows. Leah took a seat on the sofa; then it sagged beneath his weight. "We haven't had much chance to talk, have we? And I thought this weekend would be a time for getting acquainted."

"No, we haven't, but we can remedy that right now." Leah smiled. "You never talk about yourself, do you realize that?"

"I suppose that's because there's so little to say."

"Oh, that can't be true. Everyone has a story, and I'd like to hear yours."

Her easy smile, the casual tone of her voice masked

her very real eagerness. To finally learn all the things she had never known about Jim—where he'd been born, where he'd gone to school, all the mundane little details of a person's life—that was what she wanted most of all. "Just begin at the beginning," she urged. "Where were you born?"

"Right here in Phoenix. Raised here, went to school here, in another part of town. There's a shopping center where our old house used to be."

"Did you always want to be a doctor? By 'always,' I mean once you got past the astronaut or cowboy stage."

He shrugged. "I don't think there was ever a conscious decision made on my part. I simply always knew I would go into medicine. The closest I ever came to a so-called dream was thinking I'd like to be a family practitioner in a small town. It sounded romantic, I suppose."

"Why didn't you do it, then?"

"I had to take over the clinic. It was expected of me."

"Did you always do what was expected of you?"

"Always." There was no self-congratulation in his tone; rather, he seemed to be ashamed it had been so. "I never yearned to be an astronaut or a cowboy or a ballplayer, not even a fireman or a cop. Not ever. Sometimes I think there's something basically wrong with that."

In Leah's mind a picture was forming of a lonely, serious kid who had grown into an intensely private man. "Tell me about your parents," she said.

He thought a moment. "Both were intellectuals, overachievers, and they expected me to be the same."

"Were you?"

"Oh, yes. Mother thought if one was exposed to

only the finest things in life, one would grow up to demand the finest. Nothing coarse or common was ever allowed in this house. It was she who collected many of the things you see, and she whet my appetite. At the dinner table we discussed music, books and art, not batting averages or local gossip. I've often thought I took up woodworking because it was such a welcome respite from...oh, I don't know, from all that thinking." He paused to take a sip of brandy.

"It was an insulated life, really. My privileged existence cut me off from the so-called common man, a fact brought sharply to my attention during my internship and residency. Then I was forced to deal on a daily basis with all sorts of people while they were grappling with personal catastrophes. It was an education, in some ways the most important one I received. And not long after that, I was forced to deal with my parents' deaths. I had never thought of us as a close-knit family, not like some I've seen, so I wasn't prepared for how grief stricken I was or how much I missed them."

Jacob frowned, wondering what had prompted him to put together such a string of sentences. He turned to Leah apologetically. "I'm sorry. I got rather carried away. I didn't intend to be so morose."

"I don't find it morose to talk about personal things. We all have periods in our lives when we're required to make almost superhuman adjustments."

"You, too?"

"Of course."

Jacob imagined she was thinking of the split with her husband, and he didn't want Leah thinking about her husband right now. "Anyway," he continued, "that's about it, the story of my life. My father was gone by the time I had completed my residency, so I took over the clinic. Not exactly the rocky road to the top. Almost immediately I added a psychiatric unit and brought Charles in to head it up. He bought a quarter interest in the place, and . . . there you have it.''

Leah's breath caught in her throat. She knew there was more. He had to go on; he couldn't stop there. "And you've been here ever since?"

"Well, yes, except for . . . ."

Jacob hesitated. He had never discussed the blank period in his life with anyone but Charles. For one thing, he saw it as a weakness. For another, he doubted many people would be interested, and he knew there were plenty who equated amnesia with an abnormal mind, not an abnormal memory.

Leah was so different, though. She made him want to talk. Sitting there with those fascinating eyes fixed on him, she seemed to be almost demanding he talk. Soothed by her presence, he felt a kind of loosening take place within him, and the words just popped out. "Except for eight years ago when I . . . went away."

When he told her he was an amnesiac, he added, "Does that shock you?"

"Shock me?" she asked. "No, why should it?"

"It would shock some people. Most regard it as being abnormal . . . and, of course, it is."

"Please, tell me about it."

"Do you really want me to?"

"Of course. Really." Every muscle in Leah's body tensed. *Now,* she thought. *At last.* At last she was on the verge of learning just how Jim had come into her life.

CHAPTER NINE

JACOB SET HIS GLASS on a nearby end table, settled back against the sofa cushions and propped one ankle on the other knee. With surprising ease, he began telling her the story in a neutral voice.

"Eight years ago I was involved in a malpractice suit, brought on by a man I considered a friend. His daughter was gravely ill when she first came to the clinic, had been ill for some time. It was spinal meningitis, sometimes terribly difficult to diagnose, and immediate treatment is of paramount importance. Unfortunately, in this case treatment had been postponed; despite all our efforts, the girl died. Her father was grief stricken, of course. He wanted someone to blame, and I was handy. So he hired one of those wordmongers, a lawyer who specializes in malpractice suits. It was the kind of thing every doctor dreads. I subsequently won in court, but the whole unfortunate mess was in the newspapers for months, and the publicity hurt the clinic for a while.

"It hurt me, too. I was amazed at how many of my friends, even some of my colleagues, thought that where there's smoke, there must be some fire. The experience left me jaded, discouraged with the practice of medicine. It came too early in my career, you see. Had I been older, more experienced, I might have brushed it aside as an occupational hazard, but I was young and idealistic, and the scandal affected me deeply."

"Yes," Leah murmured, "I can understand that."

Jacob swallowed hard and continued. "My personal life was also at a low ebb. A woman I had loved and trusted left me during the litigation. Daphne, her name was Daphne Townsend. Isn't it strange... I honestly haven't thought of her in years. I wouldn't have now, except she was part of what was wrong with me all those years ago. Daphne was a lovely socialite with all sorts of ideas about what was proper and what wasn't. My reputation had been tarnished, at least in her eyes. She couldn't take the publicity.

"I guess Daphne was the last straw. First my parents' deaths, then the lawsuit, then her disloyalty. I was hostile and depressed. Charles was worried about me and suggested a vacation, a long one. 'Others can handle your appointments,' he said. 'Just get away from it all.' I thought about it and decided the prospect was irresistible. I remember loading my car with the idea of spending the time on my houseboat at Lake Powell, but at some point I decided to hell with it. I wasn't going to the same old place to do the same old thing. Besides, Daphne and I had spent time together on the boat, so it wasn't exactly full of fond memories. I decided to just drive until I felt like stopping. I left at night. It was April and pitch-dark—it was very late...."

Jacob paused, and a deep frown creased his forehead. "My mind just stops there, as if a switch had been turned off. I don't remember which direction I took out of the city. Charles tells me that's not unusual. Apparently few amnesiacs, even the ones ultimately 'cured,' ever recall the events immediately preceding loss of memory.

"The next thing I knew it was two years later. I was picking myself up off the floor of a bus bound for

Flagstaff. The bus had swerved to miss an oncoming truck, and some of the passengers were thrown around. I had cracked my head on the seat in front of me.''

"Wh-what did you do?'' Leah asked tremulously in a voice hardly above a whisper.

"I was dizzy for a few minutes, disoriented. I did have enough wits to announce I was a doctor and to ask if anyone was seriously hurt. Then I searched my pockets for a clue as to what the devil I was doing on that bus. All I could find was a money clip containing three hundred dollars, and—'' he gestured with his left wrist ''—I still had this watch.''

Leah wanted to scream. She clasped her hands together tightly in her lap. "You must have been so frightened.''

"Very. . .and bewildered, particularly when I saw the date on a newspaper lying on the seat beside me. I remember staring at that date for the longest time. It's impossible to describe the way I felt. I didn't know what else to do but get back to Phoenix as quickly as possible. I had plenty of cash on me, so the minute the bus reached Flagstaff I took a cab to the airport and caught the first flight. Charles almost dropped dead when I walked into the clinic.''

"And the two years? You've never remembered anything?''

He shook his head. "Sometimes something will zap in my head, as though my mind is reaching for something and just missing it, but I've never really remembered anything.''

Leah's temples began to throb. She longed to just blurt out everything, yet she wouldn't dare, not after hearing what Dr. White had had to say on the subject. "Jacob, during those two years, wasn't anyone looking for you?''

"Not for a while, I'm afraid. I had no family, and Daphne was gone. At the time I didn't feel I had many friends, apparently I didn't. Since I hadn't specified how long I intended to be gone, it was a month or more before Charles began to suspect something was amiss. He tried to find out if there had been an accident, but the one thing he didn't want to do was broadcast my disappearance so soon after the trial. Finally he convinced himself I would show up when I was good and ready."

"You mean he accepted your disappearance just like that?"

"You must remember my emotional state at the time. Charles said he frankly wouldn't have been surprised by anything I'd done."

"But what about other people, friends and colleagues?"

"Anyone who inquired was told I had taken an extended leave of absence. Apparently those who knew what I had been through believed that."

Leah was so intrigued she could almost forget what a stunning impact all this had had on her own life. "But this house, Jacob, the servants?"

"I didn't live in this house then. When my folks died, I leased it to a wealthy family from Montana. I didn't move in until I returned from...wherever I spent those two years."

"You must have lived somewhere," she persisted.

"I had an apartment, but I wasn't entirely satisfied with it. Since the lease was up for renewal about the time I left Phoenix, I had moved out and put everything in storage, thinking I would look for a newer, larger place when I got back."

"I'm surprised the storage company wasn't looking for you after a time," Leah said.

"To get paid, you mean? The clinic's bookkeeper has been paying my personal bills for years. As far as she knew, I had taken a leave of absence, and my furniture was in storage." He shook his head slowly. "It's so strange, Leah, how everything, every single thing conspired to help me vanish. Where on earth did I go, though?"

Oh, my dear, she thought miserably. *I wish I could help you.* "And you never saw Daphne again?"

He smiled slightly as he looked at Leah. "Oh, yes. She came to see me after I returned to Phoenix."

"Wanting to pick up the pieces," Leah said. It wasn't a question.

"Mmm. But I wanted no part of a woman who ran at the first sign of trouble. I understand she moved to...Hawaii, I think." A lift of his shoulders conveyed his complete indifference.

"Do those two years trouble you at all now, Jacob?"

"Yes, often. I suffered terrible headaches for a long time after I came back. I think my mind was working so hard to grasp something, anything. I spent months in therapy with Charles, but...nothing. He finally suggested I give it up, and he was right. We weren't getting anywhere. You see, during those two years I had existed in what is called a 'fugue state.'"

Carelessly Leah said, "Yes, I know."

Jacob looked at her in some surprise. "You do?"

Immediately she realized her slip. Recovering quickly, she said, "Yes, I don't know how I know, but I do. I must have read it somewhere, or perhaps I saw a show on television...."

"Well, for what it's worth, my case is almost textbook. Once a person recovers from the amnesic state, events of the fugue period are forgotten. I have to accept the fact that I may never remember or may remember only bits and pieces.''

Leah stared at her hands. A feeling of the most desolate emptiness swept through her once he had concluded his story. Now she knew, and nothing had changed. Jacob didn't remember, and realistically, she had to believe he never would. In some ways she had lost Jim all over again.

So how did she feel about that? She tried to confront her emotions head-on. Did it really matter whether he called himself Jacob or Jim? He was as desirable as ever. Couldn't she simply be glad he was back in her life and interested in her?

''I've depressed you.'' Jacob studied her pensive expression.

Her head jerked up. ''Oh, no. I was just thinking what a trauma you've been through.'' Then she asked the question she most wanted to ask. ''Do you want to remember?''

''I think so. Wouldn't you?''

''Yes, I guess I would.''

''It used to be almost an obsession with me. A few weeks after I returned to Phoenix, it occurred to me that I shouldn't have left that bus station in Flagstaff so hurriedly. I should have stayed to see if a piece of luggage had gone unclaimed. That might have given me a clue, but I was so rattled at the time, I couldn't think properly. I telephoned the station, but there was nothing. So either I had no luggage with me, or....'' His frown deepened.

''Or?''

''Or someone came for it. That worries me most of all, thinking I may have left some loose ends in the other life.'' It was on the tip of his tongue to tell her about that dream, but he thought better of it. He might already be straining the fragile beginnings of what he hoped would become a profound relationship.

Leah looked away. The suitcase Jim had taken with him on that fateful day was still in her closet, still packed. Why she had kept it she couldn't imagine. If she and Whit had left it unclaimed, Jacob might have found it and... who knew what might have happened. Damn, there were so many "mights," so many "if onlys."

Jacob drew a deep breath. "And yet, remembering might only complicate my life. There are cases on record of amnesiacs who have begun entirely new lives, learned new skills, established new relationships. Then their memories returned, and they were faced with having to choose one life or the other. You can imagine the problems."

"Yes," she said weakly. "Problems." She was recalling what Charles had said about psychological amnesia. Perhaps Jacob only thought he wanted to remember. Perhaps remembering would actually be devastating for him. The whole subject was too complex for a lay person to comprehend.

One question kept inching to the forefront of her mind, however: why hadn't Charles, with all his knowledge and interest in amnesia, been able to help Jacob more than he had? Was Jacob's case particularly complicated, stubborn—what?

"Well, wherever I was, I had been living well," Jacob went on. "I was in great physical condition. A little heavier than I like to be, but as solid as a rock. My clothes were fairly new, and I wasn't wearing a wedding ring, thank God!" At this, he looked at Leah. "Why didn't you laugh?"

"Because you didn't," she said solemnly. Jim had had a wedding ring, but once he'd gained weight it had become too tight. They had always meant to take it to a jeweler....

Jacob fell into silence, but not a troubled silence. Finally spilling all he had kept bottled up inside for so long had a disburdening effect on him. Or perhaps it was Leah who had that effect. "You know," he said after a moment or two, "I've never discussed this with another person, only Charles during therapy. Confiding in others isn't something I find easy to do. I can't for the life of me understand why I did it now."

Which wasn't all he wanted to say to her. He wanted to tell her he believed he had found a soul mate. He wanted to confess he had never felt so close to another human being in his entire life, even if that did sound absurd to his own ears. And with that confession out, he would have hoped she would have talked to him, too—told him about her husband.

But he didn't actually say any of those things, and nothing was forthcoming from Leah. She only said, "I'm glad you felt you could talk to me," and it was impossible for him to read more behind her soft, sweet expression. Right now she looked a million miles away.

Jacob longed to know if she was thinking of something else, or someone else. It was an odd sensation, this being insanely jealous of a man he had never met. Probably never would meet. Hopefully never would.

Abruptly Jacob slapped his knee and got to his feet, extending his hand. "It's late, almost one, and I've bored you long enough."

"You haven't bored me, Jacob. Far from it." Leah stood up, only to discover she was just inches from him. The lone lamp's pale light illuminated the angles and planes of his face; his eyes held her captive. For a moment they stood rooted in place. Then Jacob dropped her hand and slipped his arm around her waist, effectively holding her captive. Her breasts were crushed against the starched front of his shirt. The contact sent a thrill coursing through Leah's body, a natural, instinctive response. It had been so long, too long, and she had once known such pleasure in this man's body.

Yet for the moment her feelings weren't entirely sexual. She simply loved being close to him again. She wanted him to hold her. She wanted his warmth to enfold her.

"Leah," Jacob muttered in a low, throaty whisper. "You are such a fantastic woman."

Leah's answer to that was to slide her arms around his waist and hold him to her, letting the force of his vitality wash over her. Instead of lifting her face to receive the kiss she knew he wanted to give her, she simply laid her head on his shoulder and clung to him. Everything inside her seemed to melt. He felt so good. It was like coming out of a cold night into a warm house—a warm, familiar house. Absurdly, she wanted to cry. If he only knew how much just being close to him meant to her.

Jacob was stunned. She had walked into his arms like a lost child seeking reassurance and comfort. He didn't think anything had ever moved him so deeply. Holding her lithe body in his arms, he felt a surge of tenderness and protectiveness for her that made no sense. How did a man deal with a gentle woman like Leah? His previous experiences had been so basic and earthy, but she seemed to be asking him for something more than raw passion. He moved one hand up to cradle her head and hold it snugly against his shoulder. Alien feelings overwhelmed him. She would have to make the next move.

Leah didn't know how long they stood there with

their arms entwined around each other, not moving, not speaking. Finally one of them stirred—she thought it was she—and Leah raised her face to his. Jacob lowered his head, capturing her lips with his.

It was the sweetest sort of kiss, nothing demanding or urgent, yet it triggered a series of tiny explosions in Leah. The languid warmth she had experienced in his arms became an inferno of need. It was only natural for her to draw him closer, to open her mouth beneath his, to return the kiss with the passion and abandon they had once shared so freely.

The kiss deepened, and her body settled comfortably into the niche of his hips; they fit together perfectly. It had always seemed that their bodies had been fashioned for the express purpose of melding. Leah reveled in the feel of him, for she knew every pleasurable sinew from countless acts of love. Caught up in memories of another time and place, she moved against him invitingly.

It was Jacob who broke the kiss. Leah's eyes were still closed when he lifted his head; in that instant they flew open and looked straight into his. Full of awe, they beseeched him.

"Leah?" he gasped, unable to fully believe the message her pliant response had sent him. Did she really want him to make love to her? Was it even reasonable of him to think such a thing? *Please tell me how much you want,* he silently implored her. His mouth wouldn't form the words.

The questioning, astonished look on Jacob's face brought Leah to earth with a thud. She had entirely forgotten herself, forgotten who this man really was. For a moment she had been kissing Jim, and it would have been so easy to fall into intense lovemaking, something she wanted and needed.

But this wasn't Jim! Jacob Surratt was a newcomer to her life. A sensible woman didn't fall recklessly into bed with a man she had known a grand total of five days. At least, Leah Stone didn't. Shaken, feeling as gauche as a fifteen-year-old, unable to bear the astonished expression on Jacob's face, she looked away.

"Leah?" Jacob repeated. The arms holding her so tightly fell, and he took her chin in his hand, forcing her to look at him.

"I'm . . . sorry, Jacob."

"You are?"

"I can't think what came over me."

"Can't you?" He gave her a smile of the utmost tenderness. He thought he understood her fear and reluctance. It was tied up with her marriage and the ex-husband she couldn't forget. "I'll give you a biology lesson. I want you, and you want me. We each need what the other can give. There's nothing wrong with wanting, needing. In fact, it's natural when you've gone without it—"

"I'm not love starved, if that's what you're thinking."

Jacob sighed. "Then you're very fortunate. I am."

For a man who found confiding in others difficult, his candor with her was remarkable. Leah stepped backward; her mind was in tumult. She didn't know how to handle this. "I . . . I think I'll go upstairs now. It's been a lovely evening." An inane remark if she had ever heard one.

Jacob's hand dropped to his side. "Oh, Leah, it's such a damned shame. I can't remember, and you can't forget."

She frowned. "Forget? Forget what?"

"Your husband."

"My husband?"

"He is the problem, isn't he? You still love him."

Leah couldn't have been more surprised. She thought she had successfully avoided the subject of her husband. Was she too transparent, or was Jacob too observant? "Yes. How did you know that?"

"Oh, something strange happens to your eyes every time I say the word 'husband' or ask about your marriage." Jacob chanced stepping close to her again. Again he raised his hand, this time to gently brush it along her shimmering dark tresses, finally resting it lightly on her shoulder. "Leah, I'd be a fine one to tell you to forget the past when I'm searching for a piece of my own. And I admire loyalty. Still, the present should mean something, too. I know you're not indifferent to me. The way you kissed me told me that. The most important thing should be what you and I feel right now."

"Seize the moment, you mean?"

"Would it be so terrible? There have been damned few moments I've wanted to seize."

Jacob was confessing his loneliness. She had known crushing loneliness, too, and she supposed there was nothing wrong with two people seeking solace and comfort in each other. Or there wouldn't be, except that she and this man had once come together with absolute, shining love, and tonight she wouldn't have any idea whether she was making love to Jim or Jacob.

"It's...too soon, Jacob," was all she could think to say. "I'd be doing it for all the wrong reasons."

"Ah..." he murmured sagely. A moment of silence passed. "Leah Stone, you're an anachronism, but a charming one. Please, let me say one more thing. I think I've been looking for you for a very long time. I hope someday you'll want me as much as I want you—and I don't give a damn what the reasons turn out to be."

Leah thought she was strangling. "I'll say good night now, Jacob," she said quickly, then turned and almost ran out of the room. It wasn't until she was upstairs behind a closed door that she allowed her pent-up breath to slowly escape. Jacob had her all figured out, so he thought: she was still in love with her husband, and she had traditional values, thus her reluctance about a new relationship. Right, as far as the theory went, and she would play the role of the hesitant lover until she was certain she wanted Jacob Surratt. Only Jacob, not the ghost of her lost love.

THEY WERE ALONE AGAIN for only a minute the following day. First they had a late, leisurely Sunday breakfast, then a tour of the house to take in Jacob's extensive collection of art and antiques. After that an alfresco lunch was served by the pool, and the weekend was over. Alex went upstairs to get ready to leave; Leah stood up to follow him, but Jacob detained her.

"Must you leave so soon?" he asked quietly.

"Yes. We have to stop by my dad's to pick up Nina, and I believe Alex has a dinner engagement tonight."

"Saturday, then? I can be at your house before noon."

Leah didn't have to think about her answer. He was back in her life. She couldn't stay away from him, at least not until she knew how Leah Stone and Jacob Surratt were going to mesh. "Yes," she said. "Saturday."

"Will you please think about me?"

Leah laughed lightly. "Oh, you can be very sure I'll do that, doctor."

FOR PERHAPS THE HUNDREDTH TIME in the past five years, Leah blessed Alex for his considerate nature. There wasn't a thoughtless or callous bone in his body.

She knew he must be itching with curiosity about developments that weekend, yet throughout the drive to the Haskell farm he asked no questions. He talked about the scenery, the weather, the Surratt home, Jacob's collection—everything but what Leah knew he wanted most to talk about.

Whit, of course, was another matter. Alive with curiosity, he skillfully arranged a few private moments with his daughter.

"How was it?" he began bluntly.

"Oh, not too bad, I guess."

"Is he...at all like Jim?"

"Some. Not too much."

"I'd like to see him—I think."

"I wonder if you'd be disappointed." Succinctly Leah told him as much as she wanted him to know. She spared him the details of her palpitating heart and weak knees, but otherwise covered the visit quite thoroughly.

Her father listened with interest and concern for his daughter, and after thinking it over a moment or two, gave her the best advice he could.

"Leah, I guess you're just going to have to decide if you can let go of Jim, if you're ready for an emotional involvement with another person, because that's what Jacob Surratt is—another person entirely."

"I know, dad." She heaved a sigh. "I know."

CHAPTER TEN

FROM HER VANTAGE POINT, at her loom in front of the picture window, Leah could watch Nina and Ann Martin playing in the front yard. Every once in a while she glanced up to check on them, but for the most part her attention was riveted on her work. In a burst of creative energy, she had sketched a new design and completed her pattern draft of Jacob's tapestry the night she returned from Phoenix. Now, three days later, she was well into the work itself and feeling good about it. Back and forth the weft threads went in a steady rhythm she had perfected over the years. The joy she felt as she watched the complicated design grow right before her eyes was something only another weaver would understand, just as only another artist could appreciate the loom's ability to erase day-to-day cares.

Just then her peripheral vision caught some sort of movement in the yard; Leah looked up in time to see Sandra coming through the front gate. Her friend stopped to speak to the two girls, then looked toward the window. Leah motioned her inside.

"Don't let me interrupt," Sandra said as she entered the house. "I've come to beg, borrow or steal that divine white Mexican dress of yours. I'd like to wear it tonight."

"Sure, help yourself."

"It's the only thing you own that I could possibly

wear, since you're so disgustingly thin. But the dress doesn't have any shape, so I think it'll hide mine.''

"I don't know why you worry so much about your figure. You're just pleasingly... curvaceous."

"I guess that's one way of putting it."

"Big date tonight?"

"I'm going to dinner with Sam, so I want to look prosperous." Sandra chuckled.

Leah pulled the beater sharply forward to pack the weft tightly before momentarily turning her back on her work. "You're going to dinner with your ex-husband?"

"Uh-huh. He wants to discuss Ann's future," Sandra scoffed as she disappeared into Leah's walk-in closet. When she reappeared she was carrying the exquisite dress over her arm. "I don't know what brought on this attack of parental concern, but it's about time he shouldered some of the load. He never paid much attention to Ann, not even when we were married. Sam thought kids were 'woman's work,' and all that garbage. Now he says we ought to establish some sort of college fund for her. I couldn't agree more. Listen, Leah, I'll guard this with my life, and I'll have it cleaned before I bring it back."

"I'm not the least worried about the dress. Why don't you take my turquoise pendant, too? It's perfect with the dress."

"Oh, I couldn't."

"Nonsense. Take it."

"I know I shouldn't," Sandra said, scurrying for Leah's jewelry box, "but I will."

"Do you want to leave Ann with me?"

"No, my mom's down from Utah for a few days. Thanks, anyway."

"Are you... ah, looking forward to tonight?" Leah asked. From all accounts, Sandra's previous meetings with her former husband had been anything but pleasant.

Sandra, who was hardly ever at a loss for words, floundered for a minute. She idly caressed the turquoise pendant, then sat down in a nearby easy chair, wrinkling her nose. "I'm not sure. It's funny, but...I don't much want to fight with Sam anymore. I've proven what I needed to prove, that I wouldn't fall apart without him. Now I think I'd like us to be friends. I mean, there's Ann to consider and all. I guess what I'm trying to say is, I've turned a corner. I'm not scared anymore, and I'm no longer filled with resentment." She grinned. "Now if Sam does something horribly thoughtless, I'll just tell him to kiss off! If he doesn't like it, tough! It's nice to feel free."

"I guess so." Having never lived with a domineering personality, Leah knew she couldn't fully appreciate what Sandra had been through and had accomplished through her own indomitable spirit. "You're to be commended, not only for getting help but for sticking with it. How long did you say you were under a psychiatrist's care—two years?"

"Yeah, it takes a lot of time. A lot of time."

And Jacob had spoken of only months with his partner. How many months? After her friend left, Leah mulled over what Sandra had said, especially the remark about turning a corner. It would help if she could do that, relegate Jim to the past and regard Jacob as someone totally disconnected from any life she had known before. Whit had told her basically the same thing Sunday night.

It would be easier if Jacob would stop making those late-night phone calls. He had called Sunday night, Monday and Tuesday, too, and she was fully expecting another tonight and every night until Saturday. His calls always came after she was ready for bed, so she spoke to him, while snuggled under the covers in the darkened house. He never said anything openly suggestive—that would have been out of character—yet the sensuous quality to that familiar voice made her skin tingle and hum. Unable to see him, hearing only his voice, she was easily carried back to a time when a handsome young man had loved her passionately. Then her thoughts would turn softly erotic.

She was filled with such a desolate longing every time she hung up the phone. Desires she could name but had long since learned to subjugate surfaced to torment her, evoking dreams that were her only emotional release. She badly wanted to see Jacob again, but was it really Jacob she wanted to see?

HE ARRIVED before eleven o'clock Saturday morning. Leah had been up since dawn. Dressed in jeans, she worked first at her loom, then in the yard with Nina's "help," all the while placating her daughter, who was restless and anxious to do something. "I'm going to have company, honey. We'll have to make plans after Dr. Surratt gets here."

"That doctor who was here the other day?"

"Hmm-mmm. Did you like him. . .?"

The child looked at her mother, then shrugged. "I guess so. Are you gonna spend all day with him?" she asked petulantly.

"I really don't know how long he'll be here, honey."

"I wanted us to do something."

"Well, let's just wait and see, okay?" Leah said cheerfully. She hadn't given any thought to what she and Jacob would do. . .or to the fact that they wouldn't be alone.

She had planned to change clothes before Jacob arrived, but the time slipped away from her. Mother and daughter had gone inside to wash up when he knocked on the door. "Come in!" Leah called from the kitchen sink, and he stepped inside the house.

To her astonishment, urbane Dr. Surratt was wearing faded jeans and a short-sleeved denim shirt. The clothes only served to heighten his aura of potent masculinity and to remind her even more of Jim.

"Good morning," he said.

"Good morning."

Jacob looked at her steadily, trying not to stare but staring nevertheless. He was coming to think of her as the most-beautiful woman he'd ever known, yet it wasn't her face that came immediately to mind, but those incredible eyes. He looked into them so long she shifted uncomfortably.

Averting his gaze, he let it wander to Nina, who was sitting on a tall stool at the breakfast bar, chin resting on her hands, regarding him with six-year-old gravity. "Well, hi," he said.

"Hi." The girl's guileless eyes fastened on him.

"How're things going? Having fun this summer?"

Nina's dark curls bobbled up and down as she nodded her head.

"That's good." Jacob cleared his throat, at a loss to understand why juvenile scrutiny should be so unsettling. He looked at Leah, his eyes asking, *What do I say now?*

Leah suppressed a smile at the exchange. Amazing how few people knew how to talk to children. In all fairness to Jacob, however, she admitted her daughter had a direct, no-nonsense scrutiny that one didn't expect from a six-year-old. *Like her father,* was Leah's next startling thought. She stepped into the awkward silence. "I didn't have any idea what you wanted to do today."

"Didn't you?"

"No, so I didn't make plans."

"Good."

Leah wiped her hands on a dish towel, needlessly swiped at the counter top. On a normal Saturday she would have been working four-hour stints at her loom, Nina running in and out, back and forth from Ann's house. Nothing Jacob would find entertaining. She should have made some plans. . . .

Jacob wandered across the room to stand at her loom. "You've begun," he said.

"Yes." Useless to ask if he liked it; there wasn't enough of it for him to judge. Right now the tapestry existed only in Leah's mind's eye.

"This is exciting, Leah—viewing it from start to finished product. Sometime I'd like to watch you work."

"Anytime."

"This afternoon?"

"If you like."

Nina, apparently seeing a promising Saturday disintegrating before her eyes, piped up. "Let's go to the creek and have a picnic."

Leah and Jacob turned to look at her. "A picnic?" they chorused.

Nina nodded enthusiastically. "We can go to Slide Rock."

Leah explained to Jacob. "The creek is Oak Creek, and Slide Rock is. . . well, it's impossible to explain if you haven't been there." Then she remembered he had, several times. "H-have you been there?"

He shook his head. "I seem to have heard of it, but I've never actually been there."

"Then what do you say? How does a picnic sound?"

He chuckled. "It sounds fine to me. I can't even remember the last time I was on a picnic. It must have been before medical school for sure."

No, it was the Fourth of July before his disappearance. Leah had known him thirteen months; they had been married for six of them.

She wasn't doing a very good job of forgetting Jim, but she couldn't deny she was glad to see Jacob again. She was even beginning to think him more handsome than the man she married. Maybe that was ridiculous, since they were the same person, but she reminded herself that some men got better looking with each passing year. Jacob was going to age beautifully.

"A picnic it will be!" she said too eagerly. "Nina, find the hamper...I think it's in my closet. I'll pack a lunch."

The child scrambled off. Leah moved toward the refrigerator. "I hope you like bologna sandwiches."

"Bologna?" Jacob smiled. "The doctor in me is forced to remind you of all those nitrates, all that cholesterol. I love them! Bologna sandwiches are something else that have been sadly missing from my life for too long."

Nina reappeared. "Mama, I can't get the hamper. It's up on the top shelf."

"Let me get it for you, Nina." Jacob came to her rescue.

"You won't be able to reach it, either. You're gonna have to stand on something."

"Well, then, I have a solution. I'll put you on my shoulders, and you get it. How's that?"

Nina giggled delightedly as Jacob placed his hands under her arms and swung her up on his shoulders. Clasping him under the chin, she chortled, "Ooh, I'm up so high!"

Jacob clamped his hands firmly on her legs as he marched across the room. "Watch it. You'll have to duck when we go through the door."

Leah froze as her eyes followed father and daughter. Her mouth compressed tightly; her chest heaved in agitation. No one had yet come up with a word to express what she felt. Distractedly she opened a loaf of bread and spread slices out on the counter. *How many sandwiches could Jacob eat,* she wondered. And she supposed he preferred mustard to mayonnaise; Jim had.

She heard a light tap on the screen door; it opened to admit Sandra. She was carrying the white dress in one hand, the turquoise pendant in the other. "I just picked this up at the cleaners and wanted to get it to you before something happens to it. Sure do thank you."

"You're welcome, Sandra. Anytime."

"I'll put it in the closet. Who belongs to that fancy sports car out front?"

Just then Jacob and Nina emerged from the closet. Nina, still on his shoulders, was holding the hamper triumphantly aloft and grinning from ear to ear. "Hi, Mrs. Martin. This is mama's friend, Jacob."

Leah cast a sidelong glance in Sandra's direction. Her friend smiled politely and said, "Hello, I'm...." The words died. A second or two passed; then Sandra's eyes widened considerably. Leah thought she heard the sharp intake of the woman's breath as she stood mutely, staring at the two faces, one directly above the other. Leah's breath was suspended. Had Sandra noticed a resemblance? Tremulously she forced herself to look squarely at her daughter and Jacob, but it was impossible for her to objectively judge whether Nina looked that much like her father.

Slowly Sandra turned toward Leah. With a tilt to her

head and a lift of her brow, she quizzed her silently. Leah couldn't read the question being asked, and apparently Sandra realized no answers could be forthcoming at that moment. She turned back to stare at the man and the child with unabashed interest.

"Hang on, Nina," Jacob was saying. "I'm going to let you down." Relieved of his burden, he crossed the room and extended his hand. "How do you do? I'm Jacob Surratt."

Sandra shifted the pendant and shook hands. "Sandra Martin. I'm Leah's neighbor. I'm returning her dress. I...I'll put it in there." She hurried into the closet, hung up the dress, then closed the door behind her.

"We're going on a picnic," Nina announced.

"How nice. You have a great day for it." Sandra couldn't take her eyes off Jacob and Nina. She looked like someone who had just been dealt a severe blow to her midsection.

"Yes, very nice," Jacob agreed.

"Well—" Sandra fluttered her hands in agitation "—I guess I'd better be going." Spinning around, she faced Leah, stunned awareness in her expression. "Thanks again, Leah."

"Sure, Sandra."

"I'll be over to see you...soon." Emphasis was placed on the last word.

Leah sighed and returned to her sandwich making. Perhaps her overactive imagination was at work. It could well be that Sandra hadn't noticed any resemblance, but was only curious about Jacob. Well, whatever, she didn't doubt she was in for a grilling the next time she saw Sandra, so she'd just have to decide how much she wanted her friend to know.

OAK CREEK TUMBLED from a subalpine setting in the north to cactus country in the south. Near Sedona, the vast canyon the creek meandered widened to provide a summer playground for swimmers, hikers and campers. Halfway down the canyon, surrounded by woodlands of evergreen oaks, was Slide Rock, a series of shallow troughs carved into the creek's sandstone bedrock and coated with slippery blue-green algae. Six thousand gallons of water a minute gushed over Slide Rock. There a swimmer could sit down in the stream, let go and glide effortlessly along in the water. Scores of swimmers were doing just that that afternoon, Nina among them.

Leah and Jacob had staked out a spot on the bank of the creek where they could eat and keep an eye on the girl. All afternoon Leah watched Jacob's face for some sign that the surroundings looked familiar to him, but if anything was going "zap" in his head, he was careful to keep it from her. However, he made no attempt to conceal other thoughts. Every time their eyes met, Leah received some definitely sensuous, unspoken messages. She wondered if he had any idea how attractive he was. He was a very sexy man, and the dignified doctor surprised her with each passing moment. She guessed he might be surprising himself.

Leah was right. A queer sort of elation had taken hold of Jacob. Caring for her had made him feel bold. His thoughts turned daring and venturous. Once, when she turned to find him looking at her with undisguised hunger, she asked, "What are you thinking?"

He was astonished to hear himself reply, "I was wondering if bologna might be an aphrodisiac." Her delightful response to that was to shake an admonishing finger at him.

He was pleased that the mood between them was more relaxed than before. Still she wasn't completely at ease with him, and he didn't know what to do about that. That was probably his fault. Damn the lack of warmth and charm! How he wished for some instant charisma, anything that would make her forget the past and allow him into her life.

Nina's childish voice broke into his thoughts. "Mama! Jacob! Watch!"

He turned his attention to the girl cavorting in the water and made a big show of applauding her antics, but then he turned to Leah, clearly concerned. "Isn't that dangerous for a six-year-old?"

"Not at all," she assured him. "Nina's been slipping and sliding down Slide Rock ever since she learned to swim."

"When was that?"

"When she was two." Leah raised her arm to return her daughter's wave. With the ease of a child, Nina had ingratiated herself with a group of youngsters her own age and was having a wonderful time.

"It still looks dangerous to me," Jacob said. "You're able to treat her so casually, but I have a feeling I'd be an uptight parent."

"Oh, you learn. I was pretty uptight, too, in the early days, always worrying she'd get hurt. But kids aren't nearly as fragile as you think they are."

"I'm surprised she isn't exhausted. She's been going strong ever since we got here."

"Oh, this will make for a good night's sleep, I assure you."

Leah had spread a blanket on the ground and was sitting on it, knees pulled under her chin, arms hugging her legs. Beside her, Jacob sprawled full-length, one arm propped under his head. He was lost in a kind of euphoria, all at once lethargic and exhilarating. Thoughts of the woman beside him had distracted him all week. The regulated way of life he had created for himself no longer staved off loneliness or subdued his imagination. He, who normally welcomed the steady stream of men and women who came to him with their ailments, had been impatient with too many of them the past few days. He had always felt wretched about it afterward, wishing he could explain. But what could he say? "Forgive me, I'm daydreaming about a woman." Maybe he should have. Some of them might have understood and sympathized.

Damned if he was going to ponder and agonize over every word and move. He would say whatever popped into his head, do whatever came naturally to him and hope he got through to her. He couldn't think of another course of action.

"What time does Nina go to bed?" He hadn't known he was going to ask the question until he heard the words coming out of his mouth.

"Eight-thirty, nine at the latest," she replied absently. Then her heart tripped.

"Is she a sound sleeper?"

"Like the proverbial log."

She glanced at him and found herself on the receiving end of a devastatingly and delightfully wicked smile. It was so contagious, it demanded one in return. "Wh-why?"

"Why do you think? How long do I have to wait to make the moves I've been planning all week?"

"Jacob?" She cocked her head, looking at him as though seeing him for the first time.

"I thought I made myself clear last weekend. I thought you knew what I want. Nina's a darling girl, and I'm enjoying the hell out of the first lazy day I've

spent in years, but I want to be alone with you, Leah."
His eyes glowed into hers. "Understand?"

She flicked a tongue across her bottom lip. "Y-yes.
Don't look at me like that."

A low chuckle sounded deep in his throat. "Why
not?"

"It makes me nervous."

"Because you can feel me kissing you, can't you?
Here. . . ." He reached up and touched one corner of
her mouth with his forefinger, then the other corner.
"And here."

She took his hand and laughed lightly, enjoying the
physical pleasure of simply being close to him. Anyone
looking on would have taken them for a happily married couple on a Saturday outing with their daughter.
The day was peaceful, the mood tranquil. Now, this
minute, it would have been so easy to squeeze the
hand she was holding and say, "Jacob, I've known
you before. Your name was Jim Stone, and you married me when I was hardly more than a starry-eyed
girl."

She didn't dare, and that presented problems. Fear,
uncertainty stirred inside her. If this new relationship
continued, and she had every reason to believe it
would if she allowed it, he would expect her to tell him
about her marriage. What would she say?

She sighed audibly; Jacob frowned. "Why so pensive all of a sudden?"

"Oh, I was just thinking what an incredibly lovely
afternoon this has been."

He didn't believe her. "No, I think you're trying to
come to grips with the way I feel about you, and possibly the way you feel about me. You've been loyal to
an old relationship for a long time, and it isn't easy to
start an entirely new one."

"Doctor, you can't begin to imagine how perceptive you are."

"Relax and let it happen. I've waited so long for this." There was a pleading quality to his voice. Suddenly he jumped to his feet and held out his hand. "Come with me."

Leah took his hand without hesitation, allowing him to pull her to her feet. "Where are we going?"

"Just over here. Come on."

Leah cast a glance over her shoulder to check on Nina. The girl and her group of newfound friends were out of the water, seated in a circle on a boulder, playing some sort of game. Satisfied, Leah continued, clutching Jacob's hand. He was leading her away from the crowded bank up into the thick tangle of dark woods only a few feet away, and she would have been incredibly naive not to have guessed what he had in mind. "Jacob! There are coyotes and racoons and skunks, and I don't know what all in these woods!"

"They'll be more frightened of us than we are of them."

"But...."

In a moment they were obscured from the frolicking bathers below. Under the sheltering branches of a giant oak, Jacob stopped and, in a fluid motion, gathered her into the circle of his arms. "I guess we'll just have to make our own privacy," he said huskily. Bending his head, he covered her lips with his. And like the first time, her body simply melted against his, reassuring him that what he thought she had felt the other time was still there. Her arms slid up the hard wall of his chest and locked behind his neck, and she returned the kiss with the same ardor he remembered. For a week he had thought so often of her response to that first kiss. He wouldn't have thought it possible for arms to ache from emptiness, but his had. Holding her now was healing balm. One hand pressed her more securely against him.

Sweet warmth surged through Leah. She had always loved for Jim to hold her; in some ways it had been the nicest part of their intimacies. She parted her lips under his and accepted his gently probing tongue. Her hips against his felt so right and natural. A new name, a new set of circumstances, yet her feelings for this man were the same. Gradually Jim became Jacob and vice versa, until the two melded. *He belongs to me,* she thought. *He doesn't know it, but he does.*

When they broke the kiss, Jacob nuzzled his head into the smooth curve of her neck and simply held on to her tightly. Leah relished the closeness she could feel growing between them. For the time being, this would have to be enough, but somehow she would find time for them. She had to; she needed him.

Finally they stood apart, smiling at each other, he more shyly than she. "I just couldn't wait any longer," he said.

Those fascinating eyes caught and held his, and he read something in them, something that made his breath catch. He could hardly allow himself to believe it, but...yes, unmistakably they said, "If you want me, it's all right. I want you, too."

For Jacob it was a mind-boggling moment. He didn't know what to say. "I...guess we should get back to Nina," was what came out.

Leah smiled and slipped her hand into his. He didn't have to say anything; she knew. Holding his hand tightly, she led him out of the forest into the sunshine.

IT WAS LATE AFTERNOON when they returned to the house. As she opened the car door, Leah heard the telephone begin to ring. Nina bolted off her mother's lap and raced toward the house, yelling, "I'll get it!"

Jacob stared after the girl in wonder. "Wouldn't you think she'd be dead on her feet? What I wouldn't give for a tenth that energy!"

Leah nodded. "And she'll go and go and go until she just drops. She had a wonderful time today, Jacob. I think Nina's taken a shine to you."

"Ordinarily I don't pay much attention to kids, but Nina's different. She's easy to like."

How quickly they had warmed to each other, Leah thought. She recalled all Alex's well-meant but futile attempts to get close to her daughter. Unfortunately, Alex's overtures had been designed to please Leah more than Nina, and the child had sensed it. Not that Nina disliked Alex. She simply didn't feel one way or another about him.

It had been so different with Jacob. A quick rapport had been established between father and daughter. There might be something to blood ties, after all.

She reached for the door handle, but Jacob detained her. "Leah, what about tonight?"

"Tonight?"

"Yes. Do you suppose you could get a baby-sitter or something? I'd like to...." He felt inept. What to say? *I'd like to cart you off to a motel and make love to you all night long?* Hardly poetic stuff. Hardly worthy of Leah.

It didn't matter, since he had no chance to finish the sentence. The front door flew open, and Nina raced to the car, poking her head inside the window on the passenger side. Her eyes were bright with excitement. "Mama, it was grandpa! Bess had her puppies! He says I can come see them. Can I, mama, please?"

"Oh, Nina, honey, they'll be too little. You won't

be able to touch them. And you've had such a busy day. You need a bath, supper and bed. I know you're tired.''

"No, I'm not, really. Please! I'll just look at the puppies, I won't touch. Grandpa says we can come and have supper with him and I can spend the night. Please!''

"Nina, don't beg!" Leah said sharply. "You know how I hate that.'' Her mind raced. She wanted to be alone with Jacob, but now that the opportunity had been unexpectedly dumped in her lap, she felt guilty. Yes, guilty about considering herself and her own needs over Nina's. Had it not been for Jacob, she knew she would have said, "No, we'll wait until morning,'' and been done with it.

Expectation quickened Jacob's pulse. To have a night to themselves was what he wanted, what he thought she wanted. He couldn't understand her hesitation. Had he misread her, after all? Gently he touched her on the arm. "Please, Leah. You wouldn't want Nina to miss brand-new pups, would you?''

Why not, she asked herself sensibly. *Is it so terribly wrong to want to be alone with him?* If she had sex on her mind, so what? Nina wouldn't suffer any harm, and in Jacob's arms she could find surcease from the aching loneliness of the past six years. It would be like coming home.

"Would you like to meet my father?'' she asked Jacob with deceptive calm.

"I'd love it.''

"All right, Nina, tell your grandfather we'll be there. We'll have to change first. And, honey, be sure you tell him I'm bringing Dr. Surratt with me.'' It was best, she thought, to give Whit all the warning she could; she wondered how he would receive the news.

"Oh, boy!'' The girl was away in a flash.

Jacob opened the car door and got out. *Bless Nina and her grandfather,* he thought with a grin. And bless Bess and the puppies who, unlike so many offspring, had arrived at the perfect time.

LEAH TOOK A FEW MINUTES to change. Ducking into the bathroom, she put on fresh slacks and a blouse. When she emerged, she turned to a nearby mirror to tie up her hair. The clothes, Jacob noticed, were the ones she had been wearing the first time he'd seen her at Tlaquepaque. She was fiddling with her hair, but mainly he watched the movements of her breasts when she lifted both arms. She wasn't wearing a bra, that much he knew. He raked a forefinger across his mouth as an intense longing stirred inside him. Two weeks ago he had existed in a perpetual emotional void. Now every nerve, every cell in his body was alive and attuned to her. Leah, it seemed to him, had unearthed the very taproot of his sexuality. A man unknown to him was emerging, and he wasn't a half-bad sort.

"Jacob, tie this, please."

The girlish voice brought him up short. He looked down to see Nina standing with her back to him, holding her hair off her neck. She had changed into some sort of sunsuit, and the two straps were draped over her shoulders. He took the straps and tied them into a lopsided bow.

"That's not tight enough," the child informed him.

So he untied the straps and retied them. "How's that?"

"Fine." Nina turned and smiled. "Thanks."

"You're welcome. Always happy to come to the aid of a damsel in distress."

"What does 'damsel' mean?"

"A damsel is a fair young lady."

"What does 'distr . . . distr . . . ' "

"Distress? Well, if you're in distress, you're in trouble."

"But I'm not in trouble, am I?" she asked seriously, and Jacob laughed.

Through the mirror Leah watched them. Her heart seemed to swell to twice its normal size. What difference did it make what his name was? He belonged here, with them; she wasn't going to let anything take him from her this time.

Turning, she favored both of them with a bright smile. "Nina, did you pack your things?"

Nina nodded and pointed to a small canvas bag resting on the floor near the front door. "All right, shall we go?"

Purposely Leah directed Jacob to take the route she and Jim had always traveled to the Haskell farm. Jim had once commented that he thought he knew every pebble and bump in the road. Leah watched for any sign of recognition from Jacob, but again there was nothing.

"Beautiful country," was his only comment.

"You've never been this way before?"

"No, I fly whenever possible, and the few times I've driven north out of Phoenix I've stayed strictly to the interstate. I'm not much of a sightseer, I'm afraid, and I'm beginning to realize how much I've missed."

TWO HOURS LATER, Leah, Jacob and Whit were seated in the living room of the farmhouse, while Nina was camped in the kitchen with Tee, close to Bess and her brood. Whit's face had gone very pale when he had first "met" Jacob; now it was flushed. He kept mopping his brow, although the weather wasn't that warm, and he took countless drinks of water. Leah watched her father anxiously. She had never seen him so nonplussed. His voice was stilted, strained. Jacob seemed to notice nothing, thank God. He chatted pleasantly with the older man, and their conversation was no more awkward than any conversation between two apparent strangers.

Tee ambled in with cold beer for everyone. The housekeeper had been forewarned; Leah could tell that by the way Tee so obviously refused to look at Jácob. Only when she moved away, out of Jacob's line of vision, did she chance a full glance at him. Leah watched her covertly. Tee frowned and pressed her hand to her ample bosom, then shook her head sadly before leaving the room.

By the time supper was served, both Whit and Tee had recovered sufficiently to accept Jacob's presence. Talk flowed around the table with greater ease. Whit unfortunately called Jacob "m'boy" too often, an appellation that had suited Jim Stone perfectly but was totally inappropriate for Dr. Surratt, but Leah reminded herself that every word, every action was magnified in her mind. Jacob seemed to notice nothing but the good country food and the hospitable surroundings.

And her. Every time their eyes met, Leah felt a jolt of sensual awareness. His heart was in his eyes. The message he had been sending her all day was coming through clearer now that fulfillment was within reach. It was all so incredibly blatant and premeditated, yet she felt not the least chagrined, and all guilt had vanished.

The evening passed. Leah took a hyperactive Nina upstairs for a bath, then helped her get ready for bed. Getting the child unwound wasn't easy, but after two unnecessary trips to the bathroom and a request for a drink of water, she finally fell into a deep sleep.

Downstairs, Whit and Jacob sat engrossed in conversation, but the moment Leah appeared Jacob got to his feet. "Is she settled down?"

"Yes, thankfully."

"Want some coffee, Leah?" Whit asked.

"No, thanks. I guess we'd better be going." How casually the words came out.

Whit got to his feet, and Jacob extended his hand. "I've enjoyed it, Dr. Haskell."

The older man slapped him heartily on the back. "Whit, m'boy, Whit. Glad you could come. Hope to see you again."

"I hope so, too, Whit."

"Good night, dad." Leah stepped forward to hug her father. She thought he held her a little tighter, a little longer than usual. When they parted, the look on Whit's face was indescribable.

CHAPTER ELEVEN

THE NIGHT AIR was dry, soft and warm. Jacob led her around to the passenger side of the car and opened the door. But before she got in, he put his arms around her waist and gently held her for a moment. Only held her, that was all, but the gesture sent her pulses leaping. Wanting to do so much, she could do nothing, so she simply stood in the comforting circle of his arms without speaking.

Jacob felt her rigidity; it was out of tune with what he had read in her eyes. He wanted to tell her it was all right, everything was fine. God knows, he was no expert on people—he doubted there was a man alive who was—but he thought he knew something of what Leah was feeling. She was attracted to him, and the attraction startled her. She was having difficulty accepting it. He had to remember what a short time they had known each other. That kind of thing might bother a woman of scruples, so he would keep it in mind. He might not have cornered the market on warmth and charm, but he did have sensitivity and compassion.

Leah, of course, was thinking none of the things Jacob imagined. She was thinking that tonight would be the end of her loneliness. Had she actually only known him two short weeks, she knew she wouldn't be taking him home tonight, but....

From that point on her thoughts became more complex. She hadn't known him only two weeks. He was as integral a part of her life as Nina was, and she couldn't deny her desires and longings. It seemed something of a dream, all at once vivid and unreal. *Tonight is mine,* she mused with satisfaction, and her feeling that all was right and natural was reinforced by the knowledge that Jacob wanted her as much as she wanted him.

He released her, and she got in the car. "Air conditioner or windows down?" he asked.

"Windows down." She needed the air.

He shut the door and walked around to the other side, his spirits soaring to unparalleled heights. Sliding behind the wheel, he placed his wallet on the console between them. Leah watched him out of the corner of her eye. She had noticed him doing that earlier in the day and had remembered Jim's dislike of carrying a wallet. At supper she had spotted Jacob discreetly removing a slice of onion from on top his salad; Jim hadn't liked onions, either. More and more the two men were becoming one in her mind. He turned the key in the ignition, the engine sprang to life, and they drove away.

In all the twenty-eight years of her life, Leah had never been party to a premeditated seduction. She and Jim had drifted gradually, unknowingly into love, and the overtures to lovemaking had progressed hesitantly, inexpertly. What she and Jacob were plunging headlong toward was neither hesitant nor inexpert. She knew exactly what kind of lover he was.

The air inside the car was charged with excitement; it was an almost tangible thing. Yet somehow during the drive back to Sedona they managed light conversation.

"Your father's a nice man."

"Yes."

"He's obviously crazy about you."

"There were just the two of us for so long, and we grew very close."

"The meal was great. Tee is a fantastic cook."

"Too fantastic, I'm afraid. I'm stuffed. When I'm eating Tee's cooking, I can never remember that you're supposed to feed only your hunger, not your taste."

"But you don't have any weight worries."

All very casual and low-key, but Leah's mind was never far from what was ahead. Outwardly she remained composed; inwardly she was shaking with an exquisite torment.

The Corvette pulled to a halt in front of her house. A soft light shone from the front window like a beacon in the night. They got out of the car. They were past the need for coy amenities, so Leah didn't go through the motions of inviting him in, nor did she pause at the front door as if to tell him good night. She simply unlocked it, pushed it open, and he followed her into the house. Leah locked the door behind them.

Jacob could feel the blood pumping through his veins; his pulses pounded, his temples throbbed. He was aware of every move she made. His entire body seemed poised and alert, straining toward her. Once he had read or heard that one of the body's most erogenous zones was the mind, and now he believed it. All he could think of was Leah, the night...the long night stretching ahead of them and all the things they would do. His arousal was complete, but he would have to remember to take his time, not to rush lovemaking, to make it as perfect for her as he knew it would be for him. He wanted her to want him again and again.

Walking to the window, she pulled the drapes shut. With only a small hanging lamp on, the big room was dimly lit, as softly as if by candlelight. "Would you like some coffee, some wine, anything?"

"I don't think so. I'm going in there." He indicated the bathroom with a nod of his head.

"Sure." Leah went into the kitchen and got a drink of water. She walked out of the alcove just as Jacob emerged from the bathroom. Their gazes locked, and they smiled at each other. He closed the space between them, raised one hand and freed her hair of its confining scarf. "I like it down," he said huskily. "It's like a lovely black cloud around your face." Sliding his fingers into the silky strands, he cupped her face, bent his head and toyed with her lips, tasting, sipping. He raised his head, and the eyes meeting hers were clouded with desire.

Without a word they moved toward the sofa. Every nerve in Leah's body was tingling, and almost before she was seated she was in his arms, wrapped around him, clinging to him as though she couldn't bear to let go. His mouth as it bound to hers was so deliciously warm, his hands arousing. The blood pumping through her veins felt like molten lava—a sensation long forgotten, exquisitely sweet. She wanted more than anything to dispense with all the preliminaries and foreplay and just make love, but he wouldn't understand that. This was their first time together as far as he was concerned, so she would have to be patient, even a little shy. She imagined Jacob would be totally put off by a woman who came on strong.

Jacob's heart was pounding so loudly he was certain she could hear it. He didn't think he possessed more than an average share of caveman tendencies, and he wasn't given to ravishment, but he had reached a fever pitch of excitement and would have liked to dispense with finesse and make love to her on the floor. However, the need to move slowly with this gentle woman was uppermost in his mind. Taking a deep breath, he tried to control his racing emotions.

"How long has it been since you necked on a living-room sofa?" he asked tenderly.

"I . . . don't remember ever doing that. Did you?"

"I don't know. I must have. Something made me afraid of male parents in general. Girls' fathers always seemed so hostile."

"Possessive and protective," she corrected. "And you must remember—they knew exactly what you had on your mind."

He curved a forefinger under her chin. "I want to tell you what's on my mind right now."

"I think I know."

His expression was completely serious. "No, not that. I want you to know that I've been besotted with you since the first moment I set eyes on you, and I don't even believe in that sort of thing. Can you begin to understand how that shakes me?" Her eyelashes dipped, but he held her chin firmly. "And I flatter myself that you felt something, too, right from the start. Am I right?"

God, if he only knew! Leah opened her eyes and looked directly into his. "Yes." Her heart thumped loudly and erratically. "There are so many things. . . . Oh, Jacob, this is so difficult for me."

Because of her husband, he was sure. The man had turned out to be a greater obstacle than he'd imagined. Yet he, Jacob, had touched her in some way; she had never been indifferent to him. He had to cling to that knowledge. "Leah, I'm not asking for any breathless declarations of devotion. All I'm asking you to do is love me. . . love me tonight."

It was the easiest, most natural thing she had ever

done. Warmth, real and enticing, spiraled through her. Raising her face, she first felt the texture of his cheek against hers before his lips showered nibbling kisses on her earlobe and along her jawline. His warm breath caressed her chin. By the time his searching mouth had progressed to hers, she was ravenous for the taste of him. Her lips opened, allowing his tongue freedom to mingle with hers. It was so good to have him again.

When Jacob lifted his head, his dark eyes gleamed. "I wish I could tell you how much this means to me. How much you mean to me."

"I know." Her voice was thick.

"Do you? Maybe you do. Is that the reason you turned out to be the one, the one above all others?"

Slowly he slumped back, resting on one of the sofa cushions, bringing her with him. Now she was in a position of command, and she took advantage of it. All thought of employing shy caution was abandoned. In this, he was the novice and she the expert. She knew every sensitive receptor in his body. She had learned to drive Jim almost wild with desire, and she employed the same tactics with Jacob.

First her fingers made a sensitive foray through his thick dark hair. Then her fingernails skimmed over his neck, trailed down and slipped inside his collar to feel the smooth skin of his shoulders. Meeting resistance in the form of his shirt, she flicked open the first button, then another and another. Pushing the garment aside, Leah splayed her hands over the satisfying breadth of his chest. Her fingertips curled through the thick mat of chest hair, then moved to tease the flat nipples. Her lashes dipped, a sensuous smile curving her mouth. She was making love to the only man she had ever loved, and the hard, aching knot forming in the lower part of her body demanded assuagement. Her hands continued downward, jerking his shirt free of his pants, while her mouth placed a melting kiss on his.

Jacob gasped for air; he was suffocating. Never had a woman taken the time to initiate lovemaking with him by such gentle, tactile maneuvers. He was so overwhelmed by Leah that he could only respond with acquiescence. Her exploring fingers fumbled with the waistband of his jeans, then unsnapped, unzipped. She reached for him, her fingers closing around him possessively. As the ache in his loins threatened to erupt, he gripped her upper arms and held her inches away.

"I hope it's not crass to ask where the bed is—but where is the bed?"

"You're sitting on it."

It should have been awkward, Leah thought as they both stumbled to their feet to discard the sofa cushions. In a perfect love scene the bed would have been ready for them. He would have carried her to it. She would have been wearing something soft and flowing that could have been whipped off her in a second. Perfect love scenes didn't begin with the aroused participants having to first dismantle a bulky sofa bed, then undress each other with fumbling, trembling hands.

But the situation wasn't awkward at all. They both pulled out the bed, and their clothes just seemed to fall away. In only seconds they were lying side by side, bodies entwined, luxuriating in the feel of flesh against flesh. Their hands were never still—rubbing, petting, teasing, priming. For Leah it was a rediscovery, not only of his body but of the femininity held dormant so long. For Jacob it was an awakening of passions and desires he feared had wasted away from neglect.

He had envisioned guiding her, but she needed no guidance. Every touch she bestowed him was exciting.

Feverishly hot, fully aroused, enchanted with her sexual expertise, he again wanted her in a position of dominance. Lifting her effortlessly, he brought her down on top of him. Willingly she straddled his torso, sheathed him and began her slow undulations. Jacob was afraid to move; clenching his teeth, he fought for control. Above him her pink-tipped breasts were full and taut with desire, the nipples hard and puckered, enticing him beyond belief. His mouth took one—

And too quickly it was over. As the uncontrolled spasm shook him, his fingers bit into her soft flesh, and he cursed himself violently. It had been too long, he had fantasized about Leah too often, and he had been walking around all day in a mindless state of arousal. He groaned his dismay, his regret, his sense of inadequacy. How cheated she must feel.

"Oh, Leah," he choked. "I'm so damned sorry."

Leah, however, was undaunted. "Hush," she whispered. "Just relax." She had known him before, hundreds of times, and she knew what to do. His desire would return. She didn't allow him to withdraw, and she kept to her rhythmic pace until she felt him again, rigid and urgent. Every part of her came alive. She was attuned to his needs as if he was instructing her step by step. Thoughts and senses merged, so that they not so much made love as allowed it to happen. This time the union was joyous and mutual, as was the climax.

Never would Jacob have believed ecstasy could be so great that it was painful. This, then, was what he had wanted all these years and despaired of ever finding. Only Leah's tiny cry of a name at the moment of completion marred what was a perfect act of love.

THE HOUSE WAS HUSHED. Their labored breathing had slowed, and Leah lay next to him, her hand resting over his heart, blissful in the sweet aftermath. She snuggled against him, kissing his neck, murmuring, sighing contentedly. She thought they had been perfect together, and the release had brought such a feeling of warmth. It was good to feel positively sensual again.

"Leah?"

"Yes."

He took a labored breath. "Was your husband's name Jim?"

Leah's heartbeat slowed, then quickened. *I didn't! Please, God, I didn't call his name.* "Yes." She gulped.

"Do. . .do I remind you of him?"

"Y-yes. In some ways."

"Is that why you were attracted to me in the first place?"

"People are attracted to others for any number of reasons. You should know that," she hedged.

So that explained the instant interest. It explained her reaction to him in the gallery that first day. She hadn't been ill, she had been surprised. He reminded her of her husband, dammit! "He was your last lover?"

"He was my only lover."

That told Jacob so much about her, why she was different. There was a quality of innocence about her that made her seem vulnerable. One man in twenty-eight years. No, now two. "You called his name. Were you aware of that?"

"No. If I did, it meant nothing. A man named Jim is the only other man who ever. . .made me feel that way. Please, Jacob, not now. Must we spoil everything? I don't want—"

"Don't you think I have a right to know something about him? You've never told me a thing. Are you divorced?"

It took her a second or two to decide between a lie and the truth. "No," she said finally. "He just . . . left."

Jacob propped himself on one elbow and stared down at her incredulously. "You aren't divorced? You didn't divorce a man who left you?"

Leah huddled deeper under the covers, miserable because their sweet lovemaking had been followed by this conversation. The story she told was faltering, a mixture of half-truths. "He went away . . . there were reasons. I didn't divorce him . . . it doesn't matter. Soon he'll be declared legally dead. . . ."

Jacob's head hit the pillow again. "This is too heavy for me. Basically, I guess, I'm a simple man."

Now Leah propped up on one elbow, looking at him earnestly. "Is it really so important to you, knowing about my marriage?"

"Not unless—" he carefully considered his next words "—unless you're using me as a substitute."

"You're not a substitute, Jacob, nor a replacement. You're you, unique. Can't you accept that?"

He digested what she'd said. "Yes, I'm sorry, but I've been so curious from the beginning. I've always known you were still in love with him."

"It doesn't matter. It has nothing to do with tonight, with right now."

"What about tomorrow?"

"It has nothing to do with tomorrow, either, nor with the day after." Leah lay down, turning her back to him. She needed to talk to someone about this; she desperately needed a set of rules to follow to get her off this tightrope she was walking. Dr. White's words had been frightening: "irreparable harm." The last thing she wanted to do was harm Jacob.

Jacob touched her on the shoulder. "Have I upset you?"

"No," she said with a sigh. "But I wish you wouldn't let my marriage bother you. I wish you would put it out of your mind."

"The man left his mark on you."

"And Daphne Townsend left her mark on you."

He smiled. "You remembered her name."

"Of course."

"I'm not still in love with Daphne."

Leah chewed on her bottom lip. "Jacob, what I'm trying to say is, when it comes to you and me, the past shouldn't interfere."

"Well, it does when you can't remember who you're making love with."

She turned and smiled at him. Her dark hair splayed, contrasting strongly with the stark whiteness of the pillowcase. Their noses were almost touching. "I knew who I was making love with."

He tilted his head and nibbled at her mouth. "Say my name."

"Jacob."

"Again."

"Jacob."

Drawing her close, he sighed deeply. "I was beginning to think I'd never find you. I've waited so long."

Leah held him tightly and squeezed her eyes shut. *Oh, my darling, you have no idea what waiting is.*

WHEN JACOB AWOKE, dawn was arriving in Red Rock Country. Beside him, Leah slept soundly, the sheet pulled up tightly under her chin, one creamy thigh exposed. His fingertips itched to glide along that satiny-smooth flesh, but he didn't want to waken her. The insomniac in him envied anyone who could sleep so soundly.

Twice during the night they had reached for each

other, seeking replenishment. He had never made love before, not really. He had taken when his needs demanded it, scrupulously avoiding women who might have wanted more than he could give, but he had never made love. Not even that awful, precipitous beginning had spoiled it, thanks to Leah.

Awed, he lay still and watched her sleep. Last night he had lived out men's greatest fantasy—he had found a woman who knew exactly how to love him. The force of her passion staggered him. He, who once past adolescence had never been a so-called ladies man, had discovered the kind of love most men would die for. Jacob watched Leah a moment longer, then carefully, quietly slipped out of bed and went to the window, lifted one corner of a drape and looked outside.

A light rain had fallen during the night. The soft morning mist created a scene of ethereal beauty as the first pink rays of sunlight creeped over Gothic sandstone buttes. Jacob was experiencing an extraordinary sense of déjà vu, as if he had always known he would someday be standing naked at the window of this funny, appealing little house. That really made no sense, and he knew it.

Without warning his mind became very clear, blindingly bright; then it clouded, and shadowy images appeared. He shook his head, making the images disappear. He had experienced the dream again, and as sometimes happened, part of it stayed with him after waking. He shook his head again. Nothing was going to intrude on this perfect day, least of all his damnably unpredictable psyche. His amnesia no longer mattered, anyway. Nothing did, nothing but what he had found here. He couldn't care less about what had happened during those two years.

He turned to glance across the room at Leah, still

sleeping. It bothered him that she hadn't divorced her husband, for that meant she hadn't been able to let go. Jacob wondered if he had it in him to be the one to make her forget the past. He had to face the fact—that's what he wanted. Not an affair, not an arrangement, but a total commitment. Maybe even marriage someday, who could tell? And she wasn't free. What if her husband showed up one of these days to rekindle the flame?

Yet he himself wasn't free, either, not really. What if his memory returned? The complications that could cause were endless. Was it fair to ask a woman like Leah to share a life so fragmented?

No, he wasn't going to think about those two years. They no longer mattered.

Leah stirred just then, stretched and purred, then felt the space beside her. "Jacob?" she called softly, and he was across the room in an instant, slipping between the sheets to take her in his arms. She made a little sound, part sigh, part moan, and snuggled against him.

"Shame on you," she murmured lazily. "You robbed me of the thrill of waking up beside you."

"Sorry. I was watching the sun rise."

"Have you been awake long?"

"Not long."

"What do you want to do today?"

He chuckled. "What's wrong with what we're doing right now?"

"Good heavens, you're a lusty man!"

Lusty? Was he? A far cry from his usual aloof and reserved ways. But this morning he felt lusty, and hot-blooded, virile, potent—all those hackneyed masculine adjectives. He felt like a blue-ribbon bull in the very prime of power.

Leah smiled against his chest. She licked his skin, then kissed and nipped, then teased a nipple with her tongue. "Very lusty," she murmured, "and you taste divine." Her hand began a lazy journey along the length of his lean hard torso, pausing at his hip. Gently her finger traced the pattern of the scar there. It had faded considerably after six years.

"How did you get that?"

"From a dumb-fool kid stunt. I fell out of a tree when I was sixteen. A ragged limb sliced right through my shorts."

"Ouch," she murmured, and stored away another piece of information about the man she had married.

"That wouldn't have been so bad, but the day before the stitches were to come out, I fell off my bicycle and tore it open again. It couldn't be resutured then. Clumsy kid, wasn't I?"

"Well, thank goodness you outgrew it. You're not clumsy anymore. I love the way you do...everything." Her hands continued down his thigh, between his legs, until her fingers closed around him. The combination of her nibbling mouth, her soft breasts crushed to his stomach, her fingers on the most vulnerable part of him, sent Jacob's mind reeling, stumbling. He rose and hardened in an instant.

Leah stretched full-length beneath him and accepted him eagerly. A woman could do without this for great long stretches of time, she thought, but how wonderful to make love when one's lover was the right man.

JACOB STROLLED onto the front porch where Leah was lounging and enjoying a second cup of coffee. After breakfast he had showered and shaved, using her razor, and dressed in yesterday's clothes. Bending over her, he kissed the top of her head.

Leah tilted her face to smile up at him. She was glutted with happiness. She felt as though her bones had melted. "Hmm, you smell good."

He straightened and rubbed his chin. "I didn't have any after-shave, so I used that stuff in the green bottle. What is it?"

"Skin freshener."

"That'll wake you up quick." He sat down near her. "When will Nina come home?"

"Whenever I go get her, probably tonight, so I can work all day tomorrow without interruption. Nina would stay at dad's forever if I'd let her. And be spoiled rotten within a week, I might add."

"Will you be able to come to Phoenix next weekend?"

"I hadn't thought about it. I guess I imagined you would come here."

"There would be damned little privacy in this house if Nina was here, Leah, and I doubt you want to shuttle her off to her grandfather's every weekend. Bring her to Phoenix, and I'll turn over the entire house and all the staff to her."

Leah laughed. "And I think dad spoils her! Oh, Jacob, I'm afraid she'd get on your nerves. You aren't used to children. Nina has an attention span of twenty minutes at best. The only thing that really keeps a six-year-old entertained is another six-year-old."

"Then bring along another six-year-old."

"Are you serious?"

"Of course."

Leah pursed her lips. "Maybe Ann," she mused. "It might be a fun change for them. They'll think they've inherited Disneyland."

"Shall we plan on it?"

Her eyes sparkled; she nodded.

"I should be getting used to having a child around, don't you think?"

She cocked her head and shot him an amused, quizzical glance.

"Aren't you thinking along those lines, too? If you aren't you should be."

"Yes, I'm thinking along those lines, too," she admitted. "Once certain things are resolved."

"Yeah, I know." Briefly his eyes clouded. "I hate long-distance romances."

"How do you know? Have you ever conducted one before?"

"No, but I want to be with you all the time. Weekends aren't enough."

She reached out her hand to him. "Oh, Jacob... but they're something!"

CHAPTER TWELVE

LEAH FULLY EXPECTED to see Sandra bright and early Monday morning, and she wasn't disappointed. It was barely nine o'clock when her friend showed up, bursting with curiosity.

"I was beginning to think that red sports car was going to become a permanent fixture in front of your house."

Leah only grinned. "Want some coffee?"

"No, thanks. He was here until eight o'clock last night."

"Been checking up on me, huh?"

"Hey, I was curious as hell. And pleased as punch, I might add. The life you've been living, without men and all, isn't healthy." A second of silence passed, then Sandra demanded, "Well?"

"Well, what?"

"Oh, Leah." Her friend sighed in exasperation. "Who was that gorgeous man who spent the weekend with you?"

"His name, as you know, is Jacob Surratt. He's a doctor. He lives in Scottsdale. I'm doing this tapestry for him." She shrugged as if to say, "That's all there is to it."

"Come off it!" Sandra glanced around. "Where's Nina?"

"Still at dad's. I called her last night, and she can't

bear to tear herself away from the puppies, so I gave her one more day. I'm going to get her tonight.''

"Then we can talk. Leah, I'm not blind! When I saw that man with Nina I almost fell down. Now I know he's more than just some doctor who's commissioned you to do a tapestry. Right?''

Leah hesitated, but only for a moment. "Right. He's. . . Nina's father.''

Sandra compressed her lips and took a deep breath. "I knew it! They do have a way of straggling back, don't they? Ex-husbands, I mean.''

"It's not like that. Is the resemblance between them really that great?''

Sandra gave it some thought. "I don't know.... I always thought Nina was the living image of you, but when I saw that man.... I guess I might have been expecting to see something. Maybe that's it.''

"I hope so. You see, Jacob has no idea Nina's his. He thinks we only met two weeks ago.''

Sandra stared at her blankly. "I don't understand,'' she said weakly.

"I'm not surprised.''

"Leah, the only thing you ever told me about your ex is that he left you, that you didn't have any idea where he was. You seemed to hate talking about it, so I didn't pry. I figured you'd tell me anything you wanted me to know. But when I saw that man I immediately decided a straying husband had wandered back into the fold.''

"Wrong.''

"Do you want to tell me about it?''

Leah sighed. "I don't see why not.''

She had never known Sandra to be so quiet for so long. As the story unfolded, her friend sat transfixed, never uttering a sound. At the conclusion, she slowly shook her head. "Oh, Leah...that's the damnedest thing I ever heard! Talk about a one-man woman. Don't you just itch to tell him?"

Leah frowned thoughtfully. "Sometimes. More at first than now. The weekend Alex and I went to Phoenix for the clinic's opening, I met Jacob's partner, who's a psychiatrist. He told me things about amnesia I hadn't known before. I'm not too sure I don't want to leave well enough alone."

Sandra shook her head. "I wouldn't be able to keep quiet. I just know I wouldn't."

"Look at it this way. I've found him again, he's well, unmarried and as strongly attracted to me as when he was Jim. Wouldn't I be foolish to...complicate it?"

"Maybe. But I still wouldn't be able to keep my mouth shut."

An alarming thought occurred to Leah. "Sandra, neither Jacob nor Nina has any idea. If you're with either one of them, remember that."

"Oh, listen, when I decide to keep a secret, it's kept. What are you going to do, though? Nothing?"

Leah smiled wanly. "I guess for the time being I'll just play it by ear, take each day as it comes. We'll be seeing each other every weekend for the time being, and— Oh, that reminds me. How about letting Ann go to Phoenix with Nina and me this weekend? They can keep each other entertained, and Jacob has a house that's indescribable! I think his staff has staff. I'm sure the girls will find plenty to do."

"Sure," Sandra said without hesitation. "I was probably going to call on you for baby-sitting duty, anyway. Sam wants to take me to dinner in Flagstaff Saturday night."

"Sandra, I forgot!" Leah exclaimed, hitting her

forehead with the heel of her hand. "How was your date last week?"

"Interesting. Verrry interesting. I haven't seen Sam so charming since our dating days. Mr. Smooth." She sighed. "Why couldn't he have used just a little of that while we were married? Everything would have been so much nicer."

"Would it? Think what you've accomplished on your own. Would you have ever done that if you had stayed married to Sam?"

Sandra's head jerked quickly. "You're right. Dammit, you're right. Even my father once admitted he was proud of me. At the time I looked around to see if he was talking to someone else!"

JACOB TELEPHONED EVERY NIGHT that week, as well. There was some sort of physician's conference being held in Phoenix; not only was he a host, he was one of the principal speakers. He was busy, yet he found time to call every night.

Leah scrunched down under the covers that particular night, placing the receiver between her ear and the pillow. "You sound so important," she murmured.

Modestly he scoffed, "I'd be surprised if there were a dozen people in that auditorium who were actually listening to me. The rest were either half-asleep, dubious, or certain their own theories were far sounder than mine."

"Ah, go on. Such humility. I'll wager they all were thinking how extraordinarily brilliant you are."

He laughed. *He should do that more often,* Leah thought. *It makes such a nice sound.* "Leah, darling, the only extraordinary thing about me is the way I feel about you. If I had wanted to be eloquent this afternoon, I should have presented, to the certain astonishment of my esteemed colleagues, a dissertation on the joy you've brought to my life.''

"Oh, Jacob!" He could overwhelm her. It might be her husband's voice in her ears, but that wasn't Jim speaking. Jim couldn't have come up with words like that if his life had depended on it.

"Are the girls looking forward to the visit?" he asked.

"I'll say! Nina tells anyone who'll listen that we're going to Jacob's house this weekend. She says 'Jacob's house' as if it were the White House or Buckingham Palace."

"Waiting for this weekend has me feeling like a kid myself, waiting for Christmas."

"I know, Jacob. I feel the same way."

DAVIS OPENED THE DOOR WIDE and gave them a beaming smile. "How are you, Mrs. Stone? So nice to see you again. And these—'' he held out a welcoming hand to the two wide-eyed girls standing in front of Leah "—these young ladies must be our special guests. Dr. Surratt has asked me to take extra good care of them."

Nina and Ann stood rooted in place, presenting a charming contrast, since Ann was as fair as Nina was dark. Both girls looked as though they might explode any minute from excitement. Hesitantly they preceded Leah into Jacob's house; whispered ''wows'' and ''gees'' reached Leah's ears. Nina turned to her in astonishment. "Mama, this is bigger than school!"

Leah smiled, though she was watching Davis out of the corner of her eye. This would be the acid test, she decided. If the resemblance between Nina and Jacob was really as great as it seemed to her, surely the man would notice. But there wasn't a flicker, not a hint that he saw a thing. She relaxed somewhat. Perhaps it was true that people don't look any further than the obvious—color of the hair and eyes, shape of the mouth. Certainly in that respect Nina was enough like her mother.

Davis had everything organized. First he took Nina and Ann to the room Leah had occupied the weekend of the opening. There a tiny wren of a woman named Hilda took over. "Mrs. Stone, I'm so glad to meet you. I was on vacation the last time you were here, I believe. Now I don't want you to worry about the girls. Dr. Surratt has instructed me not to let them out of my sight, and you can be sure I'll do just that." She looked at the girls with a maternal expression. "Such lovely young things. This—" she reached out and touched the top of Nina's dark curls "—of course is your daughter. She looks so much like you. We're going to have a wonderful time, aren't we, girls?"

Nina and Ann nodded in uncertain unison.

All well and good, but Leah had some instructions of her own. "I want you girls to have fun, but please remember this isn't a playground or an amusement park. This is someone's home, and you're to treat it as such. Understand?" Containing their excitement for a moment, both girls nodded solemnly.

To Hilda, Leah said, "I've brought along an emergency kit, just in case."

The little woman frowned. "Emergency?"

"Games, coloring books, crayons. The sort of thing you resort to when all else fails."

Hilda smiled indulgently. "Well, Mrs. Stone, the staff and I hope to keep the girls so busy they won't have time for coloring books and such."

"Where's Jacob?" Nina asked.

Davis stepped forward. "Dr. Surratt had some work to do at the clinic, but he wanted me to telephone him the moment you arrived, which I've done. I'm sure he'll be here any moment." He turned to Leah. "I'll show you to your room while Hilda gets the girls settled in."

Leaving the room, Leah paused for one last word with Nina and Ann. "Remember, girls, I want some shining behavior reports."

"Please don't worry about them, ma'am," Hilda said, smiling fondly at her two new charges. "It's going to be such fun having the young ones around."

I hope she's still saying that tomorrow afternoon, Leah thought wryly as she followed Davis down the carpeted hallway. She experienced a brief moment of mortification when she saw the weekend "arrangement"—adjoining bedrooms. She was being given the room Alex had had before. It was linked to Jacob's by a beige-tiled bathroom, quite possibly the largest bathroom she had ever seen. It was completely masculine in decor, with cocoa-colored fixtures, natural wood tones and an absence of superfluous decoration, but it was also the last word in luxury. Thick nylon carpeting that looked like fur covered the floor, and a sunken tub complete with whirlpool apparatus dominated the center of the room. It was no ordinary bath; merely thinking of sharing it with Jacob was a sensuous experience.

"Thank you, Davis," Leah said stiffly, overcompensating for her embarrassment with a too-correct manner. "It's lovely."

His expression was blank. "Yes, ma'am. If there's nothing else right now, I'll go downstairs and see if Dr. Surratt has arrived."

Once Davis was gone, Leah hung up the few garments she had brought, went into the bathroom to freshen her makeup, momentarily considered changing out of her pleated shirtwaist dress, then decided to wait and see what plans Jacob had for the afternoon.

Impatient for his arrival, she crossed the expanse of the master bath to his bedroom. She had glimpsed it briefly from the hallway, but now she indulged in the luxury of really studying it. The room reflected his personality—quietly elegant, nothing ostentatious, a wealthy man's private retreat. A king-size bed, desk and chair, a recliner and reading lamp were the main furnishings. Several books lay on a bedside table; she picked them up and perused the jackets. Very intellectual stuff. Jacob apparently read more for knowledge than pleasure, whereas Jim had devoured spy thrillers.

Leah even had the temerity to open his closet door and gaze along the neat rows of clothing. Shutting the door behind her, she had started to leave the room, feeling every inch a nosy intruder, when she heard Jacob calling to her from the other bedroom. "Leah? Darling, where are you?"

Her heart leaped exultantly. "Here!" she called back, and moved in the direction of his voice. The shortest distance to him was through the bathroom. She entered from one side, he from the other; for a moment they each stood framed in their respective doorways, simply staring at each other. Then exuberantly they raced for each other like a couple of children.

She coiled her arms around his neck as he lifted her off the floor and swung her around. "Damn, it's good to see you!" he said.

"Jacob, you're making me dizzy!" she said with a laugh.

Effortlessly he swept her up into his arms, marched

out of the bathroom into his room, where he dumped her on the bed. Then he fell on top of her, a lead weight. She was the recipient of an enthusiastic kiss before he said, "I've missed you so much."

"I've missed you, too," Leah squirmed. "You weigh a ton." She tugged at the hem of her dress, which had ridden up to midthigh.

Jacob rolled off her slightly, but his hand detained hers. "Leave it where it is." He placed his palm against her stockinged flesh and rubbed sensitively. "You feel so good. What a month this week has been! I thought this moment would never come." He bent his head to kiss the pulse point at the base of her throat before searching for her mouth again.

Leah's mouth sought his as avidly. Drawing her into an ardent embrace, he kissed her again and again. His tongue explored the sweet secrets of her mouth, while his hand roamed along her thigh, pushing the dress ever higher.

"You leave me breathless," she gasped when they parted.

"For a week I've been a man with a problem," he growled, and he moved against her to prove it.

"Surely you don't...expect to solve it here and now!!"

Only Leah could make him feel so carefree, so lighthearted, happy and thoroughly reckless. "Hold on tight, darling," he whispered huskily, drawing her thighs around his hips. The dress was up around her waist by this time.

"Oh, Jacob, not here!"

"Why not?"

"Jacob, don't be ridiculous! There are other people...." It was beginning to dawn on her what a sight they would present to anyone who happened into the room, and to her knowledge no doors had been locked.

He sat back on his haunches, his eyes glittering, and his hands began a worshipful foray along the length of her slender, shapely legs. When they reached her feet, he casually flicked away her pumps and dropped them on the floor.

"This must be the finest pair of legs in all the world," he murmured reverently, his hands inching up her rounded calves, her smooth thighs. He braced an arm on either side of her, leaned over and planted a firm, warm, moist kiss on her parted lips. Gradually he settled his full weight on her.

"Oh, Leah," he muttered, "definitely . . . a problem. . . ."

"This is indecent." It was a half protest, half laugh.

"No one's going to bother us, sweetheart."

Languorously she writhed beneath him as white-hot flame curled up from the pit of her stomach. "Couldn't you please just lock some doors? I think I could get more in the spirit of this if I wasn't scared to death that someone was going to walk in on us at any minute."

"Okay," he said hoarsely, pushing himself off her, then undoing his belt buckle and unbuttoning his trousers. "I've got to get these damned pants off, anyway. Don't move."

He went to the door leading to the hall and locked it. Leah didn't move. She merely watched him. His hair was tousled, and with his belt hanging unfastened in the loops and his trousers unbuttoned, he was the perfect picture of aroused masculinity. Smiling, she flicked at the top button of her dress as he moved toward the bathroom door.

"Mama!" Nina's childish voice rent the air. It was coming from the hall, but in only seconds, Leah was sure, her daughter would wander into the adjoining bedroom, then no doubt into the bathroom, then into Jacob's room.

"Jacob!" Leah gasped in horror, leaping off the bed, trying to button her dress and grope for her shoes at the same time. He halted in his tracks and fumbled with the front of his pants. Both worked hard to steady their frantic breathing. "God a'mighty!" Jacob croaked.

"Mama?"

"In here, Nina!" Leah managed to say, smoothing her rumpled dress.

Nina and Ann appeared in the doorway leading to the bathroom. Both were wearing swimsuits and carrying inflated, doughnut-shaped gadgets. The smiling girls confronted two adults who were trying their best to look as though they had been engaged in a friendly chat. Only six-year-olds would have believed it.

"Hilda's taking us swimming," Nina announced brightly. "Wanna come?"

At that moment a rather frantic Hilda put in an appearance, hustling the girls away. Over her shoulder she threw Jacob an apologetic look. "Dr. Surratt, I'm so sorry, but they just got away from me for a minute."

"That's quite all right, Hilda. Think nothing of it."

Hilda and the girls left, but not before Nina quickly added, "Oh, Jacob, this is my friend, Ann." Jacob muttered something unintelligible as the other bedroom door closed firmly behind the trio. Leah expelled a ragged breath. Then to Jacob's astonishment, she began to giggle. Putting her hand to her mouth, she crossed the room and slumped against him, her shoulders shaking.

"What's so damned funny?" he demanded.

"Y-you should see the look on your face!"

"Damn! What a time to interrupt a guy!"

"Well, weren't you the one w-who needed to get used to having a child around...?"

"DO YOU HAVE A HEADACHE?" Leah asked seriously, sipping on her wine that evening.

"A mild one," Jacob admitted. "Nothing really."

"You're frowning, and you've been rubbing your eyes. You do that a lot."

"So I'm prone to headaches."

"Stop that, Jacob. I want to know."

They were sitting at an umbrella table beside the swimming pool, watching the sun flame and die over Camelback Mountain, enjoying a quiet, private interlude before dinner. In the distance they could see Davis driving Jacob's golf cart over the grounds. Beside him were two very happy—but surely by now—worn-out little girls who had been thoroughly catered to all afternoon. To top off their perfect day, dinner had been prepared especially for them by Jacob's cook, a robust man named George, who looked as though he had a hearty appreciation for his own cooking. At the girls' request, spaghetti had been served, but with a flair worthy of pâté de fois gras and tournedos Rossini. The trip over the grounds in the golf cart was going to be the curtain call. The moment they returned, Leah was going to get the girls off to bed. Hilda, she had noticed, wore the harried expression of a mother of five who'd just discovered the washing machine was on the blink.

"Tell me," she demanded again.

Jacob shifted in his chair and watched her. Tonight she looked ravishing; that was the only way to describe her. She was wearing some long, shimmering, emerald-green thing that seemed to be a dress, but with her legs crossed he could see it was pants. The sleeves were big and floppy, the neckline draped low to hint at the valley between her breasts, and the waist was cinched with a gold belt. Her hair hung down around her shoulders, the way he liked it. It still amazed and thrilled him that this stunning woman had been attracted to him from the beginning. It was impossible to explain what she had done for his masculine ego, but he would have liked to try. He wanted to tell her she had uncovered something in him he hadn't known existed. There was so much he would like to say to her, to talk about—almost anything but his crazy, mixed-up mind.

"Let's change the subject," he suggested softly.

Leah sighed. "I suppose so, if it bothers you that much."

"Oh, Leah, it doesn't bother me." He reached across the table and took one of her hands in his. "It just doesn't seem very interesting or important anymore. Look, every once in a while, I get these.... It's like a flashbulb goes off in my head, and I get a headache. But it always goes away fairly quickly. That's all there is to it. I don't want to think about it."

"Please, just let me ask one more question. Have you always had these headaches?"

"At first, years ago when I came out of the fugue, I had them frequently. Then they went away. They've only come back recently. Now let's drop it, okay?"

"Sure." Her thoughts were racing nevertheless. No doubt the headaches had returned since he'd met her. He was fighting the recollection. Damn, the solution seemed so simple to her untrained mind. Just fill in the blank spaces for him, and he could relax. But she didn't dare.

Jacob watched her. She had a very expressive face, and he could tell she was bothered by his "condition."

He raised her fingertips to his lips, an action that snapped her out of her reverie. His eyes strayed over her in an almost physical caress. "Leah, it's so unimportant. The headaches used to worry me, but since I met you.... I think what I'm trying to tell you is, I don't care anymore. I—"

A lump formed in his throat. It shouldn't be so hard to say, but in all his life he had only told one woman he loved her, and that had been a horrible mistake. This wasn't a mistake, though. Leah was so right for him. "I love you. I have since the moment I laid eyes on you in Alex's office."

"That's almost impossible, you know."

"It's true just the same."

Leah's lips trembled. "I love you, too, Jacob. Really I do." And she did. Everything she had ever felt for Jim had been transferred to Jacob, while Jacob heaped new sensations on the old with each passing minute.

He buried his face in her palm and kissed it, overcome with emotion. "I wish I could tell you what hearing that does to me. Here...." He placed her hand over his heart. "It's about to thud right out of my chest."

They stood simultaneously and clung to each other for a long, wordless moment. Finally Jacob stepped away from her. "Davis is coming with the girls. Let's get those two scamps in bed. The rest of the evening belongs to us. I think I'd like to take you out to dinner. It's suddenly occurred to me that we've never had an honest-to-goodness date."

THEY HAD DINNER at Trader Vic's. Jacob chose it not only for the food but for the exotic ambience, a perfect backdrop for Leah's exotic beauty. And how beautiful she did look! Before leaving the house she had changed into a swishy dress of palest apricot, with some sort of pleated furbelow at the shoulders that framed the smooth sweep of her neckline. Magically—through makeup, lighting, whatever—her cheeks had taken on the same hue as her dress. She always looked so...well, put together. He knew she wasn't a woman who spent an unusual amount of time or money on clothes, but when Leah got all dressed up, there wasn't a woman alive who could match her for style and flair.

They dined on crab Rangoon, then Indonesian lamb with peach chutney and fried rice, snow peas and water chestnuts, all washed down with a delightful chilled Chardonnay. At meal's end Leah pushed her plate slightly away from her and smiled contentedly. "It was a feast," she announced. "I'm sure I've never had a finer meal."

"I wanted it to be special."

"It's been that, all right. Very special."

"The entire day's been special. I got a real kick out of having the girls with us."

Leah chuckled. "I wonder if Davis and Hilda would say the same thing. You were really good with them."

"You sound surprised."

"You once told me you felt uptight around kids, and you looked startled out of your wits when Nina asked you to tell them a bedtime story."

"Hmm. That threw me for a while. I'm not sure anyone has ever asked me to read to them before."

"Bedtime stories are stalling tactics, don't you know that? Like drinks of water and trips to the bathroom."

"How did I do with 'The Three Little Pigs?'"

"Well...it sounded to me as if you had it confused with 'Goldilocks and the Three Bears' a time or two, but I'm not sure it wasn't more interesting that way. What difference did it make, anyway? The girls were enchanted, since they knew you had it thoroughly screwed up. They were just waiting to see how you'd extricate yourself. There's a fey side to you I haven't seen before."

He reached for her hand. "Leah, you've unearthed things in me I didn't know existed."

After leaving the restaurant, they strolled along the Fifth Avenue Shops, window-shopping before returning to Jacob's house. No one was waiting up for them, and only two small lamps had been left on, one in the foyer and one in the upstairs hall. Jacob locked the front door, turned off the foyer light, and arm in arm they ascended the stairs.

When they reached the second floor, Leah said, "Let me check on the girls."

He nodded and waited for her. She was back in a minute. "Your place or mine?" he asked.

"I think I'd like being in your bed." She walked to the door to his room and stepped inside; he followed, closing and locking it behind them. Then she was in his arms, being held, petted and kissed with a desperation that staggered her. The room was very dark. Fingers of moonlight filtering through the half-closed blinds played on the wall and across the bed.

"How do you get out of this thing?" he asked, fumbling impatiently with the apricot-colored cloth.

Quickly she undid the sash and let it fall. "There's a zipper in back," she said breathlessly.

Taking her by the shoulders, he turned her, and the zipper hissed. The garment formed a peachy puddle at her feet. He kissed her on the nape, then on both shoulder blades before turning her back to him. She stood before him in a thin wispy bra and panty hose. The muscles in Jacob's stomach tightened; the swelling in his groin made his trousers uncomfortably tight. He wondered how long it would last, this instant arousal at the sight of her, clothed or unclothed. Gently he slipped his hands around her back and undid the bra, then filled his palms with her satin-smooth breasts. "You are so...beautiful. A perfect ectomorph."

Leah's legs felt like liquid, unable to support her weight. She stumbled against him. "A what?"

"Ectomorph: slender, small boned, gentle curves. You're what all the endomorphs would like to be."

"Doctor, how romantic!" she teased. Looping her arms around his neck, she nibbled at the underside of his chin. "What are you?"

"I'm an ectomorph, too."

"Take off your clothes and let me verify that."

He complied hastily, awkwardly jerking and flinging his clothes with abandon. Then he stood before her, proud and urgent, fully aroused and eager for her. She gloried in the sight. Luxuriously she ran her hands over his chest, down his sides to his waist, which was scarcely distinguishable from his lean, hard hips. "But you have such marvelous muscles."

He swallowed hard. "Ectomorphs can develop muscles."

Her hands fluttered across his shoulders, moving to his upper arms. She slipped her arms around his waist, squeezing his buttocks with both hands. "Obviously, ectomorphs have nice buns."

His hands did some exploring of their own. "Obviously." He grinned.

One of her hands came around and down between their bellies. "And this?"

"Universal to all body types," he said on a groan. Hooking his fingers into the waistband of her panty hose, he pulled downward. "One last obstacle." She wiggled her hips to facilitate the removal.

Jacob bent and with one swift motion dispensed

with the bedspread, then guided her between the sheets. She reached for him as he joined her, and once again he marveled at how perfectly their bodies responded to each other. She slithered beneath him, slipping easily into the niche of his hips that seemed made just to fit her. Her legs locked around him, holding him tightly to her.

Even though a week had passed, neither of them was impatient for the consummation. They spent several long, leisurely minutes in stimulating exploration, each marvelously attuned to the other. Knowing hands performed their magic; not an inch of her escaped his lips. Jacob, caught in the throes of sexual readiness, nevertheless kept to an exquisitely torturous pace, stroking and priming until she cried out for the union. Levering himself above her, he withheld her request a moment and stared down at her, her eyes feverishly bright, his nostrils distended with desire.

"Please. . ." she whispered.

"All right, darling. Now. . . ." He covered her body with his and filled her completely. Her arms and legs bound him like loving ropes. Jacob buried his face in the silky hollow of her shoulder, felt her soft cheek against his, her damp hair brushing his forehead. He thrust and rotated until he felt the explosion rock her, and lifting his head, he watched ecstasy transform her face. Only when her tremors ceased and her mouth grew slack did he allow himself his own release. Certain she had been satisfied, he succumbed, and his tension broke into a shock wave of pure pleasure. Emptied and temporarily depleted, he drew her into the warm circle of his arms and, for a time, they slept.

IT WAS AFTER MIDNIGHT when they awoke. "Roll over," Leah murmured, "and I'll give you a massage."

"Sounds irresistible." Jacob rolled onto his stomach, his cheek on the pillow, and raised his arms above his head. Leah tossed the sheet away from them and knelt on the bed beside him. Tapered fingers began massaging his neck, then kneading his shoulder muscles. The ritual she performed had been perfected during her marriage and was designed to inspire and ignite, not soothe and relax.

"Feel good?" she asked after a minute or two.

Jacob's voice was muffled by his pillow. "Mmm."

"I take it that means yes."

"Mmm...."

Smiling seductively, she continued with sensitively tactile fingers, working up and down the length of him, reveling in the feel of his firm musculature. He had, it seemed to her, the perfect male physique.

"Leah?"

"Hmm?"

"Was my resemblance to your husband the reason for your peculiar reaction to me that day in the gallery?"

Her hands stopped. "Oh, God, is that what you're thinking about?"

"Was it?" he persisted.

"I...guess that was part of it."

"Do I really look that much like him?"

"I guess you do. What difference does it make?"

"None, I guess, except—" he rolled over to look at her "—except I worry that you might be making love to him through me."

Leah sat back on her heels, and her mouth compressed into a tight line of irritation. "You worry too much, doctor. Didn't anyone ever tell you that's bad for you? Why do you find it so difficult to believe I love you, just you, nobody else?"

"I'm a walking example of chronic insecurity. Haven't you discovered that by now? I'm too crazy about you, Leah. I'm not sure I could survive if you—"

"Walked out on you? Not everybody deserts. I'm not going anywhere, not unless you persist in questioning me every time we make love. If you want to talk about something, let's talk about all your old girlfriends. We've barely touched on that subject."

"All of them?" he teased.

"There were that many?"

"No," he said seriously. "Not many. Not unless you want to go back to my wild, impetuous youth, and even that was pretty tame by today's standards."

Leah didn't really want to talk about his women friends, or even the lack of same. "All right, I'll buy that. Subject closed. Now...." Grabbing the sheet, she billowed it over their heads like a tent and crawled on top of him. The percale floated down to settle around their hips. "I guess I'm going to have to try something else, since the massage obviously didn't work."

She locked her thighs against his and began moving slowly, sensuously on top of him. He groaned. "You look like an angel, but you're a sorceress, a temptress."

Bending her head, she gently captured his bottom lip between her teeth and nibbled. "I'm trying to be," she murmured. "Lie still and let me practice."

Within seconds he had caught the pace of her relentless rhythm and begun to move with her. From the beginning he had instinctively known she was not a woman of varied sexual experience, and he believed her when she said her husband had been her only lover. Yet she inspired him to new heights of sexual prowess, so that loving Leah was the easiest thing in the world. This time when the climax came it was no earth-shattering explosion, but a wonderful sensation of joy and relief and thunderous happiness. His body was glutted with pleasure.

"Leah," he said when he was capable of speech, "if you keep this up, my reproductive organs are going to be in a bottle at Harvard Medical School."

Her response was a quiet laugh of absolute triumph.

As she was preparing to leave for home the following afternoon, Jacob came into the room. "Davis and Hilda have the girls ready."

"And are counting the minutes until they see my car pull out of the driveway, I'll bet. Your staff is priceless, Jacob. This weekend they've tended to duty above and beyond the call." She snapped her suitcase shut and turned to him.

He stepped toward her, taking her loosely in his arms. "Five days is too long to be away from you."

"I know, but if we were together all the time, I'm afraid neither of us would get any work done."

His expression was intense. "I want you to do me a favor, Leah."

"Yes?" Something about the tone of his voice put her on guard.

"Think about getting a divorce."

"You dwell on that too much, Jacob."

"How else can I be sure you're ready to belong to me?"

"I belong to you."

"Then get a divorce."

"I'll. . .look into it."

"Promise?"

"Yes, I promise."

CHAPTER THIRTEEN

THE SUMMER slipped into a blissful routine. Leah and
Jacob saw each other every weekend. When he came to
Sedona, she made a point of driving him all over the
valley, thinking he might recognize something, though
whether or not he did became less and less important
to her. Together they visited the impressive Indian
ruins of the Tuzigoot National Monument and the pic-
turesque and historic old mining town of Jerome.
They spent a Saturday hiking Oak Creek's fantastic
West Fork. Touristy things mostly, because Leah
thought she had to be careful.

She couldn't risk taking him places where he might
encounter someone who had known him as Jim Stone.
At all costs she wanted to avoid doing him the irreparable harm Charles White had mentioned. For
that reason, other than for sight-seeing, they stayed
close to her house and to Whit's farm, where only her
father and Tee knew the truth and were as protective
of him as she was.

Jacob was never far from her thoughts. She was sure
she had never been happier. For the first time in her
life, Leah was being courted, wooed, and it was a
heady experience. The romance was so different from
the one that had developed between her and Jim.
Jacob was forever bringing gifts, both for her and for
Nina. He sent flowers occasionally and made those
late-night phone calls that had grown increasingly

erotic. He seemed to lose a lot of his inhibitions when talking on the phone.

Still, she balked at the idea of getting a divorce, and she had to examine exactly why. She didn't think it necessary, since she was convinced that the impasse could be resolved in a better way. Unfortunately, just what that "better way" was escaped her.

For one thing—and this was something she tried not to dwell on too heavily—divorce implied a rejection of her life with Jim. Foolish maybe, but that was the way she felt about it. Leah hated the idea of legally terminating a relationship that was still alive and well through Jacob.

So instead of immediately seeking a lawyer, she talked to Whit. She tried to visit her father at least once a week, and now that Bess's offspring were frisky and playful and nearing weaning age, Nina constantly badgered her mother to go to the farm. It didn't take much pleading, for Leah relished every chance to talk to Whit, her one true confidant.

"If Jacob persists in this divorce thing, I guess I'm going to have to go through with it, dad. He sees my refusal to get one as clinging to old memories. What do you think would be involved? Won't I have to answer a lot of questions about my husband? I can't let Jacob hear any of the answers."

By now Whit knew the whole story, and he had his own ideas on the subject. "Damned if I don't think Jacob should know the truth. Sounds to me like he's worried about the past, like he might've done something awful or some such nonsense. But we know that's not so. Between us we can probably account for every single second of Jim Stone's short life." Whit shook his head. "Sure seems to me that Jacob would feel better if he knew that."

Leah chewed on her bottom lip. "That's what I think, too, dad, but I'm no psychiatrist, and I can't forget what Dr. White said. The one thing I don't want to do is harm Jacob. I think he suffers more than he lets on."

"Well, I don't know what to tell you, but I'll send you to a fellow who might."

The fellow's name was Daniel Chapman, an attorney friend of Whit's, and most of what he told Leah she already knew. In another year, actually a few months less, she would legally be a widow. If she didn't want to wait that long she could sue for divorce on grounds of desertion. Leah winced over that one. However, Mr. Chapman went on to explain, her circumstances were a bit unusual. He would be glad to look into the case and give her a call later.

Leah left it at that for the time being. At least she could now truthfully tell Jacob she had seen a lawyer and that he was looking into it.

JACOB REGARDED MILDRED BANNISTER across the expanse of his glass-topped desk. Hiding behind his professional mask, he appeared to be listening but wasn't. He had heard Mildred's story so many times before. She had been coming to see him at least once a month for three years or so, and according to Mildred, she was in no better health now than she had been that long-ago first day. He knew that. There wasn't anything wrong with her, not medically at least, but he couldn't seem to convince her of that.

He felt sorry for Mildred, he really did, and in some ways he could empathize with her. She didn't feel good, and she wanted help. Another prescription wouldn't help her, though. Over the years he had learned a good deal about her. She was middle-aged, had married children scattered all over the country and a successful husband who spent fifteen hours a day with his work. She had a lot of money but no real interests outside the home; unfortunately, now there was seldom anyone else at home. Pity no one had come up with a pill to cure loneliness. No one knew better than he did how rotten it could make you feel.

When the woman had finished recounting her lengthy list of ailments, Jacob gave her a sympathetic smile. "Well, Mildred, the best I can do is prescribe a mild sedative to help you with your insomnia, and there are some exercises you can do before getting out of bed every morning that might alleviate that back pain. Your X-rays show no functional or structural cause for it. As for your stomach trouble...again, tests show nothing. We might have to chalk it up to that handy ailment called 'nerves.' I would suggest you lay off the antacids, however, and let your digestive system right itself."

The woman sighed with disdain. "Doctor, I can't believe that in this fancy clinic with all this fancy equipment, you can't find out what's wrong with me."

"I'm sorry. We don't know everything. If we can't see it or feel it or hear it, we're helpless."

"My sister-in-law's doctor just gives her Valium, and she says it works wonders for her."

"No, Mildred," Jacob said decisively. "Valium isn't the answer for you. Tell you what. There's another physician I'd like you to see."

"Oh?" The woman's eyes lit up.

"Yes. Dr. White."

It took Mildred a moment to realize who he was referring to. When she did, she bristled. "A psychiatrist? Do you think I'm crazy?"

"Why, Mildred! I'm surprised at you! Surely you

know there are any number of reasons for seeing a psychiatrist. I'm merely thinking your problems might stem from a less-obvious source. Emotions, perhaps. Or from external factors beyond your control.''

She gave this some thought. "Well, I can certainly understand how I'd be emotionally upset. Harry has no time for me, and he's not in the least sympathetic about my health problems. He says when I can tell him the name of what's wrong with me he'll start believing I'm sick. Wouldn't it do me a world of good to be able to tell Harry he's the one making me ill!''

Jacob reached for a note pad and pencil. "I'm going to request a consultation with Dr. White for you. Will you go?''

The idea, he could tell, was taking on more appeal with each passing second. "I certainly will, Doctor. I certainly will.''

Mildred was the day's last patient. Jacob saw her to the door, then instructed his nurse to close up shop for the day. Shutting his office door, he returned to his desk, settled into his comfortable swivel chair, propped up his feet and closed his eyes. The day had been an especially tiring one, no doubt because he had slept so poorly the night before, and the night before that.

His haunting dream was recurring with bewildering frequency. Worse, the headaches were back, the same kind he had suffered six years earlier. No longer could he pretend there was anything different about them. He had dispensed with aspirin and had begun taking a prescription medication that sometimes induced lethargy, which he hated. So far he had managed to downplay the headaches when he was with Leah, but that couldn't go on forever. She saw too much.

The past weekend in Sedona had been especially difficult for him. He thought he had successfully convinced her he had simply been working unusually long hours, until a headache all but incapacitated him. He had wasted a precious hour of their time together Saturday afternoon sleeping off the pain while she worked at her loom, and he begrudged every wasted moment.

Jacob lived for the weekends. It often seemed he was only happy and content when he was with Leah. He loved her with a mindless madness; that was the only way to describe it. She was such a quiet, addictive presence. A woman of contrasts, at once an imaginative dreamer and a serious artisan, a delightful imp and a sensuous siren. Her open passion still shook him, and he almost groaned as he thought about her.

Sometimes she came to Phoenix; more often he went to Sedona. After he had sat and watched her weave for a time, they would walk through the woods near her house or take leisurely drives through the valley. She was a great tour guide and loved the peaceful Verde. He thought he was beginning to understand why. There was something contagious about the slower pace of country life.

When Nina wasn't with her grandfather, she was with Jacob and Leah. Although the child's presence, coupled with the lack of privacy in Leah's house, were deterrents to lovemaking, Jacob never resented either. There were times when just being with Leah was enough. With her, he could relax; with her, he could be himself... whoever himself was.

He was a fortunate man, he knew. He had found the woman of his dreams, and both Leah's daughter and her father had accepted him into their lives with casual ease. Whit especially treated him as though he belonged, a fact for which Jacob was enormously grateful. Life was wonderful, and might be perfect if it

wasn't for Leah's marital status, the damnable headaches and that god-awful dream.

Thinking of Leah's husband elicited a frown. Not
even in their most private moments together had she
told him about the man. The only thing Jacob knew
for certain was that in some vague way he reminded
her of him. Nor did she ever mention the divorce, not
unless he brought it up, and then she only said some
lawyer was "looking into it." Could she possibly be
using the marriage as a crutch, something to lean on
while deciding if she really wanted to marry a man who
suffered headaches, dreams and all sorts of mental
aberrations?

The headaches had no physical cause—he had made
sure of that—so he had to accept that they were psychological. The past was trying to force its way into
the present, and he was subconsciously refusing to let
it. Why? He honestly wanted to remember, to make
sure there was nothing lurking back there in the fuzzy
recesses of his mind that could harm the future. He
wanted to be the kind of husband Leah deserved, not
some psychological freak, which was the way he saw
himself half the time. He wanted to be well and whole
and mentally sound.

Abruptly Jacob opened his eyes and swung his feet
off the desk. He walked to the window and stood with
his hands clasped behind his back. After a few minutes
of staring vacantly out over the walled-in garden at the
rear of the building, he paced restlessly around his office. He didn't particularly want to go home, but the
office walls were closing in on him. His head was
pounding, yet he didn't dare take any more medication
until he was safely out from behind the wheel of a car.

This can't go on, old man, his inner voice warned.

Removing the ever-present stethoscope from around

his neck, he stuffed it into the pocket of his white coat, then shrugged out of the coat and hung it up. He jerked his suit jacket off a hanger and slung it over his arm. Switching off the light, he walked through the empty waiting room into the silent corridor beyond. Automatically he turned toward the doctors' entrance at the rear of the building, then stopped suddenly. Acting on impulse, he pivoted and crossed the hall to the double doors leading to the psychiatric unit. It was as quiet and empty as the medical clinic, but at the end of the long hallway there was light welling from under Charles's door. Striding purposefully toward it, Jacob knocked, waited for his partner's summons, then entered the office.

Charles was standing near a bookcase. A book lay open in his hand, and reading glasses were perched on the tip of his nose. He looked up. "Ah, Jacob. Working late, I see."

"Not really. I saw my last patient a while ago. A patient I'm referring to you, by the way."

"Oh?"

Succinctly Jacob told Charles about Mildred Bannister's case. "But that's not the reason I'm here. Charles, how...how about putting me back in therapy?"

Charles frowned, regarding his partner levelly over the rim of his glasses. "What brought this on?"

"Does it matter? Can we start the sessions again?"

The psychiatrist closed the book and carefully slid it between two others in the case. He stared vacantly at the floor, not at Jacob. "I suppose that would depend on why you think you need therapy again. A lot of time has passed. I would have to guess the events of the fugue are forever buried in your subconscious."

Without being asked to, Jacob took a seat. He was

never entirely at ease with his partner, though he wasn't sure why. Charles White was one of the finest psychiatrists in the country, precisely the reason Jacob had wanted him associated with the clinic. But the two men weren't personally close, a situation Jacob often attributed to his own reserved nature. That plus the fact that Charles was less than outgoing probably made it impossible for the two of them to be fast friends.

However, it hadn't occurred to Jacob to go to anyone but his partner. He was socially acquainted with almost all of Phoenix's medical fraternity, several therapists among them, but he balked at going to any of them for help. Why, he wasn't sure; he wouldn't have hesitated to go to a surgeon friend if he needed an operation. This was different.

And he certainly wouldn't have considered going to one of Charles's younger associates. He did, after all, have a certain image to maintain in his own clinic. The other doctors referred to him as "The Man," though never to his face. They certainly didn't know he was aware of the nickname.

"That damned dream is back. The headaches, too," he told Charles. "I'll swear they're worse than before. Something's in there trying to get out. Can we begin again?"

"Is something personal bothering you? The woman?"

Jacob looked at Charles in surprise. "The woman?"

"Leah Stone."

"You know Leah?"

"No, but I met her once, at the opening."

"I'd only known her a few days then."

"Yes.... I had the feeling she was someone you were going to try to get to know better."

"Is that a fact? Charles, you amaze me. I had no idea you paid that much attention to my women friends."

"You know clinic gossip. It's quickly and effectively circulated."

Jacob frowned at the suggestion that he and Leah could be topics of clinic gossip. How could they be, since they stayed strictly to themselves? So much so that his already limited social life had been placed in virtual limbo. Lately it had crossed his mind that he should take Leah out and introduce her to some of his friends and associates. Until today he had assumed no one in Phoenix outside his household even knew of their relationship. Gossip obviously had a way of getting around. "Leah isn't in the least like any other woman I've ever met," Jacob said.

"I realize that," the psychiatrist said enigmatically. "Is she your problem?"

"Leah's no 'problem,' Charles, but I want to marry her, and I'd like to make one last stab at clearing up this damned mind of mine. I think I owe it to her."

"Headaches, hmm? As I said, a lot of time has passed. The chances aren't good, Jacob. Not good at all."

"I know," he said resignedly, "but I want to try. I've got to try."

LEAH HAD JUST TURNED OUT the lights when the phone rang. Snuggling deeper beneath the covers, she reached for the receiver. "Hello, darling," she cooed seductively.

"You're going to be very surprised some night if the call isn't from me." Jacob chuckled.

"Not nearly as surprised as the caller will be."

"How are you?"

"Fine. You?"

"Pretty good."

"What's that supposed to mean? Are you having more of those headaches you keep pretending you aren't having?"

There was a pause; his husky sigh came over the line. "Why do I ever try to keep anything from you? You're a witch."

"No, just observant. I've seen you gulping those pills. You are having headaches, aren't you?"

"Yes."

"The dream, too?" she asked quietly, for by now he had told her about the dream, and she thought she could give him a pretty good interpretation of it, if only she dared.

"Sometimes."

"Why?"

"That's what I'm going to try to find out. I'm going back into therapy. Charles all but told me it wouldn't work, but I've got to try something. I can't shake the feeling there's something in my past that needs to be cleared up."

"Oh, Jacob...."

"It bugs the hell out of me."

"I...know."

"I can't for the life of me figure out why I wasn't found for two years!"

Leah wished she didn't feel so helpless. This was awful, knowing she could tell him everything he wanted to know in ten minutes, yet having to allow him to go into months and months of therapy, possibly without results.

Did he really want to know, that was the question.

Of course he does. Otherwise, why the therapy?

That's his conscious mind going into analysis. His subconscious may still block all recollection.

If only Charles White had never mentioned psychological amnesia, she thought irrationally.

"You told me remembering didn't matter," she reminded him.

"I guess I lied. It matters."

"Well, I hope therapy accomplishes what you want it to," was all she could think to say.

"Let's talk about something else, okay? How's Nina? Is she excited about summer camp?"

"Seems to be. But it's not really summer camp, more precamp. Three days at a youth camp not far from here. It's supposed to give six-year-olds a taste of being away from home, so hopefully they'll be better prepared for a week-long stay next year. I'm not worried Nina will be homesick. She spends so much time with dad that she's not quite as tied to mama as most six-year-old kids."

"I can't tell you how I'm looking forward to this weekend. I love the little scamp, but I do want to be alone with you."

"And I with you."

They talked for their usual twenty minutes—amazing how much two quiet people could find to talk about—but Leah lay awake long after hanging up the phone. Across the room her loom stood holding Jacob's tapestry. The main body of the work was completed, as was the piece to be attached to it. Alex had stopped by the day before, pronouncing it the best work of her career. Having Jacob in her life seemed to fuel her creativity.

That wasn't all Alex had had on his mind. He could set up a one-woman show for her in a prestigious gallery in Dallas, he told her with his customary enthusiasm. Perhaps Jacob would allow her to show the tapestry before it was hung in the clinic. If it didn't prompt dozens of commissions, Alex didn't know what would. Her noticeable lack of enthusiasm sorely disappointed him, to the point where he accused her of losing interest in her career. Leah reminded him of the long hours she had been working. Did that seem to him like losing interest? Nevertheless, Alex wasn't in a particularly happy frame of mind when he left.

The thought of a one-woman show in a huge market like Dallas should have thrilled Leah, but she didn't want a separation from Jacob, not now. An odd disquiet overtook her just thinking about that, perhaps because she was remembering their last separation, six years ago. By now she was quite willing to credit any funny tricks the mind could play.

Jacob was going back into therapy, and she wasn't sure how she felt about that. In the beginning she would have been encouraged, for more than anything she had wanted him to remember being Jim Stone. That no longer seemed as important as it once had. She was happy with Jacob Surratt and thought she loved him more deeply than she had Jim. His maturity had something to do with her feelings, of course, but there was more to her change of heart than his age. Jacob was such a fascinating personality, so much more intense and interesting than Jim. Which wasn't surprising; Jim hadn't had a past to give him hang-ups.

Maybe she just feared disturbing the status quo. Things were pretty good right now. Awfully good, in fact. For the first time in years Leah was completely happy in all her roles—artist, mother, woman. And she wanted that same kind of complete happiness for Jacob, something he wasn't likely to attain until he had filled in all the blank spaces. He didn't sleep well, she knew that, and there were those headaches and that recurring dream.

Damn, it was so hard to know what to do. Watching him agonize was hard to bear when she knew all he needed to know about his past. If only she could help him....

JACOB SAT IN CHARLES'S OFFICE, perched rather tensely on the chair facing the psychiatrist's desk. He was never comfortable here, had never become accustomed to the ritual, and he vaguely wondered if that was the reason Charles hadn't been able to help him. This time he vowed he would open up, just spill anything and everything that came to mind. He would be a cooperative patient.

"I think you're right about the Bannister woman's back problem, Jacob," Charles said. "It's psychosomatic, a bid for sympathy and attention, something she certainly isn't getting from that husband of hers."

"And medication?"

"Maybe."

"Try to find out what all she's taking, will you, Charles? I know she's been to doctors outside the clinic, so she might have prescriptions at pharmacies all over town. I doubt she levels with me. She says I always 'fuss' over her, and maybe I do, but I hate to sit idly by and watch Mildred turn into a hypochondriac."

"Of course." Charles tugged at his chin as he regarded his partner. "Shall we get started?"

"I suppose so."

"Would you like to lie down?"

"I think I'll just sit."

"However you're comfortable."

Jacob settled back into the comfortable chair, stretching his long legs in front of him. He felt every bit as foolish as he had six years ago. *I shouldn't be here,* he thought. *I should be home. I'd swim a couple of laps, take a brisk shower and have Davis bring me a drink. Read awhile, have dinner, then call Leah.*

Charles's first question was to the point. "Do you have difficulty coping with the fact that you, of all people, have amnesia?"

"Yes," he heard himself saying. "People suffer blows on the head every day and don't get amnesia. Why me?"

"How do you know that's what caused the loss of memory?"

Jacob released a ragged breath. "I don't. I'm assuming. I hadn't been ill."

"Does the amnesia embarrass you?"

"A little. Not as much now as it used to."

"And why is that?"

Jacob shrugged. "I don't know. Maybe it has something to do with Leah. She accepted my murky past without a qualm."

"You've told her about it?"

"All about it."

"And she wasn't surprised, bothered, upset?"

"No, only interested."

"Did you find that odd?"

"Odd? No, I was pleased."

"Perhaps we should discuss your relationship with Leah Stone, since she apparently is the reason you're back in therapy. How did you meet her?"

"I walked into a downtown bank one morning about two months ago and saw a tapestry hanging on the wall...." How strange it now seemed to him that so much had happened because of that one seemingly insignificant act.

Talking about Leah was what Jacob did best. The words just rolled off his tongue. When he'd finished, the psychiatrist asked a surprising question.

"How do you feel when you're with her in that place...er, Sedona?"

"Feel? I'm happy...content. As relaxed as I ever get. Leah's house feels like...home. More like home than my own ever has. Leah's comfortable to be with. Strange, isn't it? Like with people. There are people in this town I've known for twenty years, yet I don't really know them. But the first time I met Leah I felt as though I'd known her all my life. I still do. We can spend hours in each other's company without saying much of anything, like an old married couple."

Charles cleared his throat. "Does she ever talk to you about your amnesia, try to get you to remember?"

"No. On the contrary, she's constantly telling me to forget it, that it doesn't matter. I wish I could. I wish it didn't matter, but it does."

"How does she feel about your going back into therapy?"

"She only said she hoped it accomplishes what I want it to. She's one hell of a woman, Charles."

When he left the office at the end of his hour, Jacob was surprised the time had passed so quickly. Surprised, too, that it hadn't been all that difficult to talk to his partner, although they didn't seem to have talked about much. He couldn't understand why dwelling on the present would help him remember the past, but he was reminded of what a complex science psychotherapy was. Best, he decided, to leave it to the experts. This time he was going to lick this thing!

As soon as Jacob left the office, Charles closed the folder he'd been scribbling in, settled back in his swivel chair and contemplated the opposite wall. For several days he had thought over Jacob's sudden decision to go back into therapy. He could sense an air of desperation behind his partner's determination this time, not like six years ago, when Jacob had been confused, frightened, disbelieving. Charles was faced with a new challenge.

He pondered the situation a moment longer. Then he reached for the telephone and dialed directory assistance.

"What city?" asked the operator.

"Sedona."

"May I help you...?"

"Leah Stone, please. I don't know the address."

CHAPTER FOURTEEN

CHARLES WHITE'S CALL took Leah completely by surprise. The psychiatrist's voice was almost conspiratorial as he told her he wanted to talk to her, and he wanted the conversation kept confidential. Jacob wasn't to know anything about it. The matter was much too complicated to discuss over the telephone. With that in mind, Charles thought it would be better if he came to see her, rather than the other way around. He could be there at ten o'clock Friday morning.

Naturally Leah agreed, her curiosity honed to a keen edge. She gave him directions to her house and stifled the urge to quiz him over the phone.

On Friday, as she waited for Charles to arrive, fresh hope stirred inside her, although she had felt downright deceitful while talking to Jacob the night before. It didn't seem right to be keeping something from him, not even if she was doing so for his sake.

The meeting with Charles would prove to be for Jacob's good; Leah just knew it. Jacob would have seen his colleague by now and would have mentioned the role Leah had played in his life. Maybe, just maybe the psychiatrist had thought of a way she could help Jacob.

After brewing a fresh pot of coffee, Leah glanced at the clock on the wall. She had been operating at a dead run since daybreak. First there had been the last-minute flurry of activity associated with getting Nina off to camp. Then she had driven her daughter to the pick-up point, where the bus had collected the youngsters at eight-thirty sharp. Afterward she had hurried back home to wait for Dr. White. The psychiatrist had informed her he would be on a tight schedule, so she knew the visit must have some real importance. She was filled with impatience and anticipation.

Just then she heard a car door slam, front-gate hinges creaking. Footsteps crossed the porch, and a loud rap sounded on her door. Leah hurried to answer it.

"Good morning, Dr. White."

"Good morning, Leah."

"Please come in. I've just made coffee. Would you like a cup?"

"Yes, thank you." Charles stepped into the house, glancing around. "Charming place."

"Thank you." Closing the door behind her guest, Leah was again struck by a certain familiar quality about the man. He definitely reminded her of someone she knew, or at least someone she had seen somewhere. She wasn't especially good at names, but she almost never forgot a face. If she'd seen him before, where or when would come to her sooner or later.

Then Charles turned to face her, and she was astonished to see he looked ill at ease. A tremor of trepidation raced through her as she dwelled on the possibility that he had come to give her some awful news about Jacob. That thought, however, was quickly dismissed. She knew so much more about Jacob than his partner did. She knew more about Jacob than Jacob himself did.

"Cream or sugar?" she asked pleasantly.

"Just black, thanks."

"Please sit down...." She indicated the most comfortable chair in the room. "This will only take a moment."

Once she had served coffee to the doctor, she took a seat on the sofa facing him. "You wanted to talk to me about Jacob?" she urged.

"Yes." Charles took a swallow of coffee, then set the cup and saucer on a small table at his elbow. Leah noticed he had some difficulty looking squarely at her. "I assume you know he's back in therapy."

"Of course."

"After talking to him this week, I happened to recall my first meeting with you—only meeting, now that I think about it. I remember that you specifically asked about amnesia that night."

"Y-yes."

"I also remember something about knowing or having known an amnesiac, right?"

Leah's heart fluttered erratically. "Yes, I did."

"Yet that night, the night of the opening, you said you had only known Jacob a few days."

"That's right."

"I also seem to recall a question regarding the wisdom of telling an amnesiac about events during the fugue. You even knew the proper term for it, which caught my attention right away."

"Yes." By now Leah had a pretty good idea what the doctor was getting at. The coincidence had become apparent to him. How many lay people would know two amnesiacs in a lifetime?

"Well, then," Charles went on, "I added that to my new knowledge concerning Jacob's recurring dream and headaches. Apparently they started up again about the time Jacob met you, and they've been happening frequently ever since."

"Jacob said that?" she asked, alarmed.

"Not in so many words. I'm sure he's unaware of the pattern that's developed. He considers the dream a warning of some kind." Charles paused, picked up his cup and sipped slowly. "I may be way off base on this, Leah, but it's occurred to me that you might know something about Jacob's fugue period."

She glanced at her hands, folded in her lap, then back at Charles. She couldn't think of a single reason not to tell him. In fact, she suspected she should tell him. He might be able to take the information and use it to help Jacob. "Yes," she said simply.

"Did you know Jacob during those two missing years?"

She nodded. "I...not only knew him, doctor, I married him."

She expected some sort of surprised reaction to that, but none was forthcoming. But then she supposed psychiatrists learned to maintain a neutral expression no matter what incredible things they heard. Or perhaps Charles had guessed some of the truth before coming to see her. He only pursed his lips and grew thoughtful. "Well, Leah, why don't you tell me the whole story from the beginning."

So again she related the story of her marriage to Jim Stone. It crossed her mind that an awful lot of people had heard about it now. For six years she, her father and Tee were the only people who had known the true story, but she had since taken Alex, Sandra and Charles into her confidence. No real harm in that, she thought worriedly, provided Jacob wasn't hurt, provided no one made a careless remark.

Charles listened without interrupting, but when she had finished he said nothing for an unusually long time. Finally he cleared his throat and asked, "And

Jacob gave no sign of recognition when he met you in that gallery?''

"None.''

"When did he tell you about his amnesia?''

"The night I was a guest in his house. The night of the opening.''

"Did he say anything specific about his earlier therapy?''

"No, only that nothing came of it, so you encouraged him to give it up.''

"Not 'encouraged' exactly,'' Charles said quickly. "I merely suggested he might be wasting his time. He responded to therapy poorly, you see, besides which, it seemed to aggravate the headaches. I suggested they might go away if he stopped trying so hard to remember. As it turned out, I was right. At that time Jacob needed to concentrate on getting on with his life. He had a lot of catching up to do.'' He shifted in the chair. "And you've told him nothing, haven't hinted you knew him before?''

Leah shook her head. "When I first saw him again in Alex's office, I was too stunned to say anything, and it was apparent he didn't recognize me at all. Later some instinct warned me against saying anything. Then I met you at the opening, and after hearing what you had to say on the subject, about adding to his confusion and doing nothing to restore his memory, about psychological amnesia...well, I wouldn't have dared say anything. The most I've done is take him to my dad's place and around the valley.''

"No recognition?''

"Not the slightest. Of course, I've been hampered in that respect. I've had to be careful and not take him anyplace where he might be recognized. Fortunately Jacob's changed just enough in six years....'' Leah moistened her lips nervously. "Dr. White, now that Jacob's back in therapy, I wondered if you've detected any change from six years ago."

"I've only seen him once, but no, I see no change. If I had to make an educated guess, I'd say his chances of regaining his memory now aren't good. The events of the fugue are probably even more deeply buried in his subconscious than they were."

Leah leaned forward, speaking earnestly. "I want you to know I personally no longer care whether or not he remembers, but I know Jacob does. He'll be happier understanding what happened, so.... Now that you have the entire story, I wanted to ask if it would be all right for me to tell him."

"No!" Charles blurted out, causing Leah to frown in confusion. The psychiatrist seemed surprised by his hasty exclamation and quickly amended, "I mean, no, not right now. I think it would be best if you gave me more time with him. I need to determine how the news would affect him."

"I realize psychiatry or psychotherapy isn't my field, doctor, but knowing Jacob as I now do, I can't help but think he would welcome the news. Those missing years bother him so. I can interpret that dream... a house, a woman. This house and I were the most important things in Jim Stone's life. I just hate seeing Jacob suffer."

Charles stood up, clasped his hands behind his back and slowly paced, head bowed. "Yes, yes. Well... we mustn't let ourselves be deceived by his apparent desire to learn about those years. It could very well be he's subconsciously fighting the recall."

"I can't imagine why," Leah persisted stubbornly, wanting so badly to convince the psychiatrist to let her follow her own instincts. "Jim Stone led a blissful two years of existence. He might very well have been the happiest person I ever knew. Not a single thing happened during those years in the valley that he need be ashamed of... or regret. Jacob would be enormously relieved to hear that, surely."

Charles paused in his pacing to give her a condescending look. "Well, Leah, as you've pointed out, you don't know very much about this sort of thing. Amnesia is complicated, since all sorts of factors come into play. Everything affects the mind, everything. As Jacob's therapist, I would strongly recommend not saying anything about any of this. In fact, I suggest you not discuss his amnesia with him at all."

Leah frowned. This was all so confusing, to say nothing of disappointing. Every time she had it all worked out in her own mind, she was reminded of psychological amnesia, and everything became a muddle again. "I really don't talk to Jacob about it. He's the one who brings it up, and I'm aware that it's never far from his thoughts. He wants to marry me. He's even more anxious to remember now, to—as he puts it—tie up any loose ends. I could so easily tell him there aren't any loose ends that need tying. Once he and Nina and I are back together again—"

"Nina?"

"Our daughter."

"Good Lord!" Charles muttered. "I'd forgotten that Jacob mentioned a child. Then she is his?"

"Yes. Nina's one reason I'd like Jacob to know the truth. I want to tell him she's his natural daughter, a continuance of the Surratt line. He'd be so pleased."

Why this bit of information, more than the rest, should be so unsettling to the psychiatrist, Leah didn't know, but she sensed it was. Suddenly she was more alert to Charles White's every move, his every expression. The doctor was ruffled. Odd but true.

"I repeat, Leah. You might do Jacob irreparable harm. He shouldn't be told these things until I'm sure he's ready to absorb them."

"And when will that be?"

"It's quite impossible for me to know that right now."

"Maybe never?"

"I really can't say."

"Then maybe you can answer this. Can you take this information I've given you and use it to help Jacob?"

"Perhaps."

He was being maddeningly noncommittal, but in fairness to him, she might be impinging on professional confidences. Leah knew she was impatient, wanting things that probably were impossible immediately. She had to think of Jacob and what was best for him. Her spirits sagged. "I suppose the only thing I can do is what I've been doing all along—taking Jacob around the valley and hoping something will trigger his memory. I suppose it would be better if he remembered on his own."

Charles jerked at the lapels of his jacket and went to sit down again. He picked up the coffee cup, then put it down without taking a sip. "I'm not sure that's wise. The more I think about it, the more....."

"Yes?" she prodded.

"It's difficult for me to say this to you, considering your relationship with Jacob, but I'm certain his welfare is your primary concern."

"Of course," she said quietly, warily.

"I'm... not sure it wouldn't be a good idea for you to stay away from him altogether, for a while, anyway."

Leah's eyes widened. "St-stay away from him?"

"For a while."

"Forgive me, doctor, but I don't see the point in that."

"Think about it, Leah. The headaches, that dream—those things had left Jacob years ago. He was living at peace with himself until you came into his life, and he's known no peace since. You're the one who confuses him, although I doubt he associates the confusion with you. Yes, I'm convinced of it, and—I'm not sure how to put this delicately—your influence undermines what I'm trying to do. I have a feeling I'll discover that the headaches and the dream plague him more after he's been with you."

Leah was totally shaken. That she might inadvertently be hampering Jacob's progress, that she might even be the one causing so much of his distress, was a theory she couldn't accept. "Dr. White, if I tell Jacob I don't want to see him for a while, he won't understand. He'll be terribly hurt. I've become the one person he feels he can trust. I couldn't do that to him." *Or to myself,* she honestly admitted, though she knew it wasn't only self-concern that made her resist Charles's suggestion.

"Not even to help him?"

Leah bristled, hating the doubts the psychiatrist was putting into her head. "That's unfair, doctor. I love Jacob and would do anything in the world for him, but I don't think staying away from him is the right thing to do."

"I realize it wouldn't be easy, but if you want to give Jacob a fair chance at restoring his memory, you should consider it."

"I. . . ." She faltered. "He would expect some sort of plausible explanation, and I wouldn't know what to say."

"You could come up with something, I'm sure. Take a trip, anything to put some distance between the two of you while I'm trying to help him. Naturally I wouldn't want you to tell him the actual reason for the separation. That would only serve to make him resent therapy, in which case I wouldn't be able to help him at all."

Leah had no intention of doing what the man was suggesting. It was unthinkable! It didn't even make sense. How could stripping Jacob of something that made him happy help him? She suspected Charles of not fully understanding Jacob's sensitive nature. Perhaps Jacob found it impossible to open up fully with his partner. In that case, he probably should seek another therapist, a stranger. She wondered if he had ever considered that.

Leah focused all her powers of concentration on Charles White. In some unexplainable way the atmosphere in the room seemed to have changed. Leah had a curious feeling the psychiatrist regarded her as an adversary, which was ridiculous. They both wanted the same thing, didn't they?

As far as she was concerned, the visit had been wholly unsatisfactory. Perhaps she had been expecting too much, but not only had the psychiatrist squelched her hopes, he had told her things she didn't want to hear. Not see Jacob at all? She wouldn't. She couldn't! She quelled a brief stab of anxiety, wishing she hadn't felt compelled to tell Charles the truth.

The psychiatrist didn't stay long after that. Pleading the pressure of his schedule, he left, but not before Leah had the chance to ask him one more question. "Dr. White, eight years ago when you first suspected Jacob was missing, you tried to find him, right?"

"Of course," he said gruffly.

"What did you find out?"

"Nothing. I came up against a brick wall. The police weren't a bit of help to me, so I decided Jacob had disappeared on purpose. Why do you ask?"

She wasn't sure, except she couldn't shake the nagging wonder that a prominent man like Jacob Surratt could vanish without a trace, even given all the coincidences at the time.

"Oh, no reason. Strange, isn't it? The police weren't any help to us, either. Apparently by the time you started looking for him, Jim Stone had given up the search."

"Apparently," Charles said. "Good day, Leah."

After he'd gone Leah roamed restlessly around the house, her thoughts whirring. She was aware of a gnawing sensation inside—nothing she could name, just a disturbing feeling that something was out of kilter.

At length, however, she shook free of it. Jacob would be with her in a few hours, and there was a long, lovely weekend ahead of them. She wasn't going to give Charles's advice another thought, and she certainly wasn't going to put any distance between her and Jacob. That was the end of it! She didn't know why she made such a big deal out of everything. Right then and there she decided to get busy and get a divorce. What did the circumstances matter? Jim Stone no longer existed. All her foolish qualms about denying Jim's existence through divorce were just that— foolish.

Leah had psyched herself up into a lighthearted mood by the time she heard Jacob's car in front of the house later that afternoon. And the look on his face when she opened the door made her heart turn over, strengthening her determination to ignore the psychiatrist's advice. How could she stay away from a man whose eyes lit up like a child's on Christmas morning every time he saw her? It was asking too much of both of them. For better or worse, Jacob had become emotionally dependent on her, and she was deeply committed to him and his peace of mind. Maybe Charles didn't fully understand that.

That afternoon Jacob was as relaxed as she had ever seen him. Leah studied him carefully without seeming to. She knew he often faked high spirits for her sake, as though he feared a sullen mood would turn her off. He wasn't faking now, though. She took heart from the loosening, disburdening effect she had on him, and thought it surely had to offset his partner's claims. The psychiatrist was clutching at straws—he had to be. Possibly he was disturbed because he hadn't been able to help Jacob.

Leah could conveniently come up with any number of reasons for ignoring Charles's words.

CHAPTER FIFTEEN

JACOB WAS USUALLY TIRED on Friday nights. For that reason, whether they spent the weekend in Sedona or Phoenix, Leah never made plans for the evening. Activities were saved for Saturdays. So tonight she prepared dinner, they ate at the dining table, then he helped her clean up. Afterward she wheeled the television set out of its hiding place, and Jacob emptied his mind by watching a noisy police drama while she spent another hour at her loom. She was in the homestretch, working on the final piece of the tapestry and anxious to finish it. The noise of gunfire and screeching tires didn't bother her at all. She honestly thought she could set up her loom in front of the state capitol in downtown Phoenix and happily weave away. Temperamental, she wasn't.

Occasionally she glanced over her shoulder at Jacob stretched out on the couch, one arm thrown behind his head. His eyes were half-closed; she couldn't tell if he was watching the show or not. A contented smile crossed her face. She so loved having him with her in her odd little house. *Where he belongs,* she thought.

Her smile faded. She liked to think that, but she wondered if it was true. Being honest, she supposed Jacob more properly belonged in that big house in Scottsdale.

Leah had long since grown used to the trappings of Jacob's wealth and was no longer awed by them, but living that way seemed so burdensome to her. Leah had never been a wealthy woman; still, her father's veterinary practice had given them a comfortable living, and now her weavings commanded high prices. She could afford many of the "finer" things in life, yet she was perfectly satisfied with her renovated schoolhouse, her sensible compact car and her orderly, uncomplicated way of life.

It had crossed her mind more than once that she might have to give up this house—not just the house, but Sedona itself and the laid-back existence it represented—and she was startled to realize that bothered her a little. Startled because she honestly loved Jacob and wanted to spend the rest of her life with him. That entailed living where he chose to live. His work was in Phoenix, whereas she could weave anywhere on earth.

Putting aside her work, she got to her feet and crossed the room to look down at him. As she suspected, he was asleep, and he looked so peaceful she was loath to waken him. After placing his dangling left arm across his stomach, she carefully removed his shoes. Then she turned off the television set and rolled it back into the cabinet. She'd leave him be and sleep in Nina's bed in the loft. Sleep didn't come that easily to Jacob.

But as she passed the sofa he grabbed her hand. "Where're you going?" he asked huskily.

"Oh! I thought you were asleep."

"Nope, just dozing on and off. I was watching you watching me."

Smiling, she knelt by the sofa, placing her hands on his chest. "You looked so peaceful."

"Sorry I've been such lousy company tonight."

"You haven't been. You never are. You don't have to keep me entertained, Jacob. I don't expect you to be at your best for me all the time, and sometimes I think that's what you try to do. I won't bolt for the door if you're grouchy and out of sorts occasionally.''

Jacob smiled softly. Lifting her hand to his lips, he gently kissed the fingertips one by one. ''That's good to know.''

''Darling, if you're too tired tonight, I can sleep in Nina's bed.''

''Don't be ridiculous. I get through the week by thinking of lying next to you on Friday night.''

She got to her feet and pulled him to a sitting position. ''Then you take the bathroom first, and I'll make up the bed.''

Once he was gone she pulled out the sofa bed and put fresh sheets on it. When he emerged and began undressing, she went into the bathroom. Undressing, she took a new champagne-colored gown off the door hook and slipped it over her head. It fell to the floor in billowing folds; the wisp of a bodice made a feeble attempt to conceal her breasts. In fact, Leah noticed as she glanced in the mirror, the gown concealed very little. It was an exquisite garment and had cost an unconscionable amount of money, but the moment she'd seen it in the boutique she had thought of Jacob and had purchased it without hesitation.

Turning off the light, she walked into the big room and found him propped up in bed, the sheet at his waist, presenting the most blatantly appealing picture of forceful masculinity she could imagine. Pausing at the foot of the bed, she drank in the sight of him while allowing him to feast his eyes on her.

He did so greedily. The expression on his face was the very one she had envisioned when she bought the gown. Tiny pinpoints of fire leaped from his eyes, and the corners of his mouth twitched. "You don't even need makeup," he observed in awe.

"You're looking at my face?" she asked in mock astonishment. "How about this gown? This is what the well-dressed, turned-on lady is wearing this season."

"Very nice," he murmured, at a loss for anything more descriptive. The gown, he noticed, was anything but "nice." Granny gowns were "nice." Leah's gown was a sexy, alluring garment designed to arouse a man, and it was doing the job. The elemental response he felt in his groin told him that.

"I thought you'd like it," she said, glorying in the desire she saw in his eyes.

"May I assume it was purchased with me in mind?"

"Of course. You should see the tailored pajamas I used to sleep in."

"Leah, somehow I imagine you're damned sexy in tailored pajamas. Wear them for me sometime." He raised the sheet. "Come here."

Smiling seductively, she slowly walked around to her side of the bed. Sliding between the sheets, she was immediately gathered in his warm embrace. His mouth covered hers in a lingering kiss, then moved to her earlobe to suck gently. One of his hands lightly traced her body's gentle curves, now so familiar to him. He ran the back of one finger over her breast, grazing, then beneath the fabric to feel the texture of the velvety mound and the puckered tip. His finger was soon replaced by his lips.

Leah slithered along his hard length and moaned his name softly. It was an incredibly sensuous experience he was giving her, completely unnecessary, for he could arouse her with a touch. From past experience, however, they knew of the exquisite pleasure awaiting them when they took their time with the preliminaries.

Finally he fumbled impatiently with her gown. "Beautiful gown," he murmured. "Pity it was destined to be worn such a short time." He quickly discarded it, and the garment fell in a heap on the floor. Sliding his tongue into the valley between her breasts, he traced a trail down her midriff to her navel, then below. The taste and scent of her skin was more intoxicating than alcohol, more stimulating than any drug ever invented. His tempting maneuvers were rewarded by a sudden arching of her hips.

"Mmm," she groaned.

He raised his head. "You like that?"

"Oh, Jacob, you're killing me!"

His heart lifted. Full and heavy with desire, he covered her body with his, thrusting for possession.

At first they made love with a quiet sort of desperation, like lovers on the eve of parting. Then he turned gentle and humble, nuzzling his face into her shoulder, moving his lips through the mass of dark hair spilling out on her pillow, kissing her breasts, declaring his limitless devotion. Jacob was a sensitive lover, for he felt things deeply. Even in the wildest throes of passion he was as concerned for her pleasure as for his own.

Each time they were together, Leah learned something new about the intimacies between a man and a woman. Jim had been carefree and uninhibited in bed, but now that she thought about it, lovemaking with him had been more of a glorious game. With Jacob it was much more profound—a heart-stopping, soul-piercing experience. They brought to each other such solace and peace. *If ever two people were meant for each other, we were,* she thought, and that didn't even seem like a cliché. Her conviction had kept her free for him all those years.

Yet tonight she clearly sensed frustration in him.

Long after he was spent from the climax, he clung to her tightly as though afraid to release her. Leah held him, crooned to him and again wished for the courage to tell him there was nothing in his past that need worry him. She cursed Charles White's advice, without trusting her own instincts sufficiently to dismiss it entirely.

Finally Jacob fell asleep. For long minutes Leah lay awake beside him simply watching him sleep. In repose, he looked so much younger, so much more vulnerable. Her heart filled with a mixture of emotions. Never in her life, not even during the marriage she had considered perfect, had she felt as much a sensual woman as she did when she was with Jacob. He had tapped the very wellspring of her femininity, making her feel alive. And she knew all too well how much she had done for him. No one would ever have called Jacob easygoing, but there had been some remarkable changes in him since they'd met in the gallery.

It just wasn't right to withhold from him all they had once been to each other....

Soon Leah also succumbed to sleep, only to awaken a few hours later to find Jacob had left the bed. Raising her head, she saw him standing in front of the window, one arm braced on her loom, the other on the wall. The dejected slump of his shoulders conveyed his inner turmoil.

"You had the dream again," she said. It wasn't a question.

"Yes," he said emotionlessly, not turning.

"Do you realize you always have that dream when you're with me?"

"No!" he said too quickly. "That isn't true."

It was, though. Leah sat up, pulled her knees up under the sheet and rested her head on them. Sighing, she allowed her mind to override her heart for once. Reluctantly she admitted that Charles might have known what he was talking about. Her presence was responsible for the dream's return and the headaches. Maybe she should back off and give the man's theory a chance. In the way of human beings, she had followed the part of the psychiatrist's advice that she could accept and chosen to ignore the rest.

"Darling," she said softly, "come back to bed. I'm sure everything's going to be all right."

He pivoted, moving as if each step was an effort. "You're right. I don't know why I let it bother me. As long as I have you, what the devil difference does that damned dream make?"

When he was beside her, she opened her arms and he went into them. "I'm going to lick this thing, Leah. I swear I am."

"You will. Of course you will."

Jacob fell asleep in her arms, his face nestled into the hollow of her shoulder, but sleep eluded Leah for most of the night. His torment was hers. What to do? Over and over she heard Charles White's voice saying, "Your influence undermines what I'm trying to do." Just as over and over she heard Jacob's voice saying, "As long as I have you...."

AT SOME POINT during the night Leah realized the show in Dallas might be the perfect excuse for a separation. It was the easy way out. The separation would be a short one, since they would only have to go for perhaps two weeks without seeing each other. Jacob wouldn't suspect it was a deliberate attempt to put some distance between them. Maybe she should at least test Charles's advice. The fact she didn't want to be away from Jacob shouldn't be a consideration.

Leah woke up unrefreshed, still thinking about Dallas. But she wouldn't say anything until Jacob was ready to leave Sunday, if indeed she said anything at all. Their limited time together was too important to them. When Jacob awoke, he showed no traces of last night's turmoil, so she didn't want to set him back, spoiling the weekend with talk of parting.

Over breakfast he suggested going to Tlaquepaque. He was in the mood to shop for additions to his collection, and his first visit to the arts-and-crafts village had been so hurried. That suited Leah fine, for she never tired of Tlaquepaque.

The place was filled with shoppers. Although Sedona boasted only nine thousand permanent residents, two million tourists a year found their way there, and most of those discovered Tlaquepaque sooner or later. Leah and Jacob spent the better part of the day browsing and poking through most of the forty-odd shops and galleries, and strolling through the tiled courtyards holding hands like a pair of teenagers. Jacob found an acrylic on canvas for himself, some turquoise jewelry for Leah and a kachina doll for Nina. Then, after delightedly gorging on frozen margaritas and enchiladas in a Mexican restaurant, they stopped in at the Trent Gallery to pay a call on Alex. It was during the visit that Jacob first spied *Gemini*.

"Don't tell me—a 'Design by Leah Stone,' " he said, studying Leah's maiden effort as a professional. "It's your style."

"Would you believe the first 'Design by Leah Stone,' " Alex said with a smile.

"I want it."

"Oh, Jacob," Leah protested, "it's not nearly the tapestry you're getting. In fact, looking at *Gemini* now, it seems rather amateurish. I've done much better things.''

"I want it, darling. The big tapestry will hang in the clinic. I want this one for the house.''

"I can do something much better for the house.''

"It's not for sale.'' Alex's tone was decisive.

Jacob turned to him with a frown. "Not for sale?''

"No, I'm afraid not. I always told Leah I wouldn't sell it in a million years, and even though she professes not to believe that, I meant it.''

Standing close to Jacob, Leah felt his body go rigid. She looked up at him. His color had heightened, and the expression on his face clearly told her he felt challenged. "Surely you'd sell it to me,'' he persisted. "To Leah and me.''

"Sorry, it's not for sale.''

"Well, if it were for sale, how much would it cost?''

Now he was grinning, and Alex was grinning. It was obvious to Leah that the two of them were sparring and enjoying every minute of it. She watched Alex as he gave the question some serious thought. Then he quoted a figure she knew was ludicrous. "Oh, Alex, that's ridiculous!'' she gasped, laughing.

Her laughter, however, quickly died when she heard Jacob say, "All right. I'll write you a check.''

"Are you serious, doctor?'' Alex asked in surprise.

"Completely.''

Leah's mouth dropped open. "Oh, Jacob, you'll do no such thing!'' Her obdurate gaze flew to Alex, who was beginning to realize just how serious Jacob was. Fun and games were over; this was real business. Leah stepped between them. "The dollar signs are in your eyes, Alex! I'm ashamed of you. You know very well that tapestry isn't worth half that.''

Alex tugged on his chin. His eyes were sparkling merrily. "My dear Leah, surely you know that a work of art is worth whatever someone is willing to pay for it. Obviously, owning *Gemini* is worth a lot to Jacob."

"It is," Jacob agreed.

"Then you just made yourself a deal. It will be delivered to your house Monday." He chuckled. "No extra charge."

Leah's hand flew to her forehead. "I don't believe this!"

Her protests did no good. With the stroke of a pen in his checkbook, Jacob became the proud owner of *Gemini*, and Alex had dispatched one of the gallery employees to see that it was properly rolled and wrapped for transport.

"Never in a million years indeed!" Leah hissed to Alex. "You have avarice in your soul."

He only smiled. "I'm a businessman, Leah, and I'd say this has been one of my better days."

She was still fuming when she and Jacob loaded their purchases into her car. Driving away from Tlaquepaque, she said, "I can't decide which one of you I'm most furious with—Alex for charging that outlandish sum or you for being foolish enough to pay it."

"I would have paid twice that, my love."

"Why?" she demanded. "It's not nearly as valuable as the piece I'm doing now, nor nearly as valuable as anything I could do for you in the future."

"I know that."

"Then why?"

"Because I should be the one who owns it. Because I didn't want Alex having it."

His honesty took her aback. "Oh, Jacob, you're not—"

"Jealous? I don't know, maybe I am a little. But I

think it's more complicated than that. I wanted it because it's a part of your early life that I don't know much about but wish I did. I've always wished I had known the young Leah." He shrugged. "I want this in my house, to look at when you're not with me. You know, when I first saw that other tapestry in the bank, it . . . called to me. Do you find that ridiculous? And *Gemini* did the same thing. It's something that can't be explained."

Leah gripped the steering wheel so tightly her knuckles turned white. She recalled the hours Jim had spent watching the beginnings of *Gemini*. There was so much lurking in the back of Jacob's mind, trying to get out. If she was the one preventing it. . . .

"You know, Leah," Jacob said thoughtfully, "it's been a long time coming, this feeling. All I've ever owned I would gladly give up in return for you. The time I have to spend away from you is agony for me. I guess what it all boils down to is—you make me happy." He grinned sheepishly. "I'm not saying this well. Maybe it's because there's so much I want to say, and I don't know where to begin."

A lump formed in Leah's throat, and she reached for his hand to give it a squeeze. "You said it beautifully."

And Charles wanted her to stay away from him! How could she? To hell with the show in Dallas. To hell with the rest of the world, for that matter. She intended to savor every minute with Jacob and to present him with divorce papers the moment arrangements could be made. A separation definitely wasn't the answer, she decided in her inexpert but very human judgment.

Their weekend from that moment on was perfect. She pulled out all the stops for dinner, presenting Jacob with a meal worthy of a French master chef. Later they made slow languorous love, with just a hint of absolutely delightful wickedness about it. Leah slept soundly that night; if he had the dream again she didn't know about it, didn't want to know about it. When they parted Sunday afternoon—Leah to pick up Nina at the bus stop, and Jacob to return home—it was with the understanding that she and Nina would come to Phoenix the following Friday. When he drove away, he looked like a man in good spirits; she hoped he was.

That night Leah worked at her loom until after midnight. She told herself everything was great, just great. It wasn't until after she was in bed that the nagging fear returned, the fear that she was an obstacle between Jacob and the end to his mental distress.

CHAPTER SIXTEEN

LEAH UNROLLED THE TAPESTRY and, with Sandra's help, hung it on two heavy wall hooks installed at ceiling height for just that purpose. By moving an armchair and the coffee table, they were able to roll the excess out on the floor. The two women moved some distance away to view the work.

"Magnificent, Leah," was Sandra's verdict. "Absolutely magnificent!"

Leah had to agree. It definitely was the best thing she had ever done. Using all shades of the red spectrum, from garnet to shell pink, with just a touch of suede gray for contrast, she had depicted rock forms that appeared to have been carved from velvet. Though some of the cliffs and buttes had edges and peaks as sharp as broken pottery, there was nothing the least harsh about the tapestry. In fact it looked strokeably soft.

"I'm very proud of it," Leah admitted. "Not even Alex can tell where the pieces were joined together."

"I'll bet you can hardly wait to show it to Jacob."

"Oh, he's seen most of it, and he's very pleased. I think it's dramatic enough. It ought to show up very well on that wall. Come on, let's have a cup of tea and you tell me what you've been up to."

The two women sat at the breakfast bar talking. Sandra was studio-bound, she declared with an air of exaggerated persecution, since she had in a weak moment promised a local gallery five new pieces within a year's time. Leah was thrilled for her, then almost choked on her tea over Sandra's next remark. "Sam's been hinting he'd like us to get married again."

"Are you serious?"

"He's definitely serious."

"Well, would you?"

Sandra was silent long enough to bring a frown to Leah's face. She couldn't help thinking of all the tales of horror she had listened to so many times before, about the terrified woman who had sought a psychiatrist's help before leaving her domineering husband.

"Would you fall down laughing if I told you I've honestly considered it? But...no," Sandra said decisively. "No, I wouldn't. It would never work. He seems to have changed—not *that* much, though. And I've definitely changed, but I don't think Sam realizes how much. I'm not the wimpy young thing he married years ago. I could never take the kind of crap I used to. My career's just beginning to take off, and it's important to me. I need time to pursue it, and in spite of what Sam says, I can't believe he'd want me taking that time. No, I'm too happy with my life the way it is now. I just can't risk it, even though—and isn't this a crock—Sam's the only man I've ever loved. Doesn't that just slay you? He's probably the most impossible person I've ever known."

Leah breathed a little sigh. "Well, I'm relieved. You're doing so well now."

"Yeah. I'm just glad Sam and I have finally called a truce. Maybe now he'll stop pestering me about it and go on and find something else, someone else. We're definitely two people who shouldn't be married to each other." Sandra took a sip of tea. "So tell me how things are going between you and Jacob. What a doll he is!"

Leah chuckled, imagining Jacob's reaction to being called a "doll." Then she sobered. "Fine, I guess. There are problems, though. He's gone back into therapy."

Sandra's brows lifted. "With the same shrink?"

"Uh-huh. This is something he did on his own."

"I keep expecting to hear you're moving to Phoenix."

"We might be one of these days, when certain things are resolved."

"I'd miss you like hell. We'd have to stay in touch."

"Oh, sure." Strange, she hadn't once thought of losing Sandra as a neighbor, or of how much she would miss her friend if that happened. The two of them would often go for days, sometimes weeks without seeing each other, but it had always been comforting to know Sandra was nearby. "Poor Nina," Leah mused. "She'd be lost without Ann."

"I know. It would be hard on the girls for a while, but thank God for the resiliency of youth. And Phoenix isn't all that far away."

"I haven't moved yet, you know," Leah reminded her with a grin.

"You will. I've seen the look on Jacob's face."

Leah nodded absently, and the disquietude that had plagued her since Sunday settled over her again. It was so easy to stick to her own convictions when he was with her, but he hadn't been gone an hour Sunday before the nagging doubt started hounding her again. Did she have the right to decide Charles was wrong, that she knew what was best for Jacob?

"Something the matter?" Sandra inquired gently.

Leah's head snapped up. "Oh. . . no, it's just that— Oh, Sandra, Jacob has so many problems, and because of them, I have problems. Last week his psychiatrist came to see me, so now I'm really confused. I want to do the right thing, but I'm not sure what the right thing is. What Dr. White tells me goes strictly against my own instincts...." She opened her hands in a helpless gesture.

"Yeah?" Sandra stared at her friend with concern. She had always thought Leah was one person who really had her act together. She'd never seen her so down. "Want to talk about it? Sometimes it helps. Believe me, you're looking at one who knows."

So Leah poured out everything. She was so intent on her story that she didn't notice her friend's changing expressions. First Sandra was interested, then concerned, then worried. Only when Leah had finished speaking did she venture an observation. "I swear, I think if I were you I'd just tell him. Sounds to me like that would solve most of his problems."

"I told you, Dr. White insists I say nothing, not only say nothing, but he wants me to stay away from Jacob altogether."

"So you said, and that bothers me most of all."

"Bothers you?"

Sandra nodded, then leaned forward and spoke firmly and confidentially. "You know something, Leah... when you first told me about Jacob, something you said didn't sit right with me—the part about Jacob's analyst encouraging him to give up therapy years ago."

"That's right."

Sandra's brow furrowed. "That doesn't make any sense. Look, I've had some experience with this sort of thing, and a good analyst simply doesn't work that way."

"I don't understand, Sandra."

"When I first went to see Dr. Graves years ago, I

naturally had to hide it from Sam. He would have put a stop to it immediately. So that meant I had to hide the forty bucks an hour it was costing me, too. And after a while it got to be too much trouble and too expensive, so a couple of times I quit. But Dr. Graves kept telephoning me and sending me little notes, and I finally went back. She was right, of course. I really needed the therapy, and in the end she did wonders for me. When I finally left analysis, I thanked her for not giving up on me, and she told me no thoughtful psychiatrist would let a patient who needed help just quit without putting up a fight. That's why this guy Jacob's seeing bothers me."

Leah shrugged. "I guess Dr. White didn't think he could help Jacob."

"How could he be certain in such a short time? Psychotherapy takes years."

"I don't know, Sandra. It's all beyond me. I wish I could help Jacob, God knows, but I have to go with the experts."

Suddenly an idea came to Sandra. "Listen, Leah, I'm getting some vibrations that aren't any of my business, so I want you to do a favor for me."

Leah's eyes quizzed her with interest.

"I have an appointment with Alicia tomorrow— that's Dr. Graves. I just wanted to touch base with her and tell her about Sam and me; she likes me to call every so often. But I can do that anytime. I'd like to ask her to give my appointment to you."

"Why on earth would I want to see a psychiatrist?"

"I'm not sure, but I think you should. Get someone else's opinion on Jacob's case."

Leah laughed lightly. "I really don't think that's necessary, Sandra."

"Please!"

The unexpected fervor of her friend's voice brought Leah up sharply. Sandra tried to explain. "Look, you said it yourself—Jacob has problems, so you have problems. You've taken this White guy's word for everything, yet I have a feeling you don't really trust him, right?"

Leah didn't deny it. "I don't know why I don't, but you're right, I don't."

"Well, if Alicia Graves told me to go jump off this house, I'd do it. Will you go see her? I'll be glad to keep Nina. What can it hurt?"

Something stirred inside Leah, prompted by a variety of things. Her own uncertainty mainly, and her unfounded uneasiness about Charles White's advice. Her unfounded uneasiness about the man himself. "Sure, I'll go. As you said, what can it hurt?"

LEAH WHEELED HER CAR into the only available parking space and switched off the ignition. For several moments she sat very still, staring sightlessly through the windshield. All at once she felt foolish and wished she hadn't made this appointment. She didn't know what to say to the woman, didn't know where to begin. But she was here now, parked in front of a low-slung brick medical building, committed to spending fifty minutes and forty dollars with Dr. Alicia Graves. Sighing, she grabbed her handbag, got out of the car and entered the building.

"Dr. Graves is waiting for you, Mrs. Stone," the neat young woman at the reception desk told her, and Leah was shown into the psychiatrist's office.

The large room looked more like someone's comfortable living room than a doctor's office. It had been furnished, the artist in Leah saw, with an eye for scale and balance. A long off-white sofa stood against a wall opposite a fireplace; a collection of mismatched candlesticks glimmered on a glass-topped coffee table. Oriental stools and silk pillows coexisted in perfect harmony with Haitian prints and paper-relief wall panels. The atmosphere was cozy. It was the sort of room that encouraged one to curl up with a cup of coffee or tea and talk, talk, talk.

Leah wasn't sure what she had expected Alicia Graves to look like—a bit stern, elderly and spectacled, she guessed. Certainly not tall, slender and fortyish as this woman was, with a sleek silver-blond chignon and warm blue eyes.

"Come in and have a seat, Mrs. Stone," Dr. Graves said. "I've been waiting for you. May I get you something to drink, coffee or tea?"

"No, thank you, doctor."

"Sandra told me almost nothing over the phone, but I take it you two are friends."

Leah sat in a chair facing the doctor's desk. "Yes, we're neighbors and have become quite close. We have a great deal in common."

"I'm glad to hear she has a good friend. I grew very fond of her while she was in therapy. She's doing well, I hear."

"Oh, Sandra's fine. I'm sure you'll be seeing her before long." Leah started to say something about Sandra and her ex-husband, then remembered that Dr. Graves would know nothing of their new truce. Certainly it was Sandra's place to tell her of the changed relationship.

Dr. Graves shuffled aside some papers, then settled back in her chair. "So Mrs. Stone...it's Leah, isn't it?"

"Yes."

"So, Leah, according to Sandra you wanted to talk

to me about your husband, who is an amnesiac, is that right?''

''I'm afraid it's a little more complicated than that, doctor.''

''Are you having some trouble coping with his illness?''

''Oh, no, it's nothing like that. You see....'' Once again Leah related the details of her marriage to Jim Stone and her subsequent meeting with Jacob. It was a lengthy story, but Alicia Graves listened carefully and with interest, and she interrupted only when something Leah said wasn't clear. Once she was certain Leah had finished her account, she leaned back in her chair and stared thoughtfully across the room.

''And you feel sure you've accepted Jacob for who he is? You no longer wish for Jim?''

Leah shook her head. ''I don't have any trouble with that anymore, I'm certain of it. That's not why I want to tell him the truth. Oh, of course it would be easier for me if he knew. I always feel like I have to be on guard, not saying anything about the past or taking him where he might be recognized. And I know he wonders why I won't tell him anything about my husband.... All that's been going on for some time now, and I can handle it. It's for Jacob's sake that I want to tell him. And for Nina's. They deserve knowing they belong to each other.'' She sighed. ''But Dr. White has been so adamant about that.''

Dr. Graves frowned thoughtfully. ''I realize that I don't know Jacob as well as his own therapist does, but from what you've told me, I see no reason he shouldn't know the truth.''

Leah's heart leaped exultantly. Exactly what she had been hoping to hear. ''Really?''

''Yes, really. I can see why it wouldn't have been

wise in the beginning, but the two of you have apparently established a mutually loving relationship, and he trusts you. Telling him about the past won't magically restore his memory, of course, but I should think the relief would be enormous.''

"You...don't think he's suffering from psychological amnesia?''

Dr. Graves looked at her in mild surprise, then pursed her lips and shook her head. "No, I don't, not at all. Jacob sounds like a textbook case of retrograde amnesia, the result of a blow to the head. Now I once had an amnesia patient who had even forgotten how to tie shoes. In fact, she didn't know what shoes were. That was psychological amnesia. The poor woman wanted to forget everything, start all over again. Once I delved into her past life, I could understand why. No, Jacob's amnesia isn't psychological at all, not from what you've told me.''

Leah thought it amazing how unquestioningly she could accept advice she wanted to hear. It was totally at odds with the advice she had received from Charles—she was beginning to realize just how much Jacob's partner bothered her—but her instincts, to say nothing of her heart, told her to trust Dr. Graves.

"Then you think I can just tell him, not mince words or lead up to it gradually?''

"I don't see why not. You see, Leah, it's been my experience that amnesiacs are usually a bit embarrassed by their condition. They see it as a weakness of character or some such nonsense. And almost all of them worry about their actions during the fugue, just as they worry that filling in the blank spaces will complicate their present lives. In Jacob's case, you can erase that worry in minutes. Peace of mind is priceless, you know.''

"I know." Leah felt as though the weight of the world had been lifted off her shoulders. She could imagine how Jacob was going to feel.

"From the expression on your face, I have to assume that telling him is going to be a happy experience," Alicia Graves said with a smile.

"Oh, doctor, you can't imagine how happy it's going to be!" Then she sobered. "I just wonder why Dr. White so specifically warned me not to. He even suggested I stay away from Jacob altogether, which would have hurt him deeply."

Dr. Graves wondered, too, Leah could tell, although all the psychiatrist said was, "Perhaps Dr. White doesn't fully understand the extent of Jacob's emotional commitment to you. It could very well be that Jacob doesn't open up with his therapist, given the nature of their working relationship. Frankly, I doubt it was a good idea for him to use his partner for an analyst. I'm surprised Dr. White took him on."

Leah's suspicions about Charles White were piling up in layers. "Why do you say that?"

Dr. Graves tried to explain. "You see, Leah, a unique and very close relationship develops between psychiatrist and patient...or should. They become very close...or should. The patient often comes to regard the therapist as the only caring person in the world. Two men who work together on a day-to-day basis...." She frowned and shook her head. "I don't see how that would work. And that business of terminating therapy six years ago—that's simply not sound psychotherapy. Continuity is of the utmost importance. If a patient discontinues therapy for whatever reason, and then returns for whatever reason, I have to start all over again."

Leah mulled this over. "If possible, Dr. Graves, I'd like Jacob to come to see you one of these days."

The doctor smiled. "And I'd like to see him. Do you know if he's ever undergone hypnosis?"

"I don't think so. He hasn't mentioned it, and I'm sure he would have."

Alicia Graves pursed her lips. "Peculiar. It can be so effective, provided the patient is a good subject. It certainly is a shortcut, too, for both therapist and patient. It's often used in battlefield conditions, where time is of the essence. I would always consider it with an amnesia case."

Leah hated thinking what she was thinking, that Jacob's partner had made no genuine attempt to help him, but she couldn't help it. Nothing about Charles White jibed... and hadn't from the beginning.

Just then Dr. Graves leaned forward and spoke earnestly. "Leah, I don't want you to get your hopes up too high regarding Jacob's recovery. Telling him the truth will help, but it won't be a magic cure-all. Once he's more relaxed about his past he might recall small random events, nothing in chronological sequence, but the chances of his regaining all memory of the fugue are, frankly, not good. Please understand that."

"Yes, yes, of course. You've given me such wonderful news nevertheless. I don't know how to thank you."

The hour had passed very quickly, and Dr. Graves bade her goodbye with, "Please stay in touch with me, Leah. I'll be so interested to know how things turn out with you and Jacob."

What an incredible woman she is, Leah thought as she backed out of the parking space. No wonder she was able to do so much for Sandra.

"WELL, THANK GOD!" Sandra had exclaimed when Leah collected Nina and told her friend about Alicia Graves's advice. Whit said almost exactly the same thing when she telephoned him. Now all she had to do was tell Jacob, and that certainly couldn't be done over the phone.

"Nina, pack your pajamas and toothbrush and something to wear for tomorrow. We're going to Jacob's house."

"Oh, boy!" the girl cried delightedly.

"In fact—" Leah hesitated briefly "—in fact, we'll be moving there permanently before long. What do you think of that?"

Nina stopped short and looked at her mother quizzically. "You and Jacob are getting married?"

Leah nodded. "How do you feel about that?"

"Okay, I guess."

"Only guess?"

"No, it's okay, really. I like Jacob. He's nice."

"And how do you feel about leaving this house?"

"Will we have to do that?"

"We might."

Nina gave it some thought. "I guess I don't mind much. I'll miss Ann."

"Yes, I know."

"But she could come to see me a lot, couldn't she?"

"Of course."

"Besides, she's going to be at her daddy's house some of the time. She heard her mama and daddy talking about it, and he lives in Flagstaff. She's glad about that." Nina shrugged with youthful resignation.

Leah placed her hand on her daughter's head and smiled down at her fondly. "I'm sure she is." Nina was young enough to have accepted the fact that her real father had gone away years ago, and she had never asked about him. Now she would have to know the truth about Jacob. Leah wasn't sure just how much a six-year-old would understand, but she would have to tell her. It was a crazy situation but not an unhappy one. Of course it would take Nina some time to accept Jacob as her daddy, but at least he wasn't a stranger to her.

Hurriedly Leah finished packing, and it wasn't until she had everything in the car and was locking the front door that something occurred to her. Another piece of unfinished business. She went into her closet, fumbled in the back and retrieved the small black suitcase she and Whit had claimed at the Flagstaff bus station six years ago. She had lost track of the number of times she had taken it out and stared at the contents. Well, no more. She would show it to Jacob, then in the trash it would go. Her days of living on memories were over. Come to think of it, they had been over since the day Jacob had come into her life.

CHAPTER SEVENTEEN

IT WAS WEDNESDAY AFTERNOON, which meant Jacob would be on the golf course. Leah didn't bother phoning ahead, merely showed up at the front door with Nina and her luggage.

"Why, Mrs. Stone, what a delightful surprise," Davis greeted her warmly. "Is Dr. Surratt expecting you?"

"No, I'm afraid he isn't."

"He hasn't returned from the club...."

"I was sure he wouldn't have. We'll just wait, if you don't mind."

"Not at all. The doctor is going to be so pleased. Let me get Hilda."

Hilda apparently had recovered sufficiently from Nina's last visit, for she hugged the girl affectionately and immediately hustled her down to the kitchen, where she could place her order for dinner. Leah was left to pace and watch the clock until Jacob arrived home.

It was five-fifteen when he did, and he burst through the front door like a whirlwind, calling her name. When she appeared at the stairwell landing, he was up in a flash, embracing her enthusiastically, his eyes as bright as a child's.

"Sweetheart, I couldn't believe it when I saw the car! Is anything wrong?"

"Nothing's wrong. Everything's wonderful, just

wonderful." Looping her arms around his neck, she nibbled on the underside of his chin. "Hmm, for a man who just came in off the golf course, you smell divine."

"I showered at the club. I only played nine holes. Too damned hot out there for more. Where's Nina?"

"In the kitchen with Hilda and George."

"May I ask to what I owe the pleasure of this unexpected visit?"

"I came to tell you a story," she said simply.

His brows knitted. "A story?"

"Mmm. Where can we talk in private?"

"Almost anywhere. What about the study?"

They descended the stairs hand in hand. "I finished the tapestry," she told him. "If I do say so myself, you have yourself a masterpiece for only the price of Alex's commission."

"Oh, no. The artist deserves her due."

"What difference does it make? We'll just put it in a joint bank account."

They had reached the study doors. Jacob opened them, almost pushed her inside, closed them and drew her into his embrace again. "You got the divorce!" he exclaimed exuberantly.

"Better than that. I . . . I think you'd better sit down. This story may knock you for a loop."

Jacob backed off and eyed her quizzically. She was being terribly mysterious, he thought, completely unlike Leah, who was as straightforward as they come. Crossing the room, he sat on the sofa and watched her as she followed and sat beside him. Her eyes were bright and excited. First she cupped his face in her hands and kissed him tenderly. Then she picked up one of his hands and idly played with his fingers. He was intrigued. Whatever this story was, she was having a hard time getting it out.

"Leah, I'm about to burst with curiosity!" he protested.

"Well, I...I...."

Then, to Jacob's utter confusion, she put her hand to her temple and began to cry quietly. Quickly he put his arm around her. "Sweetheart, what the devil's wrong?"

"N-nothing."

It occurred to him that he'd never seen Leah cry, never even seen her rattled, but she was good and rattled now. "Leah, what on earth—I can't stand this!"

"Oh, this is so st-stupid," she sobbed. "I've k-kept it bottled up so long and now I c-can't even get it out!"

Completely stumped, Jacob watched her cry for a few seconds. The only thing that prevented his being really alarmed was somehow knowing the tears weren't prompted by unhappiness. He shifted and fumbled for his hip pocket. "I don't suppose you have a handkerchief," he muttered, producing one and handing it to her. "Women never carry a handkerchief."

"Th-thanks." She dried her eyes, delicately blew her nose, then wadded the handkerchief into a ball and squeezed it. "Sorry."

"Are you all right?"

She nodded. "Yes, all right, really. Sorry for the outburst."

"You were going to tell me something?"

Again she nodded. Taking a deep breath, she rested her head on his shoulder and cuddled against him like a child. "It begins eight years ago, on a summer night. I had just graduated from college and was living with dad. One night we were sitting on the front porch after dinner, and a truck stopped in front of the house. A young man got out...."

THE LATE-AFTERNOON SKIES over Phoenix were blanketed with dark clouds; jagged streaks of lightning split them open, accompanied by deafening claps of thunder. Rain fell in sheets. It was the usual sudden and violent desert thunderstorm, descending almost without warning. The thirsty earth would greedily suck up the welcome moisture, and tomorrow everything would seem as dry and dusty as ever.

Inside Jacob's study, the two occupants were scarcely aware of the storm raging over their heads. It seemed to Leah that she had spent an awful lot of time lately relating the details of her brief marriage to Jim Stone. It took an unusually long time to tell something that had actually occupied but a fraction of her life. But this time the telling was different. She wanted Jacob to know every tiny detail, everything she could remember.

"Anyway," she concluded, "I watched that bus until it was out of sight, and. . .the next time I saw you was six years later in Alex's office."

Jacob had remained as still as a statue all the while she was talking. Leah guessed he found it almost impossible to assimilate. Small wonder. She tried to put herself in his shoes at that moment, tried to imagine what was going on in his head and found she couldn't. Oddly, her mood when she finished speaking was more fearful than anything. She couldn't assess the look on his face. Shocked? Taken aback? He might even be angry that she had let him suffer so long. But surely he'd be happy, or at least he would be when it all soaked in.

A knot had formed in Jacob's throat so tightly that he could hardly breathe. While listening to Leah's incredible story he hadn't been able to completely associate it with the two of them. He might have been listening to a piece of gossip, something that had happened to someone else. Then he looked into her lovely earnest face and reality took hold. He was stunned to the point of speechlessness. To have all the fears and worries that had plagued him for years erased within moments was more than he could grasp.

A tremor raced through Leah as she watched him. Had she been wrong to blurt the whole story out? In spite of what Alicia Graves had told her, she might have been wiser to break it to him in bits and pieces. Placing her hand on his arm, she said, "Please, Jacob... say something."

"Dear God, Leah," he croaked when he could find his voice, "why didn't you tell me this before?"

"I wanted to, from the beginning."

"Then why didn't you?"

"Charles advised me not to," she said dully. She wasn't completely sure why she had begun to despise Jacob's partner, but she had. So much of Jacob's recent turmoil, it now seemed to her, was the result of his partner's advice.

"Charles? Charles knows about this?"

Leah nodded.

"How long has he known?"

"He came to see me last Friday morning. He had telephoned earlier and asked if he could. Seems he had gotten the idea I knew something about your fugue, and of course he was right. You see, the night of the opening I had asked some questions about amnesia, and— Oh, it's all so complicated, isn't it? I wanted him to say it was all right to tell you the truth. He didn't. As a matter of fact, he suggested I ought to stay away from you altogether."

"Why would he do such a thing?"

"I don't know, Jacob. Honestly I don't." It wasn't

time yet to tell him about her suspicions regarding his partner. Maybe she never would. They were, after all, not rooted in fact.

Jacob, not surprisingly, still looked stupefied. "I think I've always known," he said in a quiet, detached voice. "I've always had this weird feeling about us, that I'd met you before or seen you before. Naturally I thought you would have mentioned it if that was the case, so I just chalked it up to my crazy, mixed-up mind." He paused. The dawning of some incredible realization was etched on his face. "The dream...a woman, a house. It was you and the house in Sedona!"

"I have to think so, darling. In fact, I know so, and I've wanted to tell you so badly. How do you feel now?"

"Now? Well, I...I'm not sure. I guess it hasn't sunk in yet. I feel...wonderful!" He began to laugh then, a quiet chuckle at first, then a full, hearty laugh that came from deep within his chest. "Wonderful! How else could I feel? It's over. Thank God, it's over."

Leah held him closer to her. "You're a married man, do you realize that?"

"Well, I'll be damned! I am, aren't I? That man you wouldn't divorce, the one I hated was me!"

"That's right. You were so persistent about the divorce, and I couldn't get one, couldn't reject the man I'd known and loved, the one I still love."

He locked his fingers into her hair and nuzzled his face into the silky stuff. "Oh, Leah, it's all so...."

"Incredible. I know. But nice, too, isn't it?"

"Nice? That doesn't begin to describe—"

At that moment the door to the study opened, and Nina burst into the room. "Mama, are you gonna stay in here all night? Hilda won't let me go swimming because of the storm, but she's gotta go to the grocery store and says I can go with her if it's all right with you.''

Leah withdrew from Jacob's embrace. "Nina, you know you're supposed to knock!"

The girl paused. "Sorry," she said contritely, "but I've seen you and Jacob kissing before."

Beside Leah, Jacob tensed. He looked at Nina across the room, and the shock hit him, slicing through him like a steel knife. His daughter! His daughter.... Pain contorted his face even as he was filled with awe, and he took a moment to wonder if every parent experienced this feeling of chest-expanding pride. He struggled for words. "Well, scamp, aren't you even going to say hello?" The words were offhand, but his voice was choked with emotion.

Nina grinned. "Hi. Can I go to the store with Hilda?" Obediently she walked into Jacob's hug.

"May I go," Leah corrected automatically. Her own emotions were barely under control. In fact, she was dangerously close to tears again.

Jacob held Nina so long the girl looked curiously over his shoulder at her mother. "Is something wrong?" she asked.

Jacob cleared his throat and released her. "No, no, everything's just fine."

"Then can—may I go to the store with Hilda?"

"Yes, that's fine," Leah said.

Jacob's eyes followed his daughter's departing figure, and he felt a peculiar choking sensation in his throat. "You did a good job, Leah."

"Thanks."

"You had to go through the last month of the pregnancy alone. I don't know how you did what you did."

"I had to," she said simply.

"Damn, I've missed so much!"

"She's still awfully young, Jacob. You'll have years and years of watching her grow up."

"I will, won't I?" He raked his fingers through his hair. "I have a lot to learn, and I want to know everything, everything about Nina, everything you and I did together, everything we said to each other...."

"Hey, that's a tall order!" She laughed. "I can't remember everything."

"I wish I could remember just part of it."

"Is it still so important to you?"

"Not as important as it once was, but I guess I still want to remember."

"Maybe, darling, someday you will."

Jacob drew her close and held her against his thudding heart. Overcome with the knowledge that everything he hadn't been able to find was now in his grasp, he found speech impossible. So he simply held her, confident that Leah, of all people, would understand what he was going through. The room grew so quiet that the only sound was the ticking of an antique clock on a nearby table.

"Oh, Jacob," Leah whispered at last, "do you know who's going to be thrilled over all this?"

"Who?"

"Dad. The two of you got along so famously, and he missed you terribly after you went away. He still says you were the best veterinarian's assistant he ever had."

"Well, damn! I should hope so!"

Leah leaped to her feet; her eyes were as bright as diamonds. "Come upstairs with me. I have something I want to show you."

"I can't stand too many more surprises, you know."

The contents of the black suitcase were just one more

startling fact of life for Jacob to come to grips with. He kept fingering the garments, staring at them. "To think you've kept it all these years."

"Dad and I claimed it, and I've gone through it dozens of times. I wonder—" she swallowed hard "—what might have happened if we had left it there for you to claim."

"I wonder," Jacob sighed, then turned to her with a small smile. "I'll never be able to accuse you of not being able to keep a secret, will I? I've said it before, and I'll say it again—I don't know how you did it. Tell me about him, darling. About Jim Stone, I mean. What was he like? How was he different from me? What was there about him that made you love him so much?"

She smiled at him with utmost tenderness. "He was a lot like you...kind, tender, a gentleman. The differences? A lot, I guess. Funny. I think I love Jim a lot more...now that he's you."

THE EVENING turned out to be a giddy, disoriented block of time. Jacob's most immediate concern was how to tell Nina. "We'll just be honest with her," Leah said. "But not tonight. Tomorrow. Let's just the two of us enjoy this happy ending tonight."

Somehow they managed to make it through dinner and Nina's bedtime with a semblance of normality, although Leah caught her daughter looking at her several times during the evening as though asking, "What's the matter with you, mama?" Leah couldn't completely contain her excitement.

Hours later Jacob was propped up in bed watching her undress. Shedding the last of her clothes, she crawled into bed and snuggled against him. He was emotionally exhausted, she could tell, so she refrained from her usual sensuous maneuvers. Peacefully she lay beside him, happy inside, knowing he was, too. Best of all, he was free.

"I hope you sleep like a baby tonight," she whispered.

She felt him kiss her temple. "That would be a new experience for me."

"I know. More reason to hope you do."

"Why am I so tired?"

"You've been through a lot today. We both have. Just sleep, darling. If you wake up during the night, wake me up, too."

"Leah, let's go to Sedona tomorrow."

"Tomorrow is only Thursday. What about the clinic?"

"I'll go early in the morning, see if I can't juggle the appointments. For sure I'll get away as soon as I can. Strange. . . I've seen the house so many times, but now I want to look at it through. . . these new eyes."

"Sure, love. Whatever you want to do."

He drifted off within minutes—a first. Normally she fell asleep long before he did, and more often than not she awoke during the night to find him sitting up in a chair or restlessly roaming. When Leah heard his shallow, even breathing, she inched away from him, settled her head on the pillow and delighted in watching him sleep so peacefully.

This, then, was what she had wanted. They were together again, there was no need to go through a divorce and maybe they could keep the house in Sedona. Nina might have a brother or sister before too long. Almost anything was possible now. Those awful years were over.

Surprisingly, she wasn't the least bit sleepy. There was too much to think about. She was perfectly content to lie there next to Jacob and go over in her mind, almost day by day, the time when he had been Jim Stone. She wasn't doing that in order to conjure up memories of Jim; now she had so much more than memories. But she wanted to remember for Jacob's sake. He was anxious to know everything, and he would be full of questions again tomorrow. Tonight they had barely scratched the surface.

Her mind raced over the early days when Jim had been nothing more to her than just a pleasant young man who worked for her father and occupied the back room. Then it settled on the days several weeks later, after she had known she was attracted to him, and she smiled softly against the pillow. Such happy, carefree days. Saturday afternoons had been their special times, when Jim's work week ended and they could leave the farm to follow their own pursuits. Those outings, she now thought, had been the beginning of whatever courtship had existed. Whit would give them the old pickup, and Leah always drove, because Jim didn't have a driver's license.

Usually they spent at least part of every Saturday afternoon at Green's Place, a café in the valley where they could listen to country music on the jukebox, drink a couple of beers, eat cooked-to-order burgers and catch up on local gossip. At Green's Place at that time, conversation had still been considered one of life's primary pleasures. It was always easy to find someone to "visit" with, either the regulars, or strangers who happened to stop in on their way to somewhere else. . . .

Leah's thoughts halted, and a frown crossed her face. She had a sudden flash of recall, and she bolted straight up in bed. Glancing down to make sure she hadn't disturbed Jacob—he was dead to the world—she put her hand to her pounding heart, and her mouth dropped open. It couldn't be!

But it was. Dear God! Events of a long-ago day came to her as clearly as if they had happened the day before. Green's Place. That's where she had first seen Dr. Charles White!

CHAPTER EIGHTEEN

DAWN WAS BEGINNING to pinken the eastern sky when Jacob opened his eyes the following morning. He awoke with a strange and pleasant sensation, the sensation of having slept a deep, untroubled sleep. Then another—the sense of freedom, release from all that had plagued his life for so long. Already he felt like a different person, and who knew what today would bring, and tomorrow, the day after?

As his mind gradually cleared, he turned to Leah, fully expecting his warm lover to be ready for the lovemaking he had been too exhausted for the night before. He groped for her, only to find her side of the bed empty. His searching eyes made a slow sweep of the room and found her, dressed in a light cotton robe, huddled in his easy chair near the window. Her knees were pulled up, and her head was resting on them. She looked very tiny and very lovely; his heart turned over as he gazed at her.

"Leah, darling," he said softly, "what's with this staring out the window at dawn? That's my bit. You're usually out like a light at this hour."

She turned to look at him, but instead of seeing her winsome smile he saw an expression that didn't seem to fit Leah. "Sweetheart, what on earth's the matter?"

Leah had slept a grand total of maybe two hours, and all in fifteen- and twenty-minute increments. Her emotions had run the gamut from uncertainty to conviction to incredulity. Now she was simply angry. "I'm too damned mad to sleep."

"Mad?" He chuckled. "What on earth do you have to be mad about?"

"He never was looking for you, Jacob," she said in an indescribably cold voice. Her mouth worked as she spat out the words. "He didn't have to. I couldn't believe it at first, but now I know. He knew where you were all the time. Oh, why can't I learn to follow my own instincts? The minute I laid eyes on that man I had this peculiar feeling—"

"What are you talking about?" Jacob threw back the sheet and, oblivious to his nudity, crossed the room to kneel beside the chair. He took one of her hands in his and was astonished to discover it was trembling. She was trembling all over, and he had never seen such an expression on that gentle face. "Leah?"

"Listen to me, Jacob, and believe what I'm telling you. Eight years ago Charles White knew where you were! He's known all along."

"What? Sweetheart, come back to bed. You've been dreaming." He got her to her feet, pulled her, unresisting, with him and led her back to the bed. When he crawled between the sheets, Leah didn't follow. She knelt on top of the bed beside him, looking down at him with blazing eyes.

"I haven't been dreaming, Jacob. I've been awake this whole night, and I know what I'm talking about. Charles White couldn't find you because he wasn't looking for you. I can't imagine why, but I do know one thing—he knew where you were!"

Jacob folded his arms behind his head and studied her carefully. He knew Leah, and he knew she never went off half-cocked about anything. As unbelievable as her accusation was, it couldn't be rash; she had given it plenty of thought. "What makes you think so?"

"I remember," she said grimly. "You had been at the farm two months, maybe a little longer. Every Saturday afternoon we'd go to a joint called Green's Place. One day a stranger came in and sat at the counter. I remember it because a stranger was always noticed in Green's Place, and later he came over to our table and asked for directions to...someplace, I forget. Then he asked you how the fishing was nearby. You said you didn't have much time for fishing, because work kept you so busy. And he asked what kind of work you were in. I remember it just as clearly as if it had happened yesterday. That man was Charles White!"

Jacob still didn't want to believe it, and had it been anyone but Leah telling him this incredible thing he would have dismissed it as the product of a wild imagination. "Darling, that was a long time ago. Charles looks like hundreds of people."

She tossed her head impatiently. "Oh, I'm right, I know I am. There have been things from the beginning.... The first time I met him, the night of the opening, my very first thought was of having seen him before. It was just as insistent when he came to see me Friday. And there have always been questions. How could a prominent physician simply disappear for two years? That always bothered me. And why couldn't Charles, who has published a paper on amnesia, help you any more than he had?"

"Leah, do you think I haven't asked myself those questions and hundreds more?"

"No!" she said vehemently, then softened her tone. "No, not like I have, because of all your hang-ups about your amnesia. It embarrasses you a little, and you've always been afraid of what lay 'back there.' Confess it now. You've wanted to remember but have been a little bit frightened to."

He sighed. "Sure I was, and I got more confused after I met you." He reached for her with a smile. "None of that matters anymore, does it? There's nothing for me to fear."

"But plenty for you to think about. Charles was adamant about my not telling you the truth, yet when I spoke to Dr. Graves, her immediate reaction was, 'Why not?' Now does it seem reasonable to you that two people in the same profession would take absolutely opposite views?"

"Believe me, it happens all the time."

She ignored him. "So many strange things, Jacob. Strange, strange things."

"God, once you get something into your head.... You're just not going to let this lie, are you?"

"Not a chance." Stretching out full-length beside him, she tried to relax and found she couldn't. She was full of concern, and her mind raced at runaway speed. At last she could give voice to suspicions that had been nagging at her for a long time, and there were plenty of them. "I don't think you've ever had the proper psychiatric care, Jacob. Sandra said the same thing."

"Oh? Where did you and Sandra go to medical school?"

"Be serious! Sandra said that nothing I'd told her jibed with what she knew about psychoanalysis, and she's been through therapy. Tell me...all the time you were seeing Charles, did you ever have the feeling that the two of you had a special relationship, that you were very close, that he was the one person in the world you could talk to?"

Jacob chuckled at the suggestion. "No, never."

"Well, you should have! Dr. Graves said so."

"This Dr. Graves has certainly made an impression on you."

Leah shot him a look of exasperation. "Then tell me something else. Did Charles ever try hypnosis?"

"No, it wasn't mentioned."

"See! Dr. Graves said she'd use it if the patient could be hypnotized. Even Charles told me it was an effective tool. Of course the reason he didn't use it with you is obvious. For some reason he didn't want Jacob Surratt to return. But once you did, he certainly didn't want you remembering the fugue. Why?"

"I don't know, Leah. I swear I don't." *But I'm damned sure going to find out,* he thought. *Later.*

"But you believe me?"

"Of course I believe you." How could he not believe that keen, sincere face? He had never seen her more impassioned.

"And you'll try to find out what it's all about?"

"I'll do what I can. The one thing I don't want is for you to worry about it, so put it out of your mind. So much heavy thinking for one morning. Take off that robe and get under the sheet with me. I want to feel you next to me. Now I realize why you always knew exactly how to love me. You did, you know."

"I know."

"Did you always know?"

"Of course not. I had to learn. I was a blushing bride. You taught me a lot of things, my love."

"Have I changed much? Am I different?"

She pretended to give it some serious thought. "Yes," she said. "You've gotten older. . .and better."

"Then come here. I haven't even properly celebrated my newfound state of connubial bliss."

Leah was unappeased, but it was dawn, and she was mentally worn-out. The mystery of Charles White could wait. Reaching out, she laced her fingers through the satisfying thickness of Jacob's dark hair. "It must be a shock to learn you're a husband and a father," she said somberly. "Now that you've had some time to let it sink in, are you glad?"

"I'm ecstatic," he said, and meant it.

"Sure?"

"Positive."

A soft smile curved her mouth. Shaking off the tiredness of her sleepless night, Leah discarded the robe, crawled under the sheet and shaped her body along the length of his, marveling at how perfectly attuned they were to each other's needs, how good he felt under her hands. Love was a gift, and hers, once lost, had been returned to her. Now the past really didn't matter. All that mattered was this—hungry mouths and hungry bodies clinging in a celebration of absolute devotion. No other man had ever, could ever, would ever....

Heat fairly radiated from their bodies as he grew turgid and sought entrance. She melted and opened to receive him. Lovemaking had always been wonderful between them, but never as wonderful as now. Finally they had found their own happy ending, except for one minor flaw....

SOMETIME LATER Jacob slipped quietly out of bed so as not to disturb Leah, who was sleeping soundly. Last night it had been impossible for him to tell her exactly how he felt; perhaps he would think of the right words later, although with Leah words were never absolutely necessary. She knew him better than he knew himself. He was thunderstruck by the way he felt, wholesome and mentally resilient. He hated leaving her now, but she might sleep for hours yet, and there was something he had to do.

He dressed quickly and walked out into the hallway. He started for the stairway, then paused and reversed direction. The door to the room Nina was sleeping in was partly ajar; he pushed it open and moved soundlessly to the side of the bed. Staring down at the small sleeping figure who was curled into an embryonic position, he was overcome by emotion.

How quickly his life had changed. This time yesterday Nina had been a cute kid, special because she was Leah's daughter. Now she was his progeny, his link to the future. Someday this child would probably present him with a grandson or granddaughter. The thought took hold of him, and he felt absurdly like weeping.

His parents had been gone a long time; only occasionally did he think about them. Now how he wished they were there to see Nina. He would have to hunt up the old family photograph albums and show his daughter some of the people she came from.

He brushed his hand across his eyes. Lord, he was getting downright maudlin! For long moments he simply stood over the bed, staring down at her. Then, resisting the urge to bend and kiss her, he left the room as quietly as he had come.

The house was very still. He hurried down the stairs and into the kitchen for a glass of juice. There, to his surprise, he encountered Hilda in her bathrobe, brewing a pot of coffee. He had no idea the household staff rose at such an early hour.

Her employer's unexpected appearance both startled and embarrassed the little woman. "Oh, Dr. Surratt. Good heavens. . . ." She cinched the nondescript robe more tightly round her waist, and her hands flew to her hair, which was stuffed into an unbecoming net.

"Don't mind me, Hilda. I'm just on my way to the clinic and thought I'd have a glass of juice. I'll get it."

"Oh, please, sir, let me." She hurried to the refrigerator, glancing at the kitchen clock as she did. "So early...."

"Yes, well...I was awake, and there are things I need to tend to," he offered by way of vague explanation. He accepted the glass of orange juice she handed him and quaffed it.

"Mrs. Stone and Nina...I guess they're still sleeping."

"Yes. If Nina wakes up before her mother does, please keep an eye on her for me."

"Of course. She's a dear little girl, doctor. I've grown very fond of her."

Jacob smiled. "That's good, Hilda, because I imagine you'll be seeing a great deal of her from now on."

There was an almost imperceptible altering of Hilda's expression. "Sir, is that something I can pass along to the rest of the staff?"

"I can't think why not. You might also tell them to get used to addressing Mrs. Stone as Mrs. Surratt."

Hilda watched the doctor leave the house by way of the back door, and she smiled a smug, satisfied smile. Oh, she could hardly wait to tell Davis and the others! Dr. Surratt's new woman friend had been the chief topic of kitchen gossip for months, and not only because of the marked changes she had wrought in their employer's personality. Mrs. Stone was a woman from his past, of that they were all sure. One had only to look at the darling child to tell that. Did Dr. Surratt honestly think they hadn't seen the resemblance?

Though now that she thought about it, Davis hadn't seen it either until she had brought it to his attention, and then he had accused her of having an overactive imagination fed by too many romance novels and soap operas.

Hilda snorted derisively. Men were such obtuse creatures, totally unobservant. Well, it was good that the doctor had decided to do what was right and marry the mother of his child. Heaven knew what kind of life that poor Mrs. Stone had been forced to lead, raising the child alone and all. Single parents had a tough time of it, and wasn't it always the woman who suffered? Knowing Dr. Surratt as she did, Hilda was surprised he hadn't done the honorable thing six years ago. But then, who could figure people when it came to affairs of the heart? Wouldn't it be interesting to know how they had happened to get together again.

This ought to shake up things in the household! Hilda snickered delightedly as she poured herself a cup of coffee. Bernice, the woman who came in twice a week to do laundry, would be there that day. *Do I have an earful for her,* Hilda thought. *This is at least as good as anything on the afternoon soaps.*

JACOB DROVE TO THE CLINIC in a mindless state, noticing only the absence of traffic at that ungodly hour. He wheeled into his private parking space, then unlocked the back door to the clinic. The building was deserted and would be for at least another half hour, which suited him perfectly.

His destination wasn't his own office or even the medical clinic, but the psychiatric unit. His master key opened every door in the place, and he used it freely, first for admittance into Records, then into Psychiatry's reception room. He didn't waste time wondering if what he was doing was ethical. He wouldn't have hesitated to pull another patient's file; certainly he was entitled to his own.

However, there didn't seem to be any records on him. Somehow that didn't surprise him at all. Locking the door behind him, Jacob walked purposefully to the office at the end of the corridor and let himself in. Charles's office, situated on the west side of the building, was dark, so he turned on the overhead light. Surveying the room, he found what he was looking for—a lone filing cabinet tucked unobtrusively into a corner behind a potted plant. He opened it, riffled through the several dozen folders he discovered and withdrew one. Then he took a seat behind Charles's desk, opened the folder and began to read. His expression at first was puzzled; then it settled into a grim cast....

SOME THIRTY MINUTES LATER Charles found him there. The light welling from beneath his door hadn't surprised him. He was forever forgetting to turn it off when he left at the end of the day. But the figure seated behind his desk prompted not only surprise but a vague rush of alarm. Charles's eyes bulged in disbelief at Jacob's temerity, so much so that he didn't waste time on pleasantness. "What the devil are you doing here?"

Jacob smiled casually. "I wanted to discuss my case with you, doctor."

"Now? Good God, Jacob, I have a full schedule this morning!" Charles took off his jacket, hung it up and shrugged into a white coat. "If there's something you want to talk to me about, we'll have to do it after office hours."

"We'll do it now."

Apparently Charles sensed something complicated was going on in Jacob's head. For a moment he stood awkwardly, looking uncomfortable. "I don't have the time," he said lamely.

"Take the time."

"I'll. . . try to work you in later."

"Now!"

Clearly agitated, Charles nevertheless mustered up an air of bravado. "Now look here, Jacob. I realize you're the head man around here, but that doesn't give you the right to barge in here and demand this and that." Then his eyes fell on the folder spread out on the desk. The bravado evaporated as his agitation increased. "What the hell are you doing?"

"Going over my case." Jacob's eyes narrowed, and in a sudden violent move he closed the folder and banged his hand on top of it. "There's not a damned thing in here, Charles! Nothing! Anyone reading this file wouldn't learn the first thing about my case. No observations, no suggestions. All jibberish. Now suppose you tell me what's going on."

Nervously Charles crossed the office to stand with his back to the desk. "It's not jibberish to me. Your case is in my head. I know how you feel about your amnesia, so I. . .thought it best not to have a written history in the clinic's files. Who knows whose hands it could fall into? I had to protect your privacy."

"Oh, bull!"

The unexpected epithet brought Charles around. "Now wait just a damned minute!"

"No, you wait just a damned minute! You knew where I was eight years ago, didn't you? You knew it all the time."

"What on earth gave you that idea?"

"The sudden recollection of a lady with a very sound memory. Leah remembered where she'd seen you before."

Charles mouth dropped open. Caught off guard, he carelessly said, "I told that woman—"

"To stay away from me, not to tell me anything. Yes, I know. Unfortunately for you, doctor, Leah is a thoughtful, inquisitive woman. She decided to seek a second opinion. Aren't we ethical medical men supposed to advise patients to do just that?"

Charles's face drained of color; he looked positively ashen. Jacob was reminded of the stricken look on Leah's face that day in Alex's office. Pressing his advantage, he went on. "The other psychiatrist Leah saw advised just the opposite, so she told me. Then and only then did she remember where she had seen you before. You came up to us in a café and asked directions. Then you asked about fishing. . . ."

"Her imagination is running rampant."

"I don't think so."

Charles turned away, obviously too shaken to say anything. Every muscle in Jacob's body tensed. Until this moment he hadn't been sure, not really, and he had harbored a faint hope that Leah was mistaken. Now he knew she had remembered correctly. The downward slump of Charles's shoulders, his hands clenched at his sides, everything about his manner told Jacob that Leah was right. He didn't know when he had felt so bitterly disappointed in another human being. Sighing wearily, he said, "That was only two months or so after I'd left Phoenix, so all that time I was gone you knew exactly where I was. Admit it."

Moving as though his feet weighed pounds, Charles walked to the window to stare bleakly out at the dawning of another bright summer day. "Yes," he said dully. "I knew."

Jacob's face twisted. A long, heavy moment of silence passed while he tried to collect himself. Storming and raging, which is what he felt like doing, would accomplish nothing. He stared at Charles's dejected figure and thought, *There has to be a reason.* "Why?" he asked hoarsely. "I just don't understand. I know we've never been close friends, but I thought we had established a mutually satisfactory working partnership. Why didn't you want me back? Was it resentment or professional jealousy, or what?"

"Oh, I resented you, all right. And envied you—your looks, your social poise, even your family background. I was a poor boy who'd worked my ass off to put myself through medical school, while everything had been handed to you on a silver platter. And even though my name was right up there beside yours, I always knew who the head man was. Everybody does. And I'll even confess to enjoying being the head man during the two years you were away. But at the same time, I was grateful to you for rescuing me from oblivion and allowing my name to be associated with a clinic that had the reputation this one does. Does any of that make sense?"

"Not much."

"It doesn't make much sense to me, either. Professional jealousy had nothing to do with my decision to leave you where you were eight years ago. In spite of what you might be thinking now, I've always been scrupulously ethical where my profession is concerned."

"Yet you didn't want me back, and once I was back you didn't want me to remember anything that had happened during the fugue."

Charles didn't deny it.

Jacob ran his fingers through his hair, shaking his head. "Why, Charles? There had to be a reason. What was it?"

The psychiatrist turned from the window to look squarely at Jacob, and the strangest smile crossed his face. He looked oddly relieved of a burden. "You know," he said quietly, "I'm actually glad it's over."

"Dammit, stop talking in riddles! The reason, Charles!"

"Probably the oldest known reason for a man to toss aside every scruple he ever had and plunge recklessly ahead. A woman. To be more specific, Daphne Townsend."

CHAPTER NINETEEN

JACOB SAT BACK in the chair as though reeling from the force of a blow. "Daphne?" he said incredulously.

Charles nodded. "Unbelievable?"

"It's more than unbelievable. *Daphne*?"

"I'm afraid so. Even I find it almost impossible to believe now, and looking back, if I could undo what I did, I would. At the time I was besotted, bewitched—call it whatever you like. I would have tossed you to the lions if it would have kept her with me."

Jacob rubbed his eyes tiredly and inhaled a painful breath. A mind could only absorb so much, he thought, and this was too much. He had been sorely tested during the past twenty-four hours. "Daphne Townsend, for heaven's sake! What in the hell did she have to do with it?"

"It's a long story. Do you want to hear it?"

"Oh, indeed I do, doctor. I'll thrash it out of you if I have to."

"I . . . think I need to sit down."

Jacob shoved himself to his feet. "Take your chair. I might have to lie down."

He didn't, however. He crossed the room and sat on the sofa, propping an ankle on his knee. With engrossed interest he eyed his partner's ashen face. In a curious way he felt sorry for Charles; the man looked positively ghastly, emotionally drained. Jacob didn't prod or probe, merely waited until Charles was ready to talk.

The psychiatrist picked up a pencil and began twirling it through his fingers like a baton. "Daphne came to see me a couple of weeks after you left Phoenix. She had been in San Francisco and had returned home to the news of your acquittal. She tried to find you, but you had moved out of your apartment, so she assumed I would know where you were. I didn't, of course, and told her as much. Then she broke down, sobbed all over the place, said how sorry she was for being so wrong about you."

"Sounds like her," Jacob sneered. "Good old Daphne, as steadfast and reliable as the weather."

"Hell, I didn't know what to do, so I took her to lunch, listened to her tale of woe and tried to calm her down. I told her to come to see me anytime she felt she needed someone to talk to. She took me up on it—once a week at first, then every few days, then every day. I grew...fond of her."

Jacob's mouth set in a tight line. Yes, he could just picture it. Daphne was a real beauty and a charmer who could turn those baby-blue eyes on you and make you feel weak in the knees. He knew, since he had succumbed to her false-hearted allure, as much as he hated admitting that. And poor Charles would have been an easy victim.

Charles cleared his throat and continued with some difficulty. "We started having dinner together, first at restaurants, eventually more often than not at my place. I knew she was using me until you got back, that she was the kind of woman who needed a man, almost any man, around. And I told myself I wasn't emotionally involved. Even after she moved in with me, I knew she'd split once you came back. I've never had a great deal of...success with the opposite sex, but when Daphne put her mind to it she could make me feel like the world's best. So I rationalized that I was just enjoying a brief, rare interlude with a beautiful woman, that I had my eyes wide open. But I think I always knew that wasn't entirely the truth. I was falling in love and doing my damnedest to make her do the same.''

Jacob's expression was passive, though he felt uncomfortable, embarrassed. It was the hardest part of his profession, listening while people poured out their heart and soul—people would tell a doctor the most incredible things—and it was doubly hard for him to sit and listen to a respected colleague.

His thoughts suddenly went into reverse. Respected? Until today, yes, highly respected. Again, as disappointed and angry as he was, pity rose in him. He felt very sorry for any man who had the bad fortune to fall for Daphne Townsend.

Charles was frowning. "One day it dawned on me that you'd been gone a helluva long time. It started preying on my mind, so I checked with the police. At first they weren't any help, but then they found a report on an accident that had happened up near Camp Verde a couple of months earlier. The report described the victim—it could have been you—and mentioned that the man had amnesia as a result of a blow to the head. Now that hit a nerve, so I decided to check it out on my own, very quietly. What I told you about not wanting any publicity so soon after that god-awful trial was true. Now, dammit, Jacob, whether you believe it or not, at that point I was genuinely trying to find you.''

"Okay, Charles, I believe you. Go on.''

"Well, I hit a dead end. No one seemed to know where you had gone once you left the hospital, but after asking around, I found a nurse who remembered your case and was sure she'd seen you recently. She didn't know where you were living or what name you were using, but at least I knew that you, or whoever it was I was tracking, were nearby. So one Saturday I drove to Camp Verde and just started moving west, looking around, stopping in stores and the like. I don't know what I thought I might find, but the whole thing was driving me nuts by then.''

He paused again to clear his throat. ''Toward afternoon I got thirsty, so I stopped in at this place for a beer. And dear God, there you were—sitting at a table with a pretty, dark-haired girl, looking like you were having a great time. I swear, that's the first time I gave any thought to the deception.''

''You came over to our table,'' Jacob prompted, unable to recall any of it but knowing it was true. Leah had remembered it correctly, almost down to the tiniest detail.

Charles nodded. ''You hadn't spotted me, but the woman had. She looked at me curiously, probably because I was a stranger, before turning back to you. It occurred to me then that the amnesia thing might have been faked. Remembering your mood when you left Phoenix, I decided you might have assumed another identity just for the hell of it. It's been done before, plenty of times. But if you had been faking it, I knew I'd see some reaction if you suddenly saw me face-to-face. Nobody's that good an actor, and I had to know for sure. That's when I approached you.''

''I didn't show any signs of recognizing you,'' Jacob said.

''Not the slightest, and I stayed at your table long enough to make sure. I saw the way the woman—ah, Leah, was looking at you with her heart in her eyes. Fascinating eyes. Incredible eyes.''

"Yes, I know."

"You told me you were working as a veterinarian's assistant. I remember damned near choking over that one before conveniently telling myself you probably enjoyed it. I knew you'd be good at it, too. All the time I stood there at that table, I was convinced I was going to tell you who you were any minute, but somehow I never did. I walked out of that café in a trance. When I got to the car I was shaking all over. Even as I drove away, I couldn't believe I was doing what I was doing. For days I thought of nothing else. I'd go back and find you, I was sure, but then...." Charles faltered.

"Then?"

"Why not leave you alone, I rationalized. You looked happier than I'd ever seen you. You and the woman obviously were crazy about each other, and you were working at something you'd be good at, something worthwhile. Why confuse your life by giving you an identity you obviously didn't want? Oh, the mind's a wonder! It can invent all sorts of convenient reasons for implausible actions. But hell, I knew the real reason for what I'd done. I knew if you came back here, Daphne would be gone like a shot. So... I left you alone."

Jacob's face was strained and taut. "I keep remembering the look you gave me when I walked into this office that day two years later. I've never seen anyone so stunned."

"Two years," Charles mused. "Two damned years. I had almost forgotten you. Your name was hardly mentioned around the clinic anymore, and I thought Daphne was happy. She had even begun considering marriage, or at least I thought she had. Until you showed up. I dislike telling you this, but for a moment I think I could have killed you. I didn't tell Daphne you were back, but she found out within days."

"She came to see me."

"I guessed as much. She moved out right after that, to Hawaii, I think. I was shattered at first, so much so that I didn't have time to think or worry about you. But then resignation set in. The whole thing had been like a dream from the beginning, anyway. I saw Daphne for what she was then—she really was a first-class bitch, you know—and I honestly think that in time I considered her departure good riddance. She was such a demanding woman, always wanting this and that...."

Jacob had placed his head in his hands. Now he quickly looked up. "Charles, why didn't you tell me then? If Daphne was the reason...."

"I had painted myself into a corner, don't you see?" he argued fervently. "I had myself in the awkward position of not having done something when I should have, of having let so much time pass that I was bound to incur your wrath. How could I tell you I'd known where you were for two entire years? I could see all this—" he waved to encompass the Surratt-White Clinic as a whole "—going down the tube. And I damned sure couldn't risk having you remember on your own, so when you asked me to put you in therapy, I grabbed the chance. There were any number of things I could have done to help you, but I didn't want your memory to come back. You might have remembered the encounter in the café."

Dazed, Jacob could only shake his head. "You robbed me of God knows how much time with Leah," he said bitterly. "And my daughter!"

"That's been the hardest part, knowing a child is involved. I'm not without conscience, in spite of what you might think," Charles said quietly; then he slipped back into the past. "Six years! Six years had passed. I thought it was all over. Then the night of the opening I saw Leah Stone, the woman I'd seen you with in that café. Hers is a face you never forget. I just stood and stared at her, feeling like I'd been punched in the stomach. But I had to risk speaking to her, staying with her long enough to make sure she didn't recognize me. She didn't, although she looked at me strangely, as though she thought she'd seen me before.

"When I learned you had just met her, when she asked me all those questions about amnesia. . . I knew. I think I knew it was only a matter of time before the whole thing blew up in my face. I fed her every piece of misinformation I could think of, even to the point of suggesting your condition might have been psychological, that remembering would do you irreparable harm. You can scare the pants off a lay person with that kind of talk. But I was only stalling, and I think I knew it. If it's any consolation to you, I haven't had a decent night's sleep since."

"It's no consolation, Charles. Neither have I. Leah said she's suspected for some time I wasn't receiving proper psychiatric care."

Charles smiled wanly. "Your girlfriend's very astute."

"My wife."

"That's right, your wife. Will you. . .apologize to her for me? She's quite a woman. All those years! It's almost unbelievable that a woman would keep a man's memory alive all those years."

Jacob said nothing. Apologize? How could anyone apologize for Leah's six lonely years? Despair was etched in his face. A searing pain had begun at his temples, but it was different than the headaches. The headaches, he imagined, were a thing of the past, as was the dream.

"You could have interpreted that dream all along," he muttered blankly.

"Without the slightest trouble."

"You compromised every principle you swore allegiance to!"

"Don't you think I know that?"

Without another word, Jacob left Charles's office. His partner probably thought his days at Surratt-White were at an end, and admittedly, at the moment Jacob's thoughts were centered on quickly and effectively canning him!

The resultant furor could be messy, though. Staff morale was good, and Jacob wanted it to stay that way. There were a lot of considerations. Did one stupid mistake negate a career? He might just keep quiet, give Charles a chance to find a position somewhere else before asking the man to resign. Jacob wasn't a vindictive person.

And he rarely did anything hastily. He would be able to deal with this more rationally in a few days. For now he wanted to concentrate on the reality of Leah and Nina and all that was ahead for him: years and years of peace and contentment. Actually, he had hope for the future all because of Leah. She had waited. His step in the corridor was brisk and springy.

The clinic was stirring to life for the day. People were pouring through the front door, filling up the chairs in the main reception room. Jacob walked into his office and was greeted by his nurse, Mary Goodwin. "Good morning, doctor. Isn't the heat awful?"

"Terrible."

"Yet you seem to be in unusually good spirits."

"I do? Well, I guess I am in a rather optimistic frame of mind. May I see today's appointments?"

"Only four, doctor, remember? The meeting upstairs at ten—"

"Cancel it. Everyone will be thrilled speechless, since they despise those meetings of mine. And tomorrow's appointments—see how many you can reschedule. The ones you can't, give to Stillman or Taylor. Something's come up. I won't be in the office until Monday.''

''Very well. Mr. Schumann's already waiting outside.''

Jacob reached for the white coat hanging on the rack. ''Give me five minutes, then send him in.''

TWO HOURS AFTER JACOB HAD GONE, Leah was awakening by slow degrees. Stretching and yawning, she opened one eye and glanced at the bedside clock, then bolted straight up. Ten-fifteen! She hadn't slept this late since weekends in college.

A far-off sound reached her ears, Nina's girlish laughter. Scrambling out of bed, Leah went to the window and looked down. Nina was splashing happily in the shallow end of the pool under Hilda's watchful eye, looking as though she was having a grand time. *The child's part fish,* Leah thought as a soft smile curved her mouth. She wasn't the least bit worried about Nina's adjustment to her new life.

Leah lifted her eyes and scanned the blue summer sky. It was a beautiful day, an absolutely gorgeous day. It was good to feel free—happy to be young and alive and in love. Jacob wasn't the only one who had been burdened these past couple of months.

Turning, she made for the bathroom and a quick shower, vaguely wondering if Jacob had been able to juggle his schedule for the day. If so, when would he be home?

The shower helped her wake up. For a few minutes she emptied her mind and let the bracing needles of water pummel her skin, then turned it off, opened the door and reached for a towel—only to find a strong hand instead. It grasped hers tightly, and she found herself being helped out of the stall. Rivulets of water were streaming down her face. Brushing them aside, she opened her eyes.

Jacob stood before her, grinning. Opening his arms, he pulled her dripping body against him and held her tightly.

"Oh, I'm getting you soaked!" She laughed.

"I can change. Let's get our daughter and go home."

"Home?"

"One of our homes. We can't ever give up the house in Sedona, Leah. It means too much. We'll divide our time between here and there, maybe use the other as a weekend retreat with an eye toward retiring there someday. I know you're not a city person."

"I can be any type person I have to be as long as I have you. But I must confess, I don't want to give up the house in Sedona. Do you have any idea how many man-hours you spent on it?"

"Now my hands are itching to pick up a hammer and saw again. I think I have a new project. The first order of business will be building on a bedroom... with a lock on the door." His grin was mischievously salacious.

She grinned back, then shivered. "Get me a towel, darling. I'm freezing!"

Whipping one off the towel bar, he wrapped it around her and dried her thoroughly. Then he knotted it around her breasts. Since the front of his shirt was soaked, he unbuttoned it, slipped it off and used it to vigorously rub his chest. "Speaking of houses, how do you feel about this one?"

"This one? Well, it's lovely."

"Really? You really like it?"

"Jacob, it's a beautiful house. What woman wouldn't like it?"

"You know, I never thought much about this house. It was just someplace to hang my hat, but now I'm starting to think of it as a home. I want to see your jacket slung over the back of a chair. I want Nina's sneakers on the stairway and her bicycle out front. I want giggling little girls spending the night. . . ."

Leah looked at him skeptically. "May I quote you on that in a few months?"

"Absolutely. My life has been too damned orderly for too damned long. You know, I think I'll clean out that exercise room I never use and turn it into a game room. She can have her friends over in a few years, and—" He stopped, and a look of absolute alarm crossed his face. "Leah, Nina's going to want to go out on dates someday. I can't allow that! I won't like any of the boys."

She laughed delightedly. "Well, don't waste your time now. There'll be plenty of other things to worry about in the meantime. So, what have you been doing this morning?"

"I saw Charles," he told her, suddenly sobering.

Leah stiffened. "Oh, Jacob!"

"You were right on all counts."

"He admitted it?"

"He didn't have a choice."

"If only I had followed my own instincts." She closed her eyes and expelled a heavy sigh. "If only I had told you months ago. Think what I could have spared you."

"You did what anyone would have done, sweetheart. You listened to what an expert had to say. I've been listening to him for six years."

"What are you going to do, about Charles, I mean."

"I don't know. I'll have to think about it, something I don't want to do today."

Pulling away, Leah looked at Jacob thoughtfully. "Why, you're not angry, are you?"

He shrugged. "I was, but it's wearing off. He was foolish over a woman. It happens to the best of us."

"A woman?"

"It's a long story. I'll tell you all about it later. Now, let's get dressed and get Nina. I guess we should tell her right away."

"Yes, let's." A rush of emotion overtook her, and she flung her arms around his neck. "I love you . . . so . . . much! It overwhelms me."

"It pretty well floors me, too." Bending his head, he kissed her eyes, the tip of her nose, her mouth. "And to think I never believed in fate. What else could have kept you free all these years? What else could have sent me into that bank on that splendid morning?"

"I've waited so long."

"I know you have."

"So many lonely nights," she murmured, melting against him, resting her cheek on his shoulder.

"I know it can't have been easy for you. We'll make up for them, I promise."

Smiling impishly, she raked her fingernails across his back, felt a little shiver race through him. "Can we start now? Hilda will keep Nina entertained. Do we have to go downstairs right away?"

"Not on your life." As he scooped her effortlessly into his arms, the towel gave way, exposing the body that drove him wild with desire. His eyes glittered in appreciation. "You have gorgeous breasts," he declared as he swept through the doorway with her.

"They're too small."

"Too small for what?" Gently he placed her on the rumpled bed, then stood over her, smiling as he dropped his trousers. "They fill up my hands. I'm more than satisfied, at least.'' As he eased himself down beside her, he showed her what he meant.

Leah sighed contentedly. ''Are the doors locked?''

''Such a worrywart. Yes, they're locked. No one will bother us, sweetheart. Relax....''

''Oh, Jacob, are we terribly wicked and love crazed?''

''Probably. Isn't it great? You make me feel like a kid.''

She smiled lovingly and reached for him. ''Oh, doctor, you're no kid, far from it. You are one gorgeous man! I'll never get enough of you, never, never.''

''Well,'' he said as their movements began, ''you can try.''

CHAPTER TWENTY

LEAH EDGED ONTO THE INTERSTATE and headed north. Beside her, Jacob was the picture of self-satisfaction. His legs were stretched in front of him as far as the car's confines would allow. His arms were folded across his stomach, his head resting on the back of the seat, and his mouth was set in a contented half smile.

In the back seat Nina had been unusually quiet. She had scarcely said a word since Jacob had explained—beautifully, Leah thought—the truth about their relationship. From time to time Leah glanced worriedly into the rearview mirror, but Nina was only staring out the window, apparently lost in thought. The child could look so grave at times, and when she did she looked so much like Jacob. Until this moment it hadn't occurred to Leah that Nina might not be thrilled about the turn of events. Perhaps she should have realized that the whole business might be more than her daughter could, or would, assimilate.

Suddenly Nina leaned forward, propped her arms on the back of the seats and spoke with six-year-old earnestness.

"If you're really my daddy, how come you didn't say anything before?"

Jacob straightened and shifted so that he could look at her. "Good question," he replied just as earnestly. "Well, Nina, the best way I can explain is to tell you I didn't know it myself."

That elicited a look of puzzled disbelief from the girl, prompting him to explain further. "You see, sometimes when people are sick they forget things, often for a long time, and that's what happened to me. Understand?"

"I guess so," she said weakly. "Did you forget me and mama?"

"Unfortunately, yes."

"And now you remember us?"

"Now I know who you are, yes."

"Are we going to live with you?"

"Oh, absolutely. Or I'm going to live with the two of you, depending on the way you want to look at it. Are you happy about that, Nina?"

There was a brief pause, causing Leah and Jacob to glance at each other apprehensively. Then Nina asked, "Are you going to let me have my puppy?"

Behind the wheel Leah chuckled. "Now how's that for getting to the heart of the matter?"

Jacob nodded in wry acknowledgment. "I guess so, Nina. One puppy might be a nice addition to the family."

"Then I'm happy about it." Nina said with a delighted smile. "Let's go to grandpa's and get Molly."

"Molly?" he asked.

"That's my puppy's name."

"You've named her already!" Jacob exclaimed in mock dismay. "Fat chance I'd have saying you couldn't have her. Well, okay, we'll get Molly. Listen though, Nina, you're going to have to take care of her. Your mother and I don't have time."

"You already sound like a daddy."

Leah grinned, looking at Jacob. "I can hardly wait to see dad. He's going to be so pleased." Studying the road ahead of her, she grew thoughtful. "Darling, I'd really like for you to make an appointment with Dr. Graves. She said she'd like to see you."

He shook his head firmly. "I've been thinking about that, and I've changed my mind. I'm through with that nonsense, Leah. No more psychiatry for me. You can fill me in on all I need to know."

"That's not a proper attitude, and you know it, doctor. You'll be happier if you remember on your own. I'll just bet Dr. Graves can help you, and I know you'll be comfortable with her."

"Let's drop it, darling. Okay?"

"No. Not okay."

Jacob began another protest, then threw up his hands. "I guess I can protest all I like, but I'm sure if you want me to, sooner or later I'll find myself seeing Dr. Graves."

"Good," she said smugly.

"Were you always this bossy? Did you tell me what to do before?"

"No, but you used to be more malleable." Leah grew serious. "You were going to tell me about Charles... something about a woman."

"Uh-huh. Daphne Townsend."

"Your old girlfriend?" Leah gasped. "The one who deserted you during the trial?"

"One and the same. When I won the case, dear Daphne apparently decided I wasn't such a bad sort, after all. She went looking for me but, of course, couldn't find me. So she went to Charles and—"

Leah grasped the situation immediately. "And he comforted her. They became... er, friendly, and one thing led to another."

"You got it. Except that he was always afraid she would split if I ever came back."

"Which she did?"

"Which she did."

"And you're not furious—livid?" she asked incredulously.

Jacob turned to her, his eyes compassionate and understanding. "Anger won't do any good. It messes up
the judgment. Charles is only human, darling, and he
did satisfy himself that I was okay, doing well, happy.
Oh, I know he'll have to leave the clinic—I don't see
how we could possibly work together now—but I'm not
sure I want to ruin him. It's occurred to me that he
could use some therapy himself. Anyway, I need to
think about it, and that will take some time."

Slowly Leah relaxed. Shaking her head, she only
said, "You're something else, darling. You really are."

"It's pretty hard for me to be angry at anyone or
anything right now. Are you bitter?"

She thought about it. "No, not really. Charles won't
be one of my favorite people, but as you said, it's pretty
hard to be mad right now. Life looks awfully good to
me."

They had been traveling for a little over an hour when
Leah chanced to look at the gas gauge. Chagrined, she
said, "Oh, oh, I should have gotten gas before leaving
the city. It's not like me to forget to check the gauge."

"No problem," Jacob said. "Turn right up here at
the next exit. There's a convenience store somewhere
around there."

"Okay, I—" Leah glanced quickly at him. "Jacob,
how did you know that?"

"What?"

"How did you know there's a convenience store
down that road? We've never been that way before. I
know I've never taken you east of the interstate."

"Well...." Straightening in the seat, he looked this
way and that. "To tell you the truth, I don't have the
slightest idea. I don't even know why I said that."

"Oh, my God!"

"Leah, stop making something out of everything. I

told you, I don't know why I said that. I don't remember a store now that I think about it, but even if one's there, I could have stopped at it any number of times.''

"No, you once told me you stay strictly to the interstate, and I know for sure you and I haven't been down that road together, not even when you were Jim Stone." She slowed and turned off at the next exit. "Well, I'm not going to sit here and wonder. I'm going to investigate."

It was there, exactly where Jacob had thought it would be. Leah's eyes misted with tears as she pulled in beside the gas pumps. "Oh, Jacob! Don't you see? You're relaxed and happy now, unconcerned about the past, so your memory's coming back, just like Dr. Graves said it might. Not all of it, of course. You'll probably never remember all of it, but bits and pieces."

"My amateur psychiatrist!"

"I don't need to be a psychiatrist. It's so obvious to me."

"Is it that important to you?"

"Yes! I want you to remember, not through my mind but through your own."

He looked at her with love and admiration. "We don't have any idea why I knew this store was here."

"I don't care. For sure I've never been here before. You did know it was here." Her eyes shone with joy and anticipation.

Grinning at her enthusiasm, Jacob grabbed the door handle. "The sign says pay before pumping. May I get you ladies something?"

"Can I have a Slurpee?" Nina asked.

"They might not have them, honey," Leah reminded her.

"What in the name of heaven is a Slurpee?" Jacob asked.

"It's sort of a slushy cola," Leah explained.

"Colas are bad for you."

Leah shot her daughter a smile. "There's a doctor in the house now, Nina. We may have to change some of our habits. But I want something cold to drink, too. Maybe they have juice."

"Well, let's all go in and you pick out what you want."

The gnarled, wizened man behind the cash register greeted them laconically. "What'll it be, folks?"

"My wife and daughter are going to get something to drink," Jacob said with aplomb, amazed at how easily the words came out. "And I want to fill the tank. I don't know what it'll hold, though."

"Don't matter. Pay after you fill up. The sign's supposed to discourage them that pumps and runs, but it don't always—" The man stopped in midsentence, squinting at Jacob. "Say, ain't you the fella.... Damned if you ain't! The one that got bonged on the noggin outside some years back! Never forget a face, I don't. Good to see you lookin' fit. Heard you wuz sick a while after."

Leah gasped and leaned against the counter for support. Her heart began to race wildly.

The man had stopped when he saw the wide-eyed look on Jacob's face. Then a tiny sniffling noise arrested his attention. Puzzled, he shifted his gaze to Leah, back to Jacob. "Mister, what's wrong with your wife? Why's she cryin'?"

Author of A SEA CHANGE

**March's other absorbing
HARLEQUIN *SuperRomance* novel**

VOWS FOREVER by Lynda Ward

Elizabeth Swenson got a shock when she drove her
Porsche into Ridleyville, Arkansas. Her estranged
husband, her big-time corporate shark, was the
minister at the Good Samaritan church!

The bigger shock was finding out she still loved
Grant O'Connor. Neither of them really believed
she wanted that divorce. They wanted each other,
desperately, and they revelled in all the new and
intimately familiar things. . . .

Two different ways of living weren't so easily
merged, however. Rediscovering grounds for marriage demanded mutual sacrifice, but Elizabeth, at
least, was single-minded . . . in business and in love.

A contemporary love story for the woman of today

These two absorbing titles
will be published in April
by

HARLEQUIN
SuperRomance

SPANGLES by Irma Walker

When she was in the cage with her cats, lion trainer
Tanya Rhodin had the upper hand. So why, when it
came to Wade Broderick, did she feel so out of
control?

The millionaire businessman had run away to the
circus to fulfil a boyhood fantasy, but when the
colour and pageantry of the travelling show faded
for him, he would leave.

The circus was Tanya's whole world. She knew it
would be folly to become involved with an outsider.
But Wade made her aware of a hundred new feelings . . . and one of them was love.

SHELTERING BRIDGES by Bobby Hutchinson

An attractive coal-mining magnate, a beautiful valley homestead and the perfect teaching job—Alana
Campbell's star was definitely on the rise!

Opening up young Bruce's silent world was the
most rewarding experience of her life—and living
with Bruce's father was the most exciting! But
communicating with the gorgeous Rand Evans was
almost as great a challenge as with his deaf son. The
man was impossibly secretive, and Alana suspected
his activities weren't strictly legal—or moral!

But she was bound to this strange yet familiar man.
They were soulmates; she felt it in his touch and
saw it in his eyes. . . .